LEGENDS
OF
WINGCHUN
EMBERS OF THE SHAOLIN

Non-Fiction by René Ritchie
Yuen Kay-San Wing Chun Kuen
Complete Wingchun
(with Robert Chu and Y. Wu)

Fiction by René Ritchie
Legends of Wingchun: Embers of the Shaolin

LEGENDS
— OF —
WINGCHUN
EMBERS OF THE SHAOLIN

A MARTIAL ARTS NOVEL BY
RENÉ RITCHIE

REMNANT-HUNTER MEDIA
Montréal

First published in Canada in 2006

Remnant-Hunter Media
POB 46511 Blvd. St. Jean, Pierrefonds,
QC, H9H-5G9
www.remnant-hunter.com

ISBN 0-9738804-0-6

Cover and interior design
and typesetting by René Ritchie

10 09 08 07 06 1 2 3 4 5

Printed in the United States
and the United Kingdom

To Wingchun
and all her myriad heirs—
many branches, one tree.

Special Thanks To

Ngo Lui-Kay and the late Grandmaster Sum Nung
for passing down the art and the tradition

Robert Chu, Hendrik Santo, and Andreas Hoffmann
for sharing their profound knowledge

Mark Wiley, Y. Wu, Eddie Chong, Garette Gee
and all those who contributed their stories for
Complete Wing Chun

Lee Man, Yuen Jo-Tong, Mok Poi-On,
William Cheung, Yip Chun, Leung Ting,
and other Wing Chun pioneers, and the great Cantonese
wuxia novelists for sharing many versions of the legend

Marty, Ray, John, Benny
and the spirit of the Friendship Seminars

Terence, Jim, Dan, David, Bob, Eric, and
all the members of WCML, KFO
and www.wingchunkuen.com

Derek, James, John, Geneviève, Ron, Ord, and Christina
for their time and effort

My parents, grandmother, and siblings
for their relentless support

And to Antony, Georgia, and Michael
for everything

Contents

Prologue

The boy stumbled through oily black smoke and crackling white flame. The square was just ahead... And his father—he had to reach his father!

"The Ch'ing have scattered the feeble remnants of your Ming Dynasty to the four winds, driven your pathetic Southern rebellion all but into the sea." The words emanated from the chaos ahead, the voice a sizzle beyond the inferno. "They have annihilated everything—everyone—that has dared stand against them. Everyone but the Shaolin..."

Constables of the Army of the Green Standard stamped around the square. Uniformed black as coal and armed with spears that glinted like polished silver, they cowered the villagers into the ground.

"The Ch'ing have razed the temples, slaughtered the monks, and yet still the Shaolin refuse to lie down, refuse to yield..."

Forbidden Bannermen tore up the road. Armored in steel plates and mounted on ebon horses, body after body tumbled in their wake—all the boy's friends, everyone he'd ever known...

"The Shaolin scurry like insects. They crawl into all the foul nooks and rotten crannies and they fester... They fester until the fire comes at last and forces them out."

The boy tripped and fell and strained through the tears and devastation for any hint of his father. But all he saw was a defiant man crouched beneath faded rags, ready to rise up even as the arms of his closest friend—of his sworn brother—stopped him.

"Only then, in death, when all that remains is char and offal, when all that remains is a stinking pile of blackened bone, are the Shaolin laid down, are they yielded..."

The Lama turned, his bone-white robes flared and, from the depths of his ashen face, his burning eyes blazed.

"Yield them."

Spears lashed out, the villagers erupted, the boy screamed...

"NO!"

And the defiant man rose, unstoppable even by the arms of a hundred friends or a thousand brothers.

"I am Leung Hong," he said, "twenty-forth generation disciple of Shaolin!" The faded rags slipped away and his muscles flexed dark. The parallel rows of dots burned into his scalp were faint now beneath black hair grown long and full, but the dragon and tiger brands still coiled and snarled bright across his arms. "I am a patriot of the Ming Dynasty that governed the Han nation through a thousand years of peace and prosperity!"

The constables crashed into Leung but he settled still as a mountain. Spears splintered against his iron skin and constables rent beneath his clawed hands.

But they had the weight of numbers behind them. They hammered and they piled until Leung was forced back.

Then his friend, his brother, rose at his side.

"I am Fong Dak!" His dark shroud fell and though no dots marked his balding pate, his tiger and dragon brands coiled and snarled every inch as bright. "I am the enemy of the Ch'ing usurpers who have corrupted our land, of the Manchu invaders who have brought only misery and despair to our people!"

The constables split their attack but Fong flowed supple as the river. Spears slipped from his turning body and constables snapped between his twisting arms.

"We are sons of Heaven & Earth," they said together. "We are brothers of the rebellion that will overthrow the Ch'ing and restore the Ming to the Dragon-Throne of China!"

The constables faltered and their lines collapsed. But then the earth trembled and the bannermen bore down, their thick-bladed, two-handed choppers assailing the night.

Leung roared and met their charge, exploded up into them with all his weight and rage.

Fong hissed. "Iron Tiger Cracks the Mountain!"

Two bannerman were shorn from their saddles and three more were sent reeling. Leung slammed back into the ground, his head down and his eyes fierce. "We are the karma that returns to you every ounce of pain," he said, "every measure of death, ten-thousand fold!"

Then a horse reared up, the long, sharp shadow of a banner captain fell over him, and steel fell with it.

Fong was too far away, he couldn't reach Leung, not in time...! But Fong scanned the wreckage, saw the broken tip of a spear lying in the dirt and flames at his feet, and he spun around and kicked it with all his speed and fury.

The smoldering blade hurtled past Leung and struck full in the face of the Banner Captain. It cut him down and sent his chopper twirling up through the smoke.

Leung claimed it.

"Come on," Fong said. "This is our chance, let's go!"

"You go," Leung said. "There's nothing left for me."

"I'm not going without you!"

"You have to." Leung tilted his gaze up the mountain. "You have no choice."

"What are you—" Fong's eyes crinkled and then his face drained white. "Buddha's name..."

"Go." Leung shoved him away and turned on the Lama—the ancient enemy that stood at the edge of the square. "Go now!"

And Leung charged.

The Lama remained still.

Leung's nostrils flared, his eyes set. The chopper leapt up.

The Lama remained still.

Leung closed until nothing but an exhalation separated the tip of the chopper from the Lama's throat.

Then the Lama's bone robes parted and his falchion split the heavens.

Leung finished his charge—his body first, his head a moment later. It bounced several times before rolling to a stop.

The banner captain staggered to his feet, his hand clutched to the ruin of his face. "Fetch the Emperor his trophy and then take this village apart—slaughter your way to the sea if you have to but find me that other monk!"

1

The Crane & the Tiger

Wingchun stood bright before the dawn, still, silent… longing for the sky. She stared through the sepia latticework of the narrow window above the Yim Family Tofu Shop, and out over the somber-shingled roofs of Lanchow. She stared until the heavens smoldered deepest red on the edge of blinding yellow conflagration, and then her gaze shifted up and out, beyond the horizon.

Past torment, prior to toil, in the tang of the morning breeze, her body remained but her spirit was set free to dream—to be anyone, anywhere… anything but a skinny little girl, in a tiny little town, stuck out in the middle of nowhere…

"Like the moon seeking itself in the shallow confines of the lake…"

The voice was stone ground.

"Father…"

The door curtain crumpled aside.

"Nightmares again?" he said.

Smoke rasped. Flame rumbled. Ghosts swarmed outside the walls, their horns polished silver. She couldn't run…

"No," she said.

The floor boards creaked close.

"No?"

Metal buckled. Wood splintered. Demons breached the gates, their hides scaled ebon. Couldn't move...

"I'm fine."

The window latches clacked shut.

"You do not have to pretend, child, not for my sake..."

A monster reared up, its body shadow, its fangs dripping with familiar blood. Could barely breathe...

"I slept well, really. Safe and sound..."

The wall charms clinked straight.

"Safe and sound... really?"

The devil turned, its robes bone, its face ash, its eyes the inferno. A single, terrible claw cleft down. Fire flared and the screams—

Wingchun fled to the corner.

"As always."

"Yet here you are up with the dawn?"

"We have a shop to run." She tucked back her pale green robes and took a seat at the burgundy-lacquered dresser "And, as you're so fond of reminding me, customers to prepare for."

"Not today."

"Not...?"

"Today," he said, "if any customers were to arrive this early, they would find the dining room fully prepared, the counter and tables already wiped, and the bowls, spoons, and chopsticks already laid out."

"Did I forget to clean up last night?"

"No more than usual..."

"Well, there's still the tofu—"

"Already freed from the press and cut and floated."

She glanced back at him. Stooped beneath his usual slate-gray robes, what little cotton-white hair remained on his head was bearded in front and braided down back.

"Why?" she said.

He plucked a long-toothed comb up from off the dresser and began to strum it through her hair.

"Must there always be a 'why'?"

"Let's see—ever since I was a little girl I've done all my own chores, all by myself, and all on time. You insisted on it, even if it meant clearing tables with one hand, wiping them with the other, and arranging the stools with both feet. All so that I would learn to—what was it?— 'achieve twice the results—' "

" 'With half the effort.' Of course, child."

"Then if it's done, all of it and already, and without me lifting the slightest finger, I think I'm entitled to a little 'why'."

"Well, not quite *all* of it," he said. "There does remain the small matter of the laundry..."

"The laundry? Today?"

"This very morning."

"But mornings are our busiest time, father, you know that. We can't just abandon shop and go traipsing off to the river and—"

"No, *we* can't."

She blinked. "You're going to let me go by myself? You're actually going to let me go someplace by myself?"

"I let you go many places by yourself."

"The kitchen doesn't count as 'many places'..."

He put the comb down. "Then without me this once, but not by yourself, *never* by yourself. Other's will be there for certain."

"How do—?"

"And you will go directly to the river, do the laundry, and come directly home. Do you understand?"

"Yes, I—"

"No. Do not simply answer, child—understand."

"I'm not really a child, father, not any more."

"You are *my* child and that means it is my duty to care for you and to protect you, and your duty simply to listen and to obey. No more, no less. You will do as I will have you do, and right now I will have you understand."

She angled a brow. "The river, the laundry, the here—all nice and direct. I think even a child could understand that."

He huffed. "So like your mother..."

"My-my mother?"

"In attitude as much as appearance!"

She looked up into the mirror atop the dresser. It was dull and chipped, and her image floated there, distant and distorted.

"I don't remember," she said. "Only the corners of her smile, the gleam of her eyes, the scent of... of...?"

"Plum blossoms."

He shifted behind her and his reflection broke, and between the cracks she saw a pain so deep she couldn't bear it.

"I understand."

He nodded.

"And, hey! At the very least, it should make for an interesting morning..."

"Child!"

"Father?"

"You know better than to tempt fate!"

"Come on..." She looked to the window, shut and warded. "No matter what the times, we live in Lanchow, and nothing even remotely interesting ever happens here."

詠 春 傳 說

Boklao strode dark past the night, swift, relentless... in search of a mountain. Salt baskets jostled from the ends of the pole across his back and dirt crunched beneath his feet as he climbed up the thinly etched path, through the endless sea of bamboo, and into the deepest backwater of Kwangsi Province. Then the breeze stirred the desiccated earth, spread it out like smoke, and the rhythm of his steps—the pace that hadn't faltered in a week—slowed and stopped.

"You come to a fork in the road."

The voice was somewhere between wind and water.

"The path you were on will not take you much farther."

Boklao's pulse quickened, his grip tightened, his eyes scanned east to west...

Birds chirped, monkeys chattered. The forest spun, stalk and leaf blurred by. Then, off to the side—a gleam...

Salt baskets thudded to the ground and Boklao's steel-tipped carrying pole scraped free. He swung it up and around and turned fully to face—

"An old woman?" His pulse slowed, his grip slacked. "Nothing but an old woman..."

She was perched cross-legged atop a rock, veiled in leaf and half-light, her small body robed and her round face capped. And in her hand gleamed coins bearing the ancient patterns of the eight trigrams that followers of the Tao believed could divine all possibilities of past, present, and future.

A smile cut across Boklao's face. "I know you."

"Do you?"

"Know your kind—fortunetellers, hucksters... One hand casts the fate while the other reaches out like the lowest of beggars."

"You know me as you know all things—by what is within you."

"Save your koan for someone more gullible. You're not getting a tael from me, old woman, not a mace, not today—not ever."

"Koan can lead closer to essential nature than you might expect, boy. They are not laid out plain for you, no, that much is true. They require something back, something more than money—they require you to think, to ponder... to work them out. By this, they offer the potential for a far deeper understanding." The old woman glanced up, a twinkle in her eye. "Such is life."

"Thank you for your insight. Here's mine—fortune favors those who stay out of my way."

"And which way is that?"

"What?"

"Not what—which? You come to a fork in the road, remember?"

Boklao adjusted the bandana wrapped over his head, looked out again to where the thinly etched path before him cleft in two, and he bit off a curse.

"You know these paths, old woman? You know where they lead?"

The old woman's cheeks rounded. "You ask the coins?"

"I'm asking you."

"The coins know better." She cast them. "They see further."

"No, I—"

"Difficulty."

"—told you, old woman, I—" He stopped and tilted his head. "Difficulty?"

"The pitfall of water above the passage of thunder. Acting in danger leads to being trapped in danger. It conceals your true strength, confuses your true thoughts, and dooms you to wander. It is the gate of Yin & Yang, the door between life and death, the endless midnight passed only when you break the bonds of your own rage—when heaven and earth are in harmony and the sun is joined by the light of the moon."

"Vague generalities couched in alchemical gibberish! Just tell me about these two paths, old women, just tell me where they lead!"

"They lead to your destination."

Boklao scoffed. "What do you know about my destination?"

"I know it is no place which you seek, no address you hope to find, no spot upon which you must stand."

"Know all that but you still can't tell me which of these paths will actually lead me there?"

"There is no duality."

"What... they join up again later?"

"Yes... and no."

"I don't understand!"

"And was that really so hard to admit?"

Boklao growled. "If you were a man, I'd grab you by your throat and squeeze until a straight answer came spilling from your lips!"

"If I were a man, you might be able to."

He snarled. "I'll just pick one then, any one, it doesn't matter! If there really is no duality then it doesn't matter which one I pick, does it?"

The old woman sighed. "Of course it does, all the more so because of it."

"Riddles and gibberish!"

Boklao grabbed his salt baskets and began towards the fork.

"If you stand atop a cliff," the old woman called after him, "can you not reach the bottom in more than one way? Can you not take the gradual way, the sure way—the winding road down the back? And can you not also take the sudden way, the fast way—the leap from the very edge?"

"And I'm supposed to believe I'm standing atop a cliff?"

"Higher than you can imagine."

"Well I'm not afraid of leaping."

"And of falling and of hitting the ground?"

Boklao's nostrils flared. "No."

The old women's cheeks flattened. "And of crushing someone else beneath you?"

"Not any of it. I have to get where I'm going. No more traveling in the rut, no more daggers hidden in smiles!"

"Such is often the way of the young." She pointed west. "Follow that path, boy. Follow it and pray you do not break too many bones when you hit the ground."

詠 春 傳 說

Eagle-Shadow crashed down the mountainside, his eyes locked on the glistening river that tore through the bamboo far below while his finger scratched along the scar that tore through his own face—across his left brow and over his nose all the way to his right jaw.

The river flowed with life and hope while his scar burned only with failure and shame perpetual as the water... Perpetual but not eternal...

"Come on." He slung his thick-bladed, two-handed chopper across his back. "We have a delivery to make."

詠 春 傳 說

The Eight Immortal Crags emerged, milky jade fringe atop the dappled turquoise sash of the Lan River. Wingchun leant against the foundations of the bridge where water raced white across the dark gray rocks, and she breathed long and deeply.

The zest of the bamboo, the richness of the mud, the... the every-thing. It was just so—

"—Deluded!"

Wingchun's nose crinkled and she glanced back.

A boy of barely a dozen years stomped up the Western Road, his per-simmon robes soiled at the hem, and the small tuft of hair on his forehead flattened against his otherwise fresh-shaved scalp.

"What are you looking at, chopstick girl?" he said, mouth full of gold-en-brown moon cake.

"Little Kung!" Mrs. Law stomped up behind her second son. Sesame-ball round, her hair was twisted and pinned, and her robe was hitched for wading. "Bad enough you made us late, but—"

"But what?" Little Kung said, bits of lotus seed and preserved yolk tumbling from his mouth. "That's what everyone calls her!"

"Not to—I mean, not..."

Wingchun turned. "Not to my face?"

Mrs. Law's ears went scarlet as her painted cheeks. She looked away, dumped her carrying pole and laundry baskets onto the banks, and planted her arms on her hips.

"Get with the sorting, boy, before my slipper gets with the flying!"

"I told you," Little Kung said. "I'm not the boy, I'm the six-armed fire giant. I set whole towns ablaze, not sort puny laundry!"

"And I told you, if you think that you're getting out of your chores again you're—"

Little Kung rolled his eyes and wiped his mouth on his sleeve. "Deluded, I know!"

"Honestly, boy," she said. "Why must you always be so much more with the hinder than the help?"

"Hey! I washed almost a whole basket last time!"

"Washed? You stomped around like a drunken monkey and knocked the basket into the river!"

"That's what I said!"

Mrs. Law reached for her slipper.

A mother and her child working together, arguing together, *being* together... Wingchun smiled, sweet and sour, and buried herself back in her work.

Piece-by-piece she took clothing from her basket, wet it down, scrubbed it with small stones, and laid it out to dry. And each time, Mrs. Law looked over and opened her mouth only to blush scarlet again, snap it back shut, and look away.

Finally Wingchun put down her laundry.

"Quiet day," she said. "I mean, most everyone goes to the big river anyway, but Mrs. Shui did stop by for water and Second-Daughter Ha to pluck some shrimp. No one really stayed very long, though. I guess... I guess they didn't feel much like talking either..."

"Miss Yim—"

"Don't worry about it." Wingchun tucked a loose tendril of hair back beneath her scarf. "What your son said—what everyone says—is true. I'm not some great beauty, round of face and full of figure like you, like all the other girls in town. You know it, I know it, and I'm fine with it, really. I'm fine with being... different."

"You're not," Mrs. Law said.

"Sorry?"

"You're not different, Miss Yim, at least not any more than you choose to be. If you just ate a little more, plaited your hair, perhaps, in the proper style... Your father never saw fit to bind your feet and he lets you work in his shop, but this far in the backwater most would probably just assume you're Hakka, one of the Guest People... If only you would try some nice long robes instead of those miserable pants I always see you in..."

"What's wrong with my pants?" Wingchun glanced down. "Lots of women wear pants."

"Manual laborers..."

"Not just manual laborers!"

"Street performers..."

"I can move freely in pants, I don't have to shuffle around, or worry about how I sit, or about the Hum brothers asking me to reach for the preserves on the top shelf... Pants are... Pants are practical!"

"Perhaps, Miss Yim, but practical is no way to assure yourself of a suitable husband."

"A suitable husband? That's what this is all about?"

"Of course, what else is there?"

"I don't know. I never really thought about it..."

"Come on, you must be over sixteen by now? When I was your age it was all I ever thought about, all my family ever let me think about—tiny feet, tiny voice, a face like a flower, and a mind to match. All so that when my appointment with the matchmaker finally came I would be paired with as suitable a husband as possible."

"An apothecary?"

"A divine horse prancing—a man of high standing who would bring me up with him. And if I had a daughter, the type of man I would prepare her for."

"Well maybe I'm being prepared for something... I don't know... Something—"

"Different?"

"Is that so impossible?"

"Not so impossible!" Mrs. Law smiled. "After all, Miss Yim, even chopsticks come in pairs."

Wingchun blinked.

Mrs. Law laughed.

And Wingchun broke down and laughed with her... until the bamboo stirred.

"What was—?"

"I don't—"

Little Kung burst out onto the banks.

"I am the three-headed, six-armed fire giant!" He brandished a lop-sided twig. "Tremble at the sight of my smoke-enshrouded sword! Flee as I set your town ablaze!"

Mrs. Law lunged. "I warned you about going into the forest, boy!"

Little Kung scampered back. "Father lets me go into the forest!"

"Only until he catches you!"

"That's what I said!"

"There are snakes in the forest, Little Kung, monkeys and leopards, and... and worse!"

Little Kung snatched up a rock and stomped in a circle. "Ha! With my gourd of ten-thousand fire crows, I defy the monkeys and leopards, and laugh in the face of the worse!"

"Gourd of—? Boy, in a minute you'll have the rear-end of ten-thousand—!"

Wingchun's nose crinkled. "Does he know how it ends?"

Mrs. Law paused. "What?"

"The story of the fire giant," Wingchun said. "Does Little Kung know how it ends?"

"No, he... he keeps falling asleep half-way through..."

Little Kung stomped over. "I do not!"

Wingchun angled a brow.

Mrs. Law smiled. "Behold! The sky princess arrives to call down the storm!"

Wingchun dipped her hand into the river and water splashed up over Little Kung.

"Mother!"

Wingchun and Mrs. Law began to laugh again.

"Never mind, boy, just be happy Miss Yim didn't have a golden pagoda to drop on your head."

"What the—!"

"That's how it ends," Wingchun said. "The fire giant loses."

"To a girl?" Little Kung's face bunched up. "No way the fire giant loses to some stupid—"

They laughed harder... until the bamboo stirred again.

Little Kung shrugged. "Don't look at me..."

And then the stir became a thrash and the laughter shattered into screams.

2

Brawl at the Bridge

Bamboo fell away and mountains rose, a verdant pommel above the azure blade of water. A covered bridge carried the path over the river, and people huddled against its stone foundations—a woman and two boys… A family—

Screaming.

Boklao slowed.

Two men crashed out onto the laundry-strewn banks. The first was no-necked as an ape, his shoulders bloated and his knuckles dragging down past his knees. The second was bandy-legged as a lizard, his face pointed and his back hunched up above his head. Their clothes were tattered and mismatched, but the long, thin blades of their sabers glinted sharply…

The woman—the mother—raised her hand, tried to steady it and point her thumb up. She didn't understand the futility…

Boklao slipped off his baskets and his steel-tipped pole scraped free.

詠春傳說

No-neck eclipsed the sun, eclipsed everything... He shoved Wingchun against the bridge. "Don't move!"

"Wait." Bandy-legs leered down at Little Kung. "Like my saber, boy? You must, you stare at it so..."

No-neck snorted. "No time for your games!"

Bandy-legs spat. "Make time. A few stray coins may still be enough for you, but not for me. Not any more..."

Mrs. Law clutched Little Kung close. "This can't be happening!"

Wingchun shook. Someone should do something...

"Call this a 'goose-quill'." Bandy-legs pressed the tip of his saber into Little Kung's cheek. "I hate that name." He drew the blade up. "Nowhere near frightening enough..."

"—can't be happening!"

Someone had to!

"Please," Wingchun said. "He-he's just a boy, he—"

"You want to go first?" Bandy-legs' sneer slammed into her. "That's always the hard part—deciding who goes first."

"Get on with it," No-neck said.

Wingchun stepped forward. "Please...!"

"Fine!"

And Bandy-legs' saber lashed out.

"NO!"

詠 春 傳 說

The dining room of the Yim Family Tofu Shop swirled with the essence of sweet fruit and smoky incense. Old Yee—as he was known to everyone in Lanchow—placed his offerings above the rounded doorway, between the square shelves, high atop the altar of General Kwan Yu. Patron spirit from the ancient days of the Three Kingdoms, the ceramic effigy stood with eyes vigilant, left arm warding, and right wielding an enormous, hook-backed halberd.

Old Yee besought the usual blessings for the peace of his town and the prosperity of his shop, and then his voice dropped low and he finished as he always did—by asking General Kwan to watch over Wingchun, to keep his last daughter secret and to keep her safe. Then he bowed three times, picked up his tray, and passed back through the indigo curtain and into the kitchen.

Master Law awaited him there against the tofu press and the old stone grinder. His mustache marked him as over fifty and yet he was still broad and bold, his hands steady and his braid untouched by gray. His silk robes were a deep copper and his bronze vest was embroidered with the subtlest of thunderbolts, yet his black cap bore no jewel. Were he Southern Han, Master Law would certainly enjoy some measure of official rank, though perhaps not as much as he already enjoyed far from officially...

"Jasmine..." Master Law lifted the crucible from atop his teacup and inhaled deeply. "The twisted leaves lend it the mellowest bite."

"Sorry to keep you," Old Yee said. "Butcher Ngao's boy would stay and eat all day if I allowed it."

"No," Master Law said. "I'm the one who's sorry."

"You? Whatever for?"

Master Law extended a small bundle wrapped in paper. "The ingredients you asked for, the mulberry root, the loquat leaf, they suggest something rather specific..."

Old Yee took it with both hands and placed it on the counter. "The slow withering of time is all."

"Indeed...?"

"Believe what you will, it matters little unless it is complete?"

"I'll have the last ingredient for you soon... a week perhaps, two at the most."

"Two weeks?"

"There remain no Tang poets to pray the rain dragons from the pool and so the phoenix is left to stoke the sun. The herbs, the roots, the water beetles... everything has faded in this drought. Even in the best of times wild ginseng would be difficult to find, but now... Now I have to scrounge twice as far for half as much, and more often than not I'm still left to barter and beg with contacts from Ngchow to well near the Yunnan border..." He leant in. "But that's probably the very reason you had to come to me at last, isn't it?"

Old Yee crossed over to the stove and began to stoke the coal. "I have no idea what you mean..."

"Really? You've been in Lanchow what, almost fourteen years now? And in all that time you've never seen fit to call on my services before. Not once, not until yesterday. I thought perhaps you were merely fortunate when it came to injury or illness, but now... Well, now I begin to suspect something else entirely..."

"Nonsense." Old Yee lifted the lid off a large wok and fussed with the soybeans inside. "But I do thank you, you and your wife both…"

"For what, keeping an eye on your daughter? Meeting you here rather than at my shop? Think nothing of it. My family knows the value of discretion more than most and… and, truth be told, I appreciate the change of scenery. I've never been fully comfortable behind an apothecary counter…"

"No?"

"I used to teach boxing…"

Old Yee stiffened. "Boxing is outlawed under the Ch'ing."

Master Law took a sip of tea. "It is."

"Yet you risked your life—the lives of your whole family—and taught anyway?"

"Even after the Ch'ing secured their hold on the South, their bans on boxing and blades never fully penetrated here, not into the deepest backwater. So I taught, yes, and the students trained hard. The mornings after brought with them the usual aches and pains, and so they would come back for liniment, sometimes a poultice. You know, the martial and the medical, flip sides of the same coin. But nothing lasts forever…"

"The Ch'ing found out…"

"Not about me, no, but about a junior of mine in Lankiang. He was a good man, a good friend. He taught for the same reason I did—so his village could protect itself from bandits and… and worse. But he had a falling out with a student and that student ran straight to the collaborators—"

"The Constabulary Army of the Green Standard…"

"—and they made an example of him… a game. They dragged him to the village square and proceeded to find out just how many punches it would take to… to…"

"To kill him and to kill the spirit of him, so that the word would spread, the warning… I remember…"

Master Law downed the last of his tea. "I gave up my school immediately, of course," he said, "and devoted myself fully to the apothecary shop. At least that side of my coin still held some value."

"It does," Old Yee said, "and now you have a good practice, a good family—a good life."

"A great practice and an even greater family, but only half a life. And now I find myself retiring even from that."

"Retiring…? You mean Big Kung will be taking over?"

"The shop at least. I must confess my first son is already twice the apothecary I was at his age."

"Green dye comes from blue but is even more highly prized."

"The student must surpass the teacher," Master Law said, "and the son, the father. We take care of them so that one day they can take care of us, and for me it seems that day approaches like the white colt over the crevice."

"Then to have such a student, such a son—perhaps your life is fuller than you realize?"

"Perhaps..." Master Law straightened his vest. "Well, my wife will be returning soon..."

"And my daughter with her." Old Yee bowed.

Master Law returned the bow and his eyes fell again on the medicine. "Have you... Have you told her yet?"

"No, not yet."

詠 春 傳 說

Wingchun's head shot up.

Death descended.

The saber moved fast, so fast it seemed to stretch out forever...

Then a growl erupted across the banks.

Bandy-legs paused.

No-neck turned.

And a stranger leapt from the bamboo, framed by the rising sun...

詠 春 傳 說

Boklao shouldn't have yelled—it ruined any chance for surprise—but he needed their attention off the family, needed them to commit, and with a bellow, No-neck did just that.

He charged at Boklao head-on and saber high, and Boklao charged back, front leg bowed and rear drawn. He cracked the steel-tipped end of his pole into No-neck's saber hand—the closest target. No-neck grunted, his other fist shot out and caught Boklao in the jaw, but Boklao went with it, spun around and slammed his pole into No-neck's head.

No-neck reeled back towards the river.

Boklao spat blood and locked eyes on the family. "Get out of here! Now!"

Bandy-legs lunged. He wasn't as big as No-neck but with a saber he didn't need to be.

Boklao angled to the side and smacked the pole down at Bandy-legs' foot. Bandy-legs dodged but Boklao followed him, smacked again and again like a blind man making his way through an alley. He needed to keep Bandy-legs moving, keep him off-balance…

His toes an inch ahead of the steel-tip, Bandy-legs scrambled, and Boklao switched directions and thrust up.

Bandy-legs should be out of position, should be open… But he wasn't—he was expecting it! He reared away at the last second, grabbed Boklao's pole, and yanked him straight into the path of his saber.

Boklao cursed, let go of his pole, and snapped down at the waist. Bandy-legs' saber shrieked by overhead. Bandy-legs swung again. Boklao leapt and the saber sliced under him. He rolled and came up into a crouch, hands clawed open.

Bandy-legs smirked and tossed the pole aside. "I'm going to impale you by inches!"

"Indahun!" No-neck clutched his head and worked his grip. "Just kill the mongrel dog and be done with it!"

They charged, their boots chomped across the banks. Boklao waited… waited for their sabers to all but taste him. And then he ducked out from in-between and swung his leg like a tiger's tail. His heel smashed into Bandy-legs' ribs, sent him colliding into No-neck, and sent them both tumbling to the ground.

"Now we'll see…" Boklao rose over them. "We'll see who the dogs are…"

A shadow reared up behind him.

"Yes, we will…"

詠 春 傳 說

They were fighting! Wingchun had never seen anything like it before, not beyond her nightmares and imagination… The man who saved them, the stranger, he moved so fast, a blur of faded blue against the dusty brown banks. A once-white bandana was wrapped above his dark, weathered face and his eyes, narrow and turbulent… But it was the way he moved, so wild, so certain, so—

"Miss Yim!"

Mrs. Law yanked her back behind the bamboo. "We have to go!"

"But—!"

A monster reared up. Its fangs dripped…

"Quickly!"

A third bandit appeared behind the stranger, not mismatched but black as shadow, a huge blade glinting in his hands…

"Wait, I—!"

"Wait? We can't, Miss Yim, not another second!"

"I have to warn—!" The bandit struck. The stranger fell. "No!"

"Quiet! Miss Yim—" Mrs. Law took a breath. "Wingchun, please, we have to go and we have to go now."

"But he was trying to save us!"

"He did." Mrs. Law gazed at Little Kung. "If we leave right now, if we get away, then he did save us. He did. But only if we leave right now!"

"Hey!" Little Kung said. "I can help! I can fight!"

"You can die, idiot boy! That's all you can do here! That's all any of us can do!"

Wingchun stared at them and then back at the stranger. "Okay, let's… let's get Little Kung out of here. You lead the way and I'll be right behind."

詠 春 傳 說

Black seared white.

Down… Boklao was down. Dirt caked his face and blood oozed from the back of his head. He'd made a mistake, underestimated them and let someone get behind him, but his bandana had taken the edge off the impact and, while he was down, he wasn't out. And that was *their* mistake.

A bark—something incomprehensible—echoed above him. Boklao's eyes slivered open. Another bark preceded a kick. Boklao clenched his teeth. He couldn't scream, couldn't let them know. Not yet…

Apish arms yanked him up from behind and cold, sharp steel bit into his throat. Boklao clenched harder.

"Stop."

The steel paused and a scarred face leered down.

"If I wanted him dead I would have hit him with the edge of my blade, not the flat." Scarface hefted a thick, two-handed chopper—the kind used to bring down horsemen. "But he's been trained to fight and that means I can cut more from him than just his head. I can cut the name of his trainer…"

No-neck snorted. "Every sick-man Southern boxer we stumble over!"

Scarface's eyes raked across at him. "You have an opinion?"

"N-no!"

"Let me slice the *lehele* open," Bandy-legs said, "and hang him from a tree. When he sees his guts dripping out, he'll tell you anything you want to know."

Scarface's eyes raked back. "Yes, I'm sure he will..."

No-neck grumbled, for the briefest moment his grip slackened...

And Boklao's eyes flew open.

He jammed his hand up between the saber and his throat, and stamped his heel down into the small bones of No-neck's foot. No-neck bleated and bent forward, and Boklao rammed his head back. The bleat became a howl.

"Pacify him!" Scarface yelled.

Bandy-legs closed fast but he wasn't the gravest threat... Boklao scanned the banks and then threw himself into a cartwheel. He spun past Bandy-legs, reached down and reclaimed his pole from off the ground, and then came back to his feet and brought the steel tip down—right onto Scarface's head.

"Now we're even, you piercing a—!"

Pain sizzled cold across Boklao's back. He jerked sideways and cursed.

Bandy-legs slashed again. Boklao blocked with pole and his breath rose hot and high. They lunged at each other. Bandy-legs slipped the pole and his saber sliced across Boklao's shoulder. Boklao swung back around but Bandy-legs was clear and No-neck was oriented again, bleating, snorting...

They circled him. Wood, water, and rock spun by. Boklao feinted towards No-neck and then twisted around and swept the pole low into the back of Bandy-legs' ankles. Bandy-legs thudded down to the rocks, and Boklao continued the motion, brought the pole up high as it would go, and then hammered it down. Bandy-legs twitched and went still. Then Boklao cross-stepped and stabbed back and up, a seated tiger flicking its tail. The pole caught No-neck mid-charge and mid-throat. He snapped in half and splashed across the edge of the river.

"This time..." Boklao's chest rose and fell. "This time you stay down!"

His legs shook, his arms prickled, but he had to focus. Scarface...
Where was—? His nostril's flared, he whipped around—
And Scarface's chopper fell.

3
Hints of Existence

Metal clanged. Thick, sticky liquid splattered. Then the coughing became all-consuming and even when he could breathe again, Old Yee's chest remained tight, a tofu cake left far too long beneath the press…

"Of all the wood handed, stone footed—!"

He stooped to retrieve the wok and clean the mess of slurry. It was getting so much harder to bear. All of it.

"Think, then, how I must feel…"

Auntie—as his daughter called her—alighted through the back door. Robed and capped the color of dew-drenched plums, she was old yet vibrant, small yet full, with a face round as the moon and eyes like silver seas, piercing and profound.

" 'Lingering like gossamer,' " he said, " 'it has but a hint of existence; and yet when you draw upon it, it is inexhaustible…' "

" 'Heaven endures,' " she said, " 'and earth yet abides; what then is the secret of their durability?' "

Old Yee wiped his mouth. "Pure stubbornness, I think at times."

"That has always been *your* secret."

He took another wok, this time filled with bluish-white soymilk, and began to fold in powdered gypsum. "Well learned, if so."

She glanced around. "Is the girl still sleeping?"

"She is at the river doing the laundry."

"Alone?"

"I let her go places a—" He huffed. "Never mind."

She arched a brow.

"I had something to attend to is all," he said, "something that need not yet concern her."

"Story of her life." She glanced at the paper-wrapped bundle atop the kitchen bench. "You could have come to me, you know. You should have."

"Your time is too precious, I would not waste it."

"It is not my time you waste, nor my awareness you escape."

"That was never my intent."

"No?"

"I would have thought that you more than anyone would understand the promise I made, the vow I must keep."

"Just as I understand that there is more than one way to keep your vow."

"Not for me. Not any more."

"Your Fifth Patriarch said—'those with sense plant seeds; seeds that will bear fruit from the ground. Without those seed there is no sense; no nature, no life.'"

"I planted seeds..."

"And then promptly buried them."

He sighed. "The Sixth Patriarch said—'the mind ground contains the seeds; with the universal rain, all will sprout. When suddenly you realize the blossoming heart; the fruit of enlightenment will naturally mature.' "

"And you think that is enough?"

"I think we both know that it is not always the universal rain that comes. Sometimes it is the fire—the inferno—and then the seeds do not mature at all, and they bear no other fruit than death."

"Is that why you are so much like the old tree," she said, "unbending and easily broken?"

"No," he said, "that is why I am so much like the old tree already bent long past broken."

"Embracing emptiness, denying its cause and effect, is reckless."

"Everything is empty, impermanent, the *Song of Enlightenment* says that as well."

"It says that emptiness cannot be grasped and so it must be let go."

"But if everything were truly empty, truly impermanent, it would not be of one nature. It would be of birth and death, and not of the essential essence that exists beyond both."

"You understand my brother's lessons well."

Old Yee bowed his head. "He had remarkable patience."

She crossed over to the window. "Yet it remains to be seen if you can transcend them."

"Sorry?"

"Last night," she said, "did you look to the heavens?"

"As I do every night," he said.

"And what did you see?"

"What you saw—the White Tiger straining to hold the Celestial Mansion while the Dark Warrior stirs and makes ready its final ascent."

"And nothing else?"

"What else was there?"

"The sixteen stars, embroidered bright as pearls across the silken black sky."

"You... you saw the Wolf of the Wood, the Walking Man...?"

"The Strider."

And he was gone, across the kitchen, and out the door.

詠 春 傳 說

Boklao wrenched his pole up and around. It cracked into Scarface's chopper and then they stood against the river and mountains, their weapons crossed and their eyes locked.

Bamboo and steel streaked through the sky and echoed up and down the banks.

Boklao kept back, out of range of the horse-chopper, and twirled the pole, jabbed and feinted—did anything he could to force the distance.

"You should have let them hang you from that tree," Scarface said. "That would have been only a single cut. Now I'm going to grant you the full two-thousand, and when you're done whimpering out the name and whereabouts of your master, I'm going to take what few scraps remain and cast them one-by-one down the river to hell."

"Right where you'll be waiting," Boklao said, "for me to kill all over again!"

Boklao thrust. Scarface slashed. The pole missed. The chopper didn't. Boklao's leg burned. Scarface laughed.

"One."

Boklao snarled and spun but Scarface caught him as he came around, kicked him and stabbed. Boklao's arm seared.

"Two."

The world narrowed red, Boklao's nose filled with the smell of salt and his mouth the taste of iron. He swung the pole low. Scarface cut high. Boklao's ear stung.

"Three."

And then Scarface brought the chopper back up and around and it hung over Boklao's head.

Boklao growled and jammed the pole tight against the chopper's crosspiece, barred it before it could begin its descent.

Scarface pressed. Boklao dropped down to one knee. The pole groaned and Boklao's arms wavered. Scarface bent his full weight behind the chopper. The pole splintered, Boklao blasted back through the mud, and Scarface loomed over him, chopper glinting.

"I want you to know something," Scarface said. "I want you to know that after you're dead I'm going to track down that family—the one you tried so righteously to save—and I'm going to send them to hell after you. I'm going to grant you that final failure."

"They're—" Boklao's breath tore through him and the pain lanced from joint to joint. "They're gone. They got away from you..."

Scarface laughed again. "They couldn't have gotten far."

"They didn't."

詠 春 傳 說

Wingchun was still hidden, wasn't she? She had to be. She couldn't be moving, could she? If she was moving, she'd know it. She'd be crying out. She'd be screaming...

Apart, she saw herself step from the bamboo. Detached, she heard the echo of words escaping her lips. Numb, she felt the rock smash down.

A scarred face cringed and yelped out. Then the distance closed, the rock tumbled to the ground, haze consumed the corners of her vision, bitterness the back of her throat, and a dull rush swallowed all other sound.

She collapsed back, ready to shatter into a ten-thousand pieces...

詠 春 傳 說

"*Aii*—!" Scarface staggered and his chopper clanged off the rocks.

Boklao roared and exploded up. His clawed hand smashed into Scarface's jaw.

Teeth flew and blood splattered. Scarface spun up into the air and smashed back down into the dirt.

And behind him... behind him Boklao saw a boy crumpled against the bamboo. No... not a boy—*the* boy, the one from the family he'd tried to save... But he should be long gone, why would he—

Boklao tilted his head. Though a scarf veiled the hair, the beige jacket and pants betrayed the hint of curves...

Not a boy—"A girl..."

She stared back up at him. "What did you say?"

"I—" Fire spat up his leg only to race cold down his arm. "I said you should go."

"You're hurt..."

He backed away. "Just a scratch."

"A deep one."

"They're all deep."

He peeled off his sash and shucked his jacket.

She gasped. "Those scars..."

They crisscrossed his torso, some short and straight, others long and jagged. "Like I said..."

He clenched his teeth, tore his sash into thin strips, and began to bind them around his waist and arm.

"Here," she said, "let me help you."

"You want to help me, get gone."

"Please." She took the ends and tied them off. "You came to my rescue. You saved me, you saved all of us. You... you were like a martial hero right out of the epics."

"Is that what you think?"

"That's what I know."

"Not everything is what it seems." Boklao pulled away and stumbled over to the bodies. He kicked No-neck's legs together, took a deep, searing breath, and began to drag him away. "When I get back, you're gone. Know that."

詠 春 傳 說

Bandy-legs went next and Scarface last. Boots, body, and finally hands, consumed by the bamboo until only the blood remained... blood so red it drained the color from everything else...

Wingchun's head churned and her stomach curdled. She dropped back against a large rock and balled herself up, face buried in her knees. And she cried. She cried until *he* was back...

"I told you to go," he said, "to get back to whatever hut or hovel you call home and lock yourself in. It's not safe out here."

She glanced up. "You're out here."

"Exactly."

"And it's a town."

"What?"

"It's not a hut or a hovel, it's a town." Wingchun wiped her face and poked her chin towards the Western Road. "Back that way."

"I just came from back that way and I didn't see a whole lot of anything but bamboo."

"There's this shortcut, an old riverbed just passed this outcropping of rocks. It's not obvious—you have to know what you're looking for."

He turned and stared. "I usually do. Your home must be very well hidden..."

"Shut away is more like it. And it's not my home, it's not where I come from, not really."

"What are you saying, that you come from, the water?"

"From the water? What—? No, I..." She sighed. "I don't know. My father doesn't like to talk about it, about anything before... before my mother died..."

"It's a terrible thing to grow up without a mother."

"It is." There was something about him, something so familiar... "It really is."

"Listen, miss...?"

"Yim. Yim Wingchun."

He tilted his head. "Wingchun?"

She nodded.

"Your name is Wingchun?"

"As opposed to…?"

"Boklao."

She bowed.

He returned the bow but then groaned and doubled over—

"Mister…?"

—and began to fall.

"Boklao!"

She caught him and lowered him down. He felt cold…

"Keep away!"

"Who…?" Wingchun looked around and then her father was beside her, his eyes gleaming but his face dark as the storm. His fingers prodded her wrist.

"Are you okay?" he said.

"Okay?"

"The blood, are you injured?"

"No, it's—" She looked down and saw her plain beige jacket splattered dark and wet. "It's not me, it's not mine. It's him, it's Boklao. We… we have to do something. We have to help him!"

Her father shook his head. "The only thing we have to do is get you home."

"But he—!"

"No. No he, no him." Her father grabbed her by the wrist and dragged her up. "Just you. Now come on…"

Boklao toppled to the ground and began to convulse.

Wingchun pulled back. "He's dying!"

"Child…!"

"Father, please—he saved my life!"

詠 春 傳 說

The sun smoldered down behind the mountains, and the old priest crossed the covered bridge and fell upon the banks.

"Blood lingers in the air…" He sniffed. "Saturates it…"

He bowed towards the riverbanks. "Footprints twist and turn, a dance of fist and foot and pole and saber. Four fought… No—five… the skills as different as Yin & Yang, as us and *them*…"

The old priest sniffed again and then broke into the bamboo, to a fissure sullied with corpses. The first was bandy-legged, the second no-necked. The old priest flung them aside to reveal the scarface beneath.

詠 春 傳 說

Four round bamboo bowls clacked down onto the sandalwood counter. Tofu squares sloshed inside and water spilled up over the edges. Wingchun fumbled lids onto each one and then hurried across the dining room to fetch four more.

"I'm sorry."

She wiped her eyes, sniffed, and shook her head. "No need."

"Sorry to keep you, that is."

"You're not, Mr. Lee. I—"

"Uncle Lee." He shifted, his indigo cowl swayed, and the floorboards moaned. "Please, must I keep telling you?"

There was a twist to his accent, something he ascribed to his hermitage—*"High among the Miu and Yao peoples who settled the mountains long before the first Han came south."*

"Uncle Lee." She nodded. "I was just going to say that you may be the last customer of the day but you're also the biggest."

Bushy white brows flattened across Uncle Lee's sallow, bean-bald head. "You mean the size of my order—?" He grabbed the large folds of his stomach. "—or of my belly?"

"What? No! Your order. I—"

Uncle Lee rolled out a smile. "I'm joking. I do that, remember? My ingratiating face aside, it's the most essential part of my charm."

"Of course." Wingchun sighed. "It's just… It's been a long day."

"It seemed about the same length as yesterday to me… Perhaps even a little shorter than the day before…"

"Seemed twice as long to me, I'm afraid."

"Are you really?"

"I…" She angled a brow. "You're joking again?"

"It's been a long day or so I heard." He stroked his stringy, off-white beard. "But then we live in interesting times…"

"Interesting…?"

"Sounds like just a word, doesn't it?"

"That's what I thought, but…" She gazed up along the ceiling beams, towards the back of the house.

"But?"

"But you're a customer." She finished tying up his order and pushed the eight bowls across the counter. "You're here for the tofu, not for me and my whining…"

"I'm an old hermit, Miss Yim, and on those rare occasions when I do come into town, you can be certain it's for more than just tofu." His arms swirled out, the cord unraveled, and four bowls dropped and hung from each of his hands. "No matter what the size of my order."

"You're too polite..."

"Nonsense, You—" His eyes shot past her and then the smile rolled off his face. "You're right, it's late and I still have so much to do." He inclined his head. "We'll finish this some other time."

The wooden chimes rattled and the double doors closed. Wingchun dropped the iron-bound locking bar into place and turned back towards the kitchen. And then she stopped and her eyes went wide.

"Auntie!"

"Who was that, girl?" Auntie said.

"Who was who? You mean Uncle Lee?"

"Uncle Lee...?" Auntie came around the counter.

"Wait, what are you doing here? When did you get into town? Why didn't—?"

"One at a time, girl."

"Does father know you're here?"

"Of course."

"Then you've seen him? Did... did you see Boklao too? I mean, is he... Is—"

"Your father has done all he can," Auntie said, "applied his every skill."

"And?"

"And what?"

"And how is he?"

"He is *dark*, girl, obscure and uncertain. The mountain rises now above the water and blocks out all light. The Yin injures the Yang, the primordial culminates and the conditioned appears. The original spirit is hidden, essence is disturbed, and life is destabilized. It is like being born ten-thousand times in a single day only to die again just as many... It is a dangerous stagnation but it may yet be helped. He may yet revert to the fundamental and return to the origin."

"Wow," Wingchun said. "All that and to think I still have absolutely no idea how he actually is!"

Auntie shook her head. "The bleeding has stopped but he has a host of internal injuries, some recent, others quite old. He has yet to awaken and that is not likely to change for some time."

"I should probably check on him…"

"You have work of your own to do," Auntie said.

"The cleaning can wait until morning."

"And the grinding, girl, can that wait as well?"

"The grinding…?"

"You still have a shop to run and customers who will arrive tomorrow expecting not only clean bowls but fresh tofu to fill them. The boy needs time to rest, your father needs time to tend to him, and you need to give that time to both of them."

Wingchun puffed, crossed her arms and slumped over the counter. "Fine."

"Really?"

"Sorry?"

"It occurs to me," Auntie said, "that with all your concern for the boy, we have yet to discover how *you* are."

A chill coursed through Wingchun and then a fiery surge. Her fingers stung and her mouth parched. Tears threatened to rain down and laughter to rumble up. She took another breath and fought it all down.

"If you deny your feelings," Auntie said, "if you bury them, they will consume you."

"I'm not denying my feelings, and I'm not… I'm not burying anything. I'm—"

"Fine?"

Wingchun's head dropped into her arms. "Really."

詠 春 傳 說

"You stir…" The voice was a writhing whisper. "What is it you call yourself now… Eagle-Shadow, is it?"

"*Wema…?*"

"Ah, the pain makes you revert to your native tongue…"

Eagle-Shadow groaned. "Who… who are you?"

"Fate."

"I… I don't…"

"You don't believe in fate? And yet here you are in the deepest backwater…"

Eagle-Shadow's eyes blistered open. Beneath robes black as the night emaciated flesh crawled in wrinkled layers over a grossly distended belly, and an eight-trigram medallion glinted with ancient menace.

"Look at you," the old priest said. "Destitute, disgraced, the last re-fuse that would follow you finally laid waste... How could there be fate? How could there be anything but the most profound bitterness of hap-penstance, savage and capricious, punishing the righteous and rewarding only the cowardly and the treacherous? How could there be any connec-tion beyond what you force there to be?" A taloned finger scratched its way down the scar that split Eagle-Shadow's face. "Is that what you have come to believe?"

"Yes..."

A terrible presence rolled over him.

"Then you will believe in me."

4

The Fist & the Heart

Boklao bolted up. Blankets… he was covered in blankets and—pain… He clutched his head. His bandana was gone and thick layers of poultice were in its place. Smoke billowed up from a ceramic censor on the table beside him. Strong and bitter, it cut through him. It was… it was too much…

He needed space. He needed air. He stumbled to his feet, his legs wobbled and the floor spun beneath him. He grabbed onto the window lattice for support.

The sky was blue-black but framed in the half moon was a light, lithe silhouette that rose from the stone-tiled courtyard below like a lily from the water.

The arms lifted, slowly, deliberately.

Boklao tilted his head.

"Ten fingers, one heart…"

They crested and overturned, closed into fists and sank back.

"Ming will overcome…"

They twined up and down, closed and overturned again.

"Through crossed knives of Heaven & Earth, Ming will overcome…"

Boklao's knuckles strained white against the dark lattice.

They twisted out and turned until the fingers pointed up as though in prayer.

His teeth clenched and the memories rumbled up inside him.

Clawed hands stamped down. The hall shook with the force of a monsoon. Boklao peeked around the corner. "What is that?"

The body joined the arms, turned side-to-side as the hands wove back and forth. A leg pierced the night.

Fifth-Son Bil chuckled. "Don't you know, Little Lao?"

The memories swirled around the silhouette but they didn't fit... The movements were too soft, too subtle. Where was the strength of muscle and bone, where was the rending, the tearing?

"Don't you know? Did my father really never tell you?"

Where was the intent?

Bil laughed. "It's the secret fist, the rebel fist—"

The movements below ended but the memories surged.

"—the Fist of the Elders!"

Boklao slipped, the lattice creaked, and the silhouette glanced up, captured in all the light of the moon. He saw grace and beauty, power and passion. His heart stopped. The world stopped. Everything, every other thought, every other desire fell away until only she remained. Only—

"Wingchun..."

Then the floor streaked up at him. Boklao tensed, braced for the blood and darkness that would follow... But he wasn't falling down—he was falling back across the room and into the bed. He had to stop, had to get to her, had to see her again! His hand grabbed onto cloth, a sleeve tore, and beneath it something coiled bright.

"I..." Boklao's strength failed and the room faded. "I saw—"

"Nothing."

"Nothing...?"

"Nothing but a dream."

詠 春 傳 說

Wingchun whisked her hands side-to-side and then sank them back down in front of her. She shifted, scissored them up and down, pushed and pulled each one back and—

"What in Buddha's name are you doing, child?"

"Father...?" She pushed her hair back out of her face. "I came out to fetch another bag of soybeans for the grinder and then... Well, I just started to do the old breathing exercises. You know, the ones you taught me when I was little and the night terrors came..."

"But you are not little anymore and the terrors are no longer confined to the night."

"What does that mean?"

"It means... It means that it is late and you have had a... a long day. You need to rest."

"But the tofu—"

"Will be seen to. Once you are inside—once you are safe—I will see to it. I will see to everything."

She nodded and turned towards the stairs—

Smoke rasped and flame rumbled.

Blood fell like rain.

Her father was at her side. "What is it, child?"

"I was... I was just thinking that with what happened today, well—"

Then something gleamed, bright and cold.

Flame flickered and smoke fled.

"—that maybe I should learn how to fight."

Her father stiffened. "What did you say?"

"That maybe Boklao could teach me."

"Boklao?"

"When he's better, I mean—"

"No."

"But—"

"Fighting fragments and separates, child. It is losing as much as winning. It is against the Tao."

"You're not a fighter, father, not like Boklao. You wouldn't understand..."

"I understand more than you know. I understand that it is the nature of a weapon to turn against its wielder. I understand that if you know how to fight, you will fight, and if you look for trouble, you *will* find it."

"I wasn't looking for trouble today and it found me anyway, didn't it? I wasn't looking to be attacked at the river, and it still happened. If Boklao hadn't been there—"

"Boklao? Enough Boklao! You are my daughter, you will do as I will have you do, and I will *not* have you fight."

"And when it happens again?"

"It will not."

"How can you know that?"

"Because I will not allow it."

She crossed her arms. "Because you won't ever let me out of your sight again?"

Her father crossed his right back. "I *will* protect you."

"You can't, father, not from everything and not forever. I need to be able to take care of myself. If more bandits—"

"Bandits?"

"Yes, if more bandits—"

"You think this is about bandits?" His eyes crinkled east. "There are more terrible dangers in this world than bandits, child. Far more terrible."

詠 春 傳 說

Ngchow, Gateway to the West, Pearl of the Frontier Treasure, trembled. Drums beat and gongs clanged, doors slammed and windows clacked shut, stragglers and drunks fled for deeper shadow.

The Constabulary Army of the Green Standard turned and snapped their spears to attention and, from his balcony above the square, the Mandarin pulled at the damp silk collar of his robes.

Then the gates opened, jazerant flashed in the lantern light, and steel-shod hooves tore up the central road.

Men of the Bordered Yellow Banner, guardians of the Forbidden City itself, entered Kwangsi, and all eyes and terror were upon them—all eyes but the Lama's.

The Lama cared nothing for the pageantry or parade, nothing even for the latest imperial trophy the bannermen flaunted high atop a spear. The only thing he cared about was the *next* trophy—the next Shaolin whose head he would cleave and whose spirit he would condemn down the river of hell. And the Lama's eyes flared west.

詠 春 傳 說

Old Yee raced to the shelves in the far corner of his room, slid aside the statue of Koon Yam, thousand armed Goddess of Mercy, that perched atop them, and took down the box hidden beneath.

His fingers traced through the dust, across the smooth black lacquer, over the glazed semblances of cranes at play in their mountain grotto, until he found just the right spot... He pressed, a seamless lid clicked open, and he was struck by silk, white as mourning, so peaceful, so final... How could he disturb it?

Then coughs racked his body, the silk shifted, and cold steel sliced across his finger.

"The nature of the thing."

Old Yee snapped the lid shut. "I should tie chimes around your neck!"

Auntie arched a brow. "Need chimes now, do you?"

He huffed and reached up to return the box.

She caught his hand, her touch light but inescapable. "You're bleeding..."

"Yet I remain tranquil."

"Like water the instant before it boils."

He pulled away. "Have you spoken to Wingchun?"

"Have you?"

"Of course."

"And?"

"And she is holding up well."

"Is she?"

"She is not weeping, not collapsed in some corner. She faced adversity and she endured. I could ask no more."

"No, I don't suppose you could..."

He hissed. "What is it you would rather hear? That no matter my reasons, my intentions, I sent her out there—that I put her in harm's way? Fine, you've heard it. But that she survived, that she is still standing, still strong, is all I have right now. So please forgive me if I take some small solace in that."

"Take the smallest solace you can, but do not give in to delusion."

"I am most certainly—"

"Your daughter is not 'holding up well' as you so conveniently put it. She does not know and so does not fully comprehend what transpired. She emerged unscathed and so she does not truly appreciate what could have happened."

"I know. I appreciate."

"You walk a dangerous path."

"I walk the center, I walk the mean."

She came up beside him. "And that is enough?"

He glanced back at the hidden box. "For now."

詠 春 傳 說

Boklao floated alone in the dark, faster, farther... Then a voice called out, honeyed and spiced. It called out to him... Called him back...

Firecrackers burst bright, the sparks seared into a single, undying ember, and a face blossomed, graceful and beautiful. Boklao hurtled towards it.

"Morning," he said.

"Afternoon," she said.

Wingchun was draped in teal robes embroidered with birds and flowers, and the shiny black strands of her hair were plaited now. They framed her face, porcelain-pale, and set off her eyes, dark and luminous as jade...

Boklao shook his head. "After—? How long was I out?"

"About a day and a half."

"Whoa..."

"Feels like longer?"

"Feels like a lifetime."

She lowered her gaze and turned away. "Drink tea?"

"No, thank you."

"Please, no need to be polite."

She warmed a ceramic pot and wet it down, drizzled in the straight, taut leaves and drowned them with hot water. Then she discarded the first steeping and poured the second. Steam wafted, the smell fermented...

"Black dragon?" Boklao said.

She nodded, put down the cup, and passed him a round bowl filled with a large square of tofu. "I thought you might be hungry as well."

"Thank you." He took a heaping spoonful and swallowed it down, and then another and another.

"You might want to stop when you hit bowl..."

"Why," he said, "is there meat coming?"

"Sorry, we only ever make tofu and vegetables here."

"Then no promises. This is some of the best I've ever had. Maybe *the* best."

"The secret is in the grinding, at least that's what my father says."

"Must take a whole heard of oxen to grind up something smooth as this..."

She bowed. "At your service."

"What... you?"

"Is that so hard to believe? You just have to know how to stand, how to keep your knees and elbows in."

"Knees and elbows in?"

"So your bones can brace with the ground, borrow its stability and lend it your direction."

"What—?"

The door curtain rustled.

"Feeling better, I see."

Boklao glanced past Wingchun. "Thanks to you... Master Yim?"

"Old Yee, boy. Just Old Yee."

He shuffled into the room, stooped beneath robes gray as slate, his movements slow, almost measured, and Wingchun surrendered her seat immediately.

"You're Bokchao?" Old Yee said.

"Bok*lao*."

Old Yee nodded, checked his eyes and tongue, and then his pulses. "From Fatshan, I take it."

Boklao blinked. "I grew up in Siuhing, but that's very close. You must have passed through the Pearl River Delta?"

"No."

"Really, because—" Boklao reached out to set his bowl down on the table but pain flashed across his face, and the bowl slipped from between his fingers and plummeted towards the hard wooden floor.

Old Yee glanced at it.

Boklao leant in...

But Old Yee's hand didn't so much as twitch and the bowl shattered across the floor...

"Sorry," Boklao said. "My mistake."

"No, the mistake was ours." Old Yee stood and looked at Wingchun. "We should have seen to your health before your stomach. If you will excuse us, we'll correct this oversight."

"I should probably just clean this up first..." Wingchun ducked down and began to sweep the sharp white shards off the dull brown floor.

"Later, child, I—"

"You know," Boklao said, "my ear's not nearly as good as yours, Master Yim, but for a moment there I could have sworn I heard a tinge of Fukien dialect..."

"I've been coming down with a slight cold is all…" Old Yee coughed. "That must be what you think you heard."

Boklao smiled. "Must be."

Old Yee smiled back. Then he plucked a long, fat pill from his pocket and jammed it into Boklao's mouth. "That will help with your internal. I'll be back in a moment to take care of the rest."

Boklao sputtered, grabbed for his tea, and gulped it down. Then he poured another cup and then another…

"Whoa…" He stretched his mouth. "They say the stronger, the more bitter. If that's true, then your father's medicine must be the strongest under heaven."

"I know what you mean," Wingchun said. "When I was eight years old I tried to climb over the back fence and I fell and hit my head on the tiles. My father gave me a pill just like that and sometimes… well, sometimes I still think I can taste it." She crinkled her nose. "Which I guess might have been the point…"

"Bean-grinding, fence-climbing… And to think where I come from all the girls ever did was wait around for the boys to catch them crickets…"

"I only ever got one cricket and that was a long, long time ago." She stood and wiped her hands and then turned back to him. "You… you mentioned Fukien before…"

Boklao nodded.

"Where is that?"

"Along the coast, north of Kwangtung and east of Kiangsi. Why?"

"You think my father sounds like someone from there?"

"From the southern part."

"Wow, you can tell that?"

"Spent some time there. They have their own dialects, Northern and Southern Min. The way your father speaks—the tang of it—is Southern Min."

"You know so much…"

"Just traveled a lot."

"It sounds so romantic, all those different places, all those new and exciting people …"

"Sleeping in the dirt, never seeing the same face twice… Sounds romantic to you?"

"To be out there all on your own with the whole world in front of you?"

"As opposed to being in here with a family and a place to call home?"

"I told you, I don't call this place home."

"Then you don't understand what a home is."

The strong, bitter taste surged up Boklao's throat again. He scrambled for the teapot. She reached for it at the same time and their hands touched.

Then the teapot was shoved aside, a tray filled with medicine and bandages slammed down, and Old Yee was between them.

"Watch the shop," he said to Wingchun. "This will not take long."

"But—"

"Now, child."

Wingchun bowed and went to the door, but her eyes lingered on Boklao until the curtain swayed closed.

Old Yee unwrapped the bandages from Boklao's head. "You seem rested."

Boklao shrugged. "A few strange dreams aside."

"Dreams?"

"Not that I can remember much…"

"Perhaps that is for the best."

Old Yee applied a fresh batch of dark, thick paste.

Boklao's nostril's flared. "Smells like a powder I tried once in Yunnan Province," he said. "Cattail pollen and pseudo-ginseng? Doesn't sting as much though…"

"Fukien to Yunnan," Old Yee said. "One end of the South to the other. That's quite a distance…"

"I'd travel twice that far and back again if I had to."

"Even when you suffer so much along the way?"

"Hasn't it been your experience that nothing of value in life can be obtained without a little suffering?"

"My experience has been that it depends entirely on what exactly you seek to obtain."

"Enlightenment, Master Yim. Only enlightenment."

"Enlightenment is like the sword."

"It has two edges?"

"It demands blood."

"A price I'm willing to pay."

Old Yee huffed. "The delusion of youth."

"Lucky for all of us then, I'm still young."

"I do not doubt your courage, boy. You put yourself between my daughter and those so-called bandits at the river—"

"So-called…?"

"Come now, their manner, their methods—their weapons. They may not have had their banners raised but we both know what they really were."

"You seem to know a great deal…"

"I know the Ch'ing are savage in avenging the deaths of their own."

"They were rogues, they had to be. They won't be missed much less avenged."

"Why? Because you think you hid the bodies better than their comrades will search for them?"

"I'm not unskilled…"

"That is precisely what concerns me." Old Yee sat back. "Your actions, no matter how righteous, could very easily bring the wrath of the Ch'ing down upon you and everyone around you, including my town and my daughter. And that I will not allow."

"Will not allow…?"

"Don't test me, boy. You do not wish to discover just how far I would go to protect her."

Boklao straightened. "Say what you have to say."

"You saved my daughter's life and for that I thank you. Ten thousand times thank you. But now I must ask you to keep that life safe." He leveled Boklao with his gaze. "You are strong and resilient like few I have ever met, strong enough to travel again…"

"Travel? You mean leave… You're asking me to leave?"

"I'm telling you. For my town."

"But—"

"For my daughter."

"I still have some business to attend to here…"

"Not any more." Old Yee trickled coins down onto the table in front of him. "That's three times what you would have made for your salt even this far from the sea, enough to hasten you back to Siuhing, all the way back to Fukien if you so wish it. Make arrangements for tea—for anything that gives you reason to get back on the road—and make them quickly. And while you do, stay away from my shop and from my daughter."

5
Of Lanterns & Light

Wingchun bowed her head and offered up one of their finest bowls, glazed with red meander around knotted green circles that framed the inky black characters of the four seasons.

Mrs. Law scowled. "It will take more than even your father's famous silken pudding to make up for what you did."

"Fried curd?"

"Miss Yim—"

"Preserves?"

"Wingchun!"

"I said I was sorry!"

" 'Right behind.' I believe that is what you said."

"I *was* behind just not so right…"

"If it hadn't been for… what was his name again?"

"Boklao."

"Yes, Boklao… If it hadn't been for him, well, you'd be as gone as our laundry, now wouldn't you?"

"For the ten-thousandth time, I'm—"

" 'Sorry', yes. And what happened to him anyway, this Boklao? Where is he now?"

Wingchun glanced up.

Mrs. Law glanced after her. "Here?"

"I…"

"Oh, how *very* convenient…"

"He was injured and I—I mean, my father, he—"

"Of course, of course…" Mrs. Law looked her up and down. "Nice robes… And look at your hair, plaited so suddenly right and proper… Why, next thing you know, you'll be pinning it back with some nice bodkins and your cheeks will be red as paint."

Wingchun flushed and her hands flew to her face.

"And so they are!"

Mrs. Law laughed, put down the bowl, and bowed her leave. The door closed and the wood chimes rattled in front of Wingchun just as the curtain rustled behind.

"Father…?"

He leant against the round lattice frame, stooped beneath his usual slate-gray robes. No… his but not him…

"Boklao!"

Her father's robes hid the bandages on his body and the bandana, white as cotton, covered the poultice on his head, but pain still lurked deep in his eyes.

"What are you doing up?" she said.

"Trying to remember how to walk…" He eased around the counter, past the long scrolls that hung down between the windows, and the miniature trees that sat on the thin-legged tables beneath. "What's with your cheeks?"

"N-nothing…" She dipped her head and pulled a stool out for him. "Sit. I'll bring you some more tea and we can—"

"Thank you, but no more tea for me, not for a while."

"More tofu then?"

"No, I… I have to get going."

"Going? You can barely make it across the dining room, where do you think you're going?"

"I have something I need to finish."

"Can't it wait?"

"It has," he said, "for far too long already."

"Fine," she said. "Give me a minute and I'll accompany you."

"No need."

"It's polite, you know, to walk a guest at least part of the way home."

"You have customers to attend and, besides, I'm not going all the way home."

"My father will attend to the customers and, good, because I'm not walking you all the way to the Kwangtung border..."

He smiled and their eyes met again, and then the ceiling creaked overhead. He turned back towards the door.

She moved to follow but he stopped her.

"Boklao..."

"Really," he said. "Don't."

She stared at him. "Fine. I... I understand."

"Listen, I—"

"Really," she said. "Don't."

"Wingchun..."

She flicked her sleeves and turned away.

"Go."

詠 春 傳 說

Old Yee stood in the dark and watched through the lattice of his daughter's window until the boy was swallowed by the crowd that wound its way down West Glory Street.

"So?" he said.

"So you no longer require chimes?"

"So what did you find at the river?"

Auntie stepped up beside him. "Bodies, but only two of them. And what's more—Manchu pure."

"Forbidden Bannermen? But what were they doing here, now, in the deepest backwater?"

"A secret only the next life can tell."

"I would give anything if that were so..."

She turned and looked out. "This used to be a place of dragons. They embraced the town in their coils. But then the Ch'ing came and the heavens wept, and by the time the flood receded, the river had changed course, the town had changed name... Everything had changed."

"And now threatens to change again..."

"Has it already begun?"

"Last night she... she asked me about fighting. She wanted that boy to teach her." He huffed. "For protection..."

"And you told her that you would protect her, while even in your heart you knew you couldn't, not forever."

"That's what she said." He closed his eyes. "If only I could be certain!"

"There is no duality," Auntie said. "The past is a lantern that illuminates what will be, the future a light that gives purpose to what was."

"Yet I can no more make one than I can unmake the other. They remain ungraspable."

"You do now because of what was done before and, in so doing, you determine in part what will be done next. You cannot escape the past but you can accept it and then do what you must."

"And you," he said. "What must you do?"

"I cannot remain here," she said.

"No, your presence will only increase the risk."

詠 春 傳 說

Big Kung set the big-mouthed, floppy-eared, horn-topped lion's head, in all its indigo-papered, red- and gold-fringed glory, back onto the altar. "Keep it."

Five-Metal Yang's shaggy face knotted up. "I wouldn't have offered if you, boy," he said, "not if you hadn't earned it."

"If I had the slightest interest in it you wouldn't have to offer, would you? My father would be more than happy to parade the whole town out into the square and present it to me himself, wouldn't he?"

"Master Law knows your potential. We all do."

"My father knows only what he wants to know. But I'm not him, not in face or feat, so don't think you have to kowtow to me like—"

A gong reverberated through the Azure Mountain Hall. It made Big Kung's right eye pucker and his left bulge. He spun around and glared at his second brother, Little Kung, hand flourishing a beater, face the spitting image of their father...

"If you don't want the lion's head," Little Kung said. "I'll take it."

"You'll take yourself back home where you belong," Big Kung said. "hiding behind mother's skirt and crying into your tiny octagonal pillow!"

"Now just hold on," Yang said.

"I'm a martial hero," Little Kung said. "I fight bandits and save families, not hide behind soggy pillows!"

He twirled the beater up to strike the gong again but Big Kung snatched it away. "You do what I tell you to do."

"Hey!" Little Kung said. "That's mine!"

"No, this was grandfather's, and then it was father's, and then it was *mine*. It was only sloughed off on you when it became just another in the long line of things that held no interest for me."

Little Kung glared up at Yang. "Why even offer him the head when he already makes such a perfect ass!"

"Little Kung!" Yang said.

"I was wrong." Big Kung shoved the beater back at his younger brother. "I'm the one who doesn't belong here."

"Big Kung!"

The Azure Mountain Hall's double doors slammed shut behind Big Kung. They cut off the noise and the stench... They cut off the burden.

Big Kung paused atop the wide stairs guarded on either side by massive stone lions, the mother's paw clutched around their cub, the father's, a pearl. "What are you looking at?"

Then he slipped down the steps and disappeared into the crowd.

詠 春 傳 說

Boklao had been wandering for too long. He'd forgotten what it was like—the meander on every stitch of cloth, the key-lock on every edge of stone, the symmetry of the buildings and the huge matching arches of the Market Gates that proclaimed Lanchow itself... Everything in town built with such strict order only to be filled by the chaos of shrimp and fish and chicken and pig and ox and cart and peddler and haggler and beggar... only to be filled by the townsfolk.

He turned off West Glory Street, away from the Jade Garden Teahouse and the Azure Mountain Hall that dominated its south side, and plowed headlong through the market to Central Mountain Main Street and the Five Treasure Guesthouse of its northeast corner.

Inside, the owner cowered mouse-like behind a desk strewn with countless statues of gods and godlings. Another man, shrouded beneath strangely mottled robes and a wide-brimmed, coarsely woven hat, stalked him like an alley cat, his voice gratingly familiar—

"—Cover what you owe, Tsui. Not by half."

"P-please, Kwai," the owner, Tsui said. "Give me one more day, just one. My luck will change, you'll see. Tell Panther-King—"

Boklao stepped up between them. "I need a room."

"Busy just now," the other, Kwai said. "Come back never."

"Anything you have," Boklao said to the owner. "I don't care."

"Can't you take a threat, boy?"

Boklao scoffed. "What threat, vagabond?"

Kwai looked up and his eyes flashed. Then he lunged.

Boklao wheeled around and blocked.

Their clawed hands crossed.

Tsui stiffened. "Not here!"

Kwai hesitated and Boklao grabbed him by the arm and tossed him back across the entryway towards the door. He rolled and came up in a crouch, and something sharp and metallic shimmered between his fingers.

"No!" Tsui dove beneath his desk. "Not in town, Kwai! You know what Master—" He glanced at Boklao. "You know what *he'll* do when he finds out!"

Kwai growled, the sharp metal disappeared, and he stood and straightened. "I'll be back tomorrow for the rest of the coin, Tsui." His eyes locked on Boklao. "And the moment you set so much as one foot outside of town, boy, I'll be back for you as well..."

"Can't wait..." Boklao stayed on Tsui. "My room?"

"W-what room?" Tsui fussed with his statues. "Autumn Moon is less than a week away, all of our rooms have been closed for over a month!"

"Un-close one."

"Listen, I d-don't want any more trouble..."

"No..." Boklao let coin after coin clink down onto the desk. "Just this, right?"

Tsui scurried through the arrangements and then called for the Little Misses to escort Boklao upstairs.

They were young and lush and reeked of flowers.

"Fragrant bath, mister, to wash the road from your back? Oiled massage to rub the weariness from your bones? Pleasant company to help pass the night?"

Boklao handed them more coins. "Clothes, dark as you can find... And two sashes."

One door closed but could another open? He paced back and forth. He had to be careful now, he couldn't just go up and knock and beg to

tell his tale and hope it was finally to the right person and the right end...
No, he had to think...

The age fit and the tributes, both subtle and profound... What he'd heard and more—what he'd seen! If he'd really seen it, if it hadn't been just some dream, some delusion...

Boklao cursed.

Even if it was the right person there was no way of knowing the end. What if he was lied to? What if he was lied to just to buy time for another flight, another escape? Boklao couldn't take that chance...

The Little Misses returned with cotton indigo as the night. Boklao slipped on the jacket and pants, tied one sash around his waist, and then wrapped the other over his head and across his face until it shrouded everything. Everything but his eyes.

May his ancestors forgive him, it was the only way. The only way to know for sure.

詠 春 傳 説

The Yim Family Tofu Shop was hot and loud, full with the chatter and clatter of customers, their mouths open and their hands thrust out.

Wingchun circled the square tables, cleared with one hand, served with the other, and kicked aside the endless stream of litter with both feet.

She set fresh bowls down in front of Lai Bang and Chao Jeet and then crossed over to Boy Ngao.

"Sorry," she said. "That was the last of the preserves. We're all out."

"Did you check in back? Maybe the new batch is ready?"

"And if it is, that just means you'll have less tomorrow..."

"I know, I know, but... Please?"

Wingchun nodded, picked up his empty bowl, and nudged her way through the curtain and into the kitchen.

Her father stooped there beside the stove, his head hung and his mouth buried in a rag. She rushed to his side. "Father, are you—?"

"Fine." He fumbled for his teacup. "I'm fine."

She picked up the pot and poured for him. "No you're not, not at all."

"I'm fine if I say so, if I believe so. I'm fine, like you. Both of us—fine."

"Are we? I thought so before but now I... I don't know... I never realized how completely the world could change. How it could sweep you up from muted despair into blinding hope only to dump you back down every bit as quick—"

"Stop, child..."

"— worse, leave you dangling between the two, knowing what you never—"

"Stop!"

He slammed his hand down. The teapot leapt and a stack of trays clattered to the ground. "You... you must stop, child," he said. "If you do not learn to control your feelings they will come to control you. They will consume you."

"Auntie said that it's when you deny your feelings, when you bury them, that they consume you."

"Yes, well, she has many opinions..."

"What's that supposed to mean?"

"It means—"

The curtain rustled. "Any luck back there? Any more preserves?"

"Curse that butcher and his progeny," her father hissed. "A shop stunk full of meat, yet his son has a stomach bottomless for tofu!" He plucked a jar off the top shelf and handed it to Wingchun. "Give him these."

Dark brown wedges jostled in yellow-green brine.

"Ah... don't you think these are just a little rancid looking?" she said.

"I think, perhaps, just enough to wean him for a night..."

"Father...!"

"Go on," he said. "And when you're done and the shop is locked, come find me in the courtyard."

"The courtyard? What are you going to be doing out there?"

"What I have to..."

"Sorry?"

"The old exercises, child," he said. "It's long past time you had a review."

6

The Lesson

Big Kung crossed beneath the arch of the North Market Gate to the southwest corner of Central Mountain Main Street where familiar brown brick and green shingle sat aglow in the last rays of the setting sun. The carved and painted Dragon & Phoenix Poles that flanked the double doors seemed to come alive in the twilight, when the bright gilded, dark nielloed sign above most proudly proclaimed the name of the Vast Beneficence Apothecary Shop—of Big Kung's home.

"Mrs. Pang's treatment went well this morning," he said the moment he passed through the door, "but I'm still scarring too much with the moxibustion." He rolled up his sleeves and reached for the mugwart. "I need more practice."

Piebald Chan brushed grassy black characters down a smooth, white-flecked scroll. "You already have the lightest touch I've ever felt, Big Kung." he said. "Lighter even than your grandfather if that's at all possible..."

"I can do better. I would be doing better if I didn't have to waste half my day prancing around the Ancestral Hall like a—"

"Dutiful first son who respects the tradition of more than three generations of his family? The *complete* tradition?" Chan's upside-down egg of a face soured. "Damn Kwaichow paper is sucking the very spirit out of my work... I'm going to fetch something in a vermillion, I think, and when I return back, we'll see to your moxibustion, yes?"

"Yes..."

"Good."

Chan plunked his long, thin brush back onto its short, squat inkpot and shuffled off into the storeroom.

Big Kung shook his head. Then he tensed his arm, lit the small cone of mugwart, and breathed out as it began to smoke and sizzle. When it was done, he looked down and sighed. "Maybe next time I should try removing it just before it finishes—"

A tightly wrapped bundle of cloth thudded onto the counter.

"—burning."

"You the apothecary?"

"I didn't hear you come in." Big Kung stared at the bundle. "What's this?"

"What you sent word all the way to Yunnan for—wild ginseng."

"Wild—?" Big Kung looked up. The man wore tattered black and his face was lost beneath a hood... Lost but for a jagged scar that glistened in the lamplight. "You managed to hunt down wild ginseng this quickly?"

"The least of my skill."

Big Kung opened the package. "The quality is exceptional... My father will insist on checking for himself, of course, but he's otherwise occupied right now. If you come back in the morning—"

The man snatched the bundle back. "My mistake, I thought this was urgent..."

"It is, it is!" Big Kung leapt up. "I'll get you your coin and then I'll take the medicine right over. There's no reason to keep the old tofu-maker waiting."

The man's scar twisted. "Tofu-maker, you say...?"

詠 春 傳 說

Night changed everything. It caused streets and alleys to shift, and landmarks to disappear as if they were no longer required to provide direction. But as much as it obscured, the darkness also made clear, like the stars hidden behind the light of day...

Boklao crossed back from North Gate to South, passed East Glory to West, circled around to Red Fortune Alley, and stopped. There it was at the end, walls dark but windows bright—the Yim Family Tofu Shop.

The wooden doors were barred and the stone fence high, but not as high as the tree in the corner...

Two steps and Boklao was on a barrel, off a stack of crates, and up into the gnarled branches.

The courtyard inside was washed silver-blue, silent but for a thousand muted sounds, and empty but for the old man who stood beneath the shadows of the balcony...

Boklao flexed his frame, clawed his hand open and closed, and made ready to jump down, to cast his coin and embrace his fate.

But then his nostrils flared and he paused.

She was there...

詠 春 傳 說

Crickets chirped. A dog barked. Something shifted in the back alleys. Wingchun took a breath, and then another and another. "Father...?"

His head hung and his eyes were closed.

"Father, are we still going to do this?"

He nodded and pointed her to the center of the courtyard. "Begin."

She brought her feet together and her arms slowly up.

"Chin down," he said. "Relax."

She rotated her toes out, and then her heels, until her feet were angled in at shoulders' width. Then she sunk down, back straight, until her knees were a fist apart.

"Do not force the Yang Clamping Posture, settle into it."

"I am. I was just wishing I had a goat to—" She chopped her hand down. "—you know..."

"I know that amused you when you were... what—eight, child? But you are older now, old enough to understand that Yin & Yang are the core alchemy of the Tao. They form the great extremes of male and female, up and down, dark and bright, of everything in nature. We open the legs but keep them adducted—"

"Yes, father."

"—because the Yin line is broken in two parts, disconnected. The Yang line, however, is one. Like Yang, you align your meridians to connect your body—to make it whole."

She rolled her eyes. "Yes, father…"

"I've told you this before?"

"Only about a hundred times since I was… what—eight?"

He circled behind her. "Then you know it?"

"I—"

He placed a foot on the inside of her knee and stepped up to stand with his full weight on her calf.

"—do!"

He switched to her other leg. "Knowledge comes in degree."

She gulped.

He stepped down.

"You used to watch me, to mimic me," he said. "That gave you the external, the skin and bones. The internal, the marrow, you must cultivate on your own."

"How do I do that?"

"Keep quiet for starters and let your mind become tranquil. Then look forward and extend your left hand until your Yin palm is shoulder height—"

詠 春 傳 說

Boklao watched her body twist and turn, flow—

"Like a snake coiling through the bamboo…"

It hadn't been a dream or a delusion, but it wasn't real either. The way she moved… he couldn't reconcile it, not with his memories or experiences, not with anything. It just didn't fit. It didn't make any sense.

The meridians, the essential channels of the body that Old Yee spoke of, were useful enough for medicine but what good were they for fighting? And what good were those narrow, awkward postures and short, constricted bridge-arms? What good was any of it!

Where were the classic steps, the deep, square postures and the long, bold bridges? And where was the intent, the lethality?

Could Old Yee have seen him spying and somehow changed everything, somehow made up a crippled shell to hide the true seeds and instantly gotten Wingchun to go along with it?

Boklao shook his head. That was ridiculous, the stuff of old folk stories. There had to be something more, something he was missing… But what?

He stayed hidden up in the gnarled branches until Old Yee called an end to the training and ushered Wingchun back inside. He stayed until the last lantern flickered out and the shop settled fully into the night, and only then did he slip back down into the alley below.

"I came for answers and leave only with more questions!"

Mouths tell ten-thousand tales but the fist comes straight from the heart… People can hide many things but they can't hide the way they move… But he never saw Old Yee move, only Wingchun, and her movement told him nothing at all!

Boklao growled. "I'll come back tomorrow night, see if they're training again, see her. I'll… I'll come back every night…" He looked up at the dark outline of the shop. "And if I have to, I'll force Old Yee to move. I'll force his fists to pound into me every single answer I seek!"

詠 春 傳 說

Old Yee sipped the wild ginseng tea, the strongest, bitterest liquid he'd ever known, and gazed down at his daughter.

She tossed and turned behind the gossamer veil of her bed, asleep but not at peace. Never at peace…

"I cannot accept the past," he whispered, "any more than I can escape it. All I can do now is pray…"

He turned back to the window. West Gate Street was empty, the crowds gone and chaos paused. Yet something stirred in the shadows…

A chill shot through him and bit down to the bone.

He looked up to the heavens. The Strider was obscured by the first clouds of the season, but a new constellation had risen—the three stars of the Swallow of the Moon, the Crouching Man—

"The Danger."

詠 春 傳 說

Eagle-Shadow shrank deeper into the alley. His finger scratched down his hook-shaped scar but his eyes remained locked on the window above the tofu shop and the old man betrayed within.

"Perpetual but not eternal…"

詠 春 傳 說

Days flared only to burn back into night, and the moon turned gibbous only for its glare to cost Boklao the details of her movement.

She remained always in the center of the courtyard facing her father at its edge, but the embroidered robes were gone again and her hair was tucked back once more beneath a plain beige scarf.

"Trace the great-ultimate circle with all five fingers," Old Yee said. "Good. Now, Snake Parts the Water—the Dispersing Arm..."

Was her hand moving along her side? Boklao bit off a curse, clenched the gnarled branch, and slid just a little farther out...

"Extend," Old Yee said. "Twist more... More... Take your time with it, with the precision of its measure and the path of its movement—it is the essence."

She paused. "The essence?"

"One dispersing arm to..."

"To...? To what?"

"It's getting late, child, and I digress."

"Father...?"

"Continue. Turn your wrist and point your fingers up toward the heavens. Transform into the center, half-Yin, half-Yang. The power must balance both ways, retract slowly but keep the intent forward... No, no need to rush. Speed is an illusion."

"And that means...?"

"What use is speed if you miss the doorway and smash into the wall? Concentrate on precision and path. The fastest way is the shortest way and the shortest way is the straight line."

"To where?"

"Sorry?"

"The shortest way to where? Where exactly am I going?"

"Right now, to the second section."

"But—"

"In the first you found your center and learned to keep your alignment as you contracted and expanded. In the second you must learn to maintain that center and alignment as you move and—"

Old Yee stopped and spun around, and his eyes gleamed.

Boklao stiffened. His breath caught but his pulse raced. He'd spent the last week spying on them but now was he the one revealed?

Foulness spread from the pit of his stomach to coat the back of his throat. Cowardly, dishonorable... unworthy of a brave man and true! He should be ashamed but there was no time for that now. He swallowed and savored the bitterness, and set himself for what was to come...

But then Old Yee turned back. "The white clouds have become gray as dogs..." He hurried Wingchun inside. "We are done for the night."

"Close..." Blood trickled from where Boklao's nails had clawed deep into the branch. "Too damn close. What—?"

Then he felt it, a terrible presence rolling out from the bamboo...

詠 春 傳 說

Mist curdled up from the river. A leopard turned from its kill, sniffed the night air, and ran. A hawk shrieked, surrendered its prey, and took off for the mountains. A greater predator had taken hunt.

The old priest undulated through the bamboo, his shroud cast aside and his essential nature laid bare in the full obscenity of its power.

Then the wind changed, strummed as though by endless wings.

The old priest paused and a spirit with ancient grace alighted in his path.

Trackless, traceless, they circled until the old priest's talons fisted and his white eyebrows flattened. Then he fled and, with a brief glance back at the town, the nun took chase.

詠 春 傳 說

The Lama's bone robes billowed, his burning eyes flared, and his falchion cleft down atop the tattered swirl of black.

Eagle-Shadow felt the weight of it come to rest against his neck but he remained crashed down on one knee, his hand slapped against the ground in Manchu salute.

"Master..."

"No longer," the Lama said. "You have broken your banishment, severed the last slender thread that held you in this life."

"Master, I've found him."

"Him?"

Eagle-Shadow glanced up and the scar twisted across his face. *"Him."*

"It's been years..."

"Almost fourteen. I know, master."

The falchion bit down but Eagle-Shadow didn't flinch.

"I saw him, I saw his eyes. They haven't changed, master, not in fourteen years. They would not change in forty!"

"And he did not see you? He did not see you see him, and is not now fleeing even further into the putrid south?"

"He did not see me, master. I stake what's left of my life on it."

"No." The Lama turned, his bone robes fell closed, and he stalked off towards the stables. "What you stake now is the next."

詠 春 傳 說

The moon rounded full and Wingchun's silhouette thinned against its silver glare.

"The third section," Old Yee said. "You have found your center and your alignment, you have moved and turned them, now you must remove and return them."

Her elbow... was it coming up or sinking down?

Boklao bit off another curse.

"Focus," Old Yee said. "Your intent is vital. It must move your breath and cultivate your spirit. It must allow you to flow like the river, bound to the earth yet open to the heavens."

One of her hands darted to the side... or was it both?

"Twin Snakes Pierce the Bamboo. They must be flexible, feel and adapt..."

"Feel?" She stopped. "I don't understand half of what you're saying, father, do you realize that? I'm trying to, I really am, but feel what? I'm doing this all by myself, so tell me just what exactly I'm supposed to feel?"

"Start with what comes. That is the key."

The key? Boklao clenched the gnarled branch and slid out just a little farther...

"What comes?" Wingchun said.

"Yes, you must receive what comes and..."

"And...? And nothing, right?"

Old Yee huffed. "Focus, child. No more interruptions."

"I'm only interrupting you because you keep interrupting yourself! How can I focus through that?"

"You must. These exercises are important."

"So important that we just suddenly stopped doing them after a few years?"

"After what happened in Lankiang village…"

"What happened in Lankiang village? And what happened two weeks ago to make us start again? Is… is this my punishment for asking about fighting? Are you trying to breathing-exercise me into a stupor?"

"Punishment? Buddha's name, child…"

"Then what?"

"Things change."

"I know, I'm one of them! These exercises, they're… they're building something inside me. *That* I can feel. I just don't know what that something is."

"Nonsense!"

"It's not nonsense, father, and you know it. You know so much but tell me so little. My whole life it's been that way. I know who I am but nothing else, not where I come from, not what I'm doing here, nothing!"

"None of that matters."

"It matters to me!"

"You don't understand…"

"How can I when you never explain? Receive what comes and…?"

Boklao clenched tightly with both hands and leant out far as he could.

"And—"

And the branch cracked.

詠 春 傳 說

Wingchun's head snapped up. The old tree in the corner shook, a large branch came crashing down, and a stranger, indigo as the night, came crashing with it.

"Spy! Thief!" Her father sprang at the stranger, grabbed him by the collar, and yanked him around.

The same dark cloth concealed the stranger's face, concealed everything but his eyes, narrow and turbulent…

"You came for a lesson?" her father said. "Here it is!"

The stranger seized her father by the wrists, flared his elbows, and tried to wrench himself free.

"Your power is rigid." Her father's arm twisted and the stranger tumbled back. "True power is wrapped in softness."

Her father folded both arms behind his back and paced at the edge of the courtyard.

The stranger punched the ground and then shot at him again, feinted left, angled right, and kicked straight up between her father's legs.

"Your movement is obvious." Her father's waist turned, and the stranger flipped up and over and thudded back down in the middle of the tiles. "True movement is cloaked in stillness."

Her father turned away.

The stranger growled and kipped back up, his hands clawed open, and he lashed out at her father's head.

"Your intent is scattered." Her father smiled, and the stranger twirled across the heavens and smashed into the stone fence. "True intent cleaves the center."

The stranger's breath wheezed thin and ragged.

"There's your lesson, boy." Her father reached down and took hold of the indigo sash that concealed the stranger's face. "Now we end this—"

"NO!"

The stranger roared and exploded up.

Her father hissed. "Iron Tiger Cracks the Mountain!"

Then his body flowed, twisted and turned right through the attack.

The stranger flew across the courtyard, bounced off the balcony rail, tumbled down the back steps, and collapsed at Wingchun's feet.

She looked to her father. He opened his hand and shreds of indigo fell from his fingers. Then she looked back at the stranger, the shadows slipped from his face, and her heart plummeted.

"Boklao…"

He stared back at her, his voice silent but his eyes screaming.

"What are you doing?" she said. "Sneaking in the trees like some kind of forest demon? If you wanted to talk to me—"

"Go inside," her father said to her. "Now."

"What, why?"

"No, no more 'why'. No more argument. You are *my* daughter—"

"Yes," Boklao said. "Daughter of Fong Dak."

Her father stopped dead.

"Who's Fong Dak?" Wingchun said.

"A ghost," her father said. "A myth."

"A hero," Boklao said. "A legend."

Her father grabbed her and pulled her up the stairs and through the kitchen.

"You're hurting me!"

"I'm protecting you!"

"Father, he called you a hero!"

He pulled her all the way into the dining room and then he stopped. "What some call heroes are simply those with the luck—good or ill—to survive that which destroys everything else around them. And those made wise by such fate do not tempt it further. They let it go."

"They don't." Boklao stumbled after them. "They can't. Not me, not you. Not completely."

"You don't know what you're talking about."

"I know you taught your daughter the boxing. You slowed it down, hid its true purpose, but she still has the movements inside her. And the name—you traveled more than half-way across the south and it still leaves your lips every day."

"What boxing," Wingchun said to her father. "What name?"

"Don't," her father said to Boklao.

"Your name," Boklao said to her. "The name of the daughter of Fong Dak, hero of Fukien Province and legend of Wingchun County."

"Father...?"

"Child..."

"I'm not a child anymore! I see the pain in your eyes, father, but I'm sorry, I'm not changing the subject, not again, and I'm not burying the questions, not anymore. You're my father and I know it's your duty to raise me as you see fit and mine only to listen and obey. I know all of that but that's all I know. Nothing about you, about our family. Nothing at all about where I come from!"

"What you seek is what I have spent your whole life protecting you from..."

"But you can't protect me, father, not from this. Don't you understand? I need to know."

"You need? You...." Her father stared at them both and shook his head. "You have no idea, not either of you, but you will... you will. Listen and I will tell you..."

7
Small Enlightenment

The fruit had turned sickly, the incense to ash, and the statue of General Kwan was lost now in the deepened shadows. Wingchun's father stood away from her, hunched before the dining room windows, the heavens dark beyond.

"I was born Fong Dak," he said, "in a coastal village just outside Wansiu. The Ch'ing hoards had butchered their way south decades before and we'd long since been under their control.

"My father came from a proud line of Ming Dynasty officers. He tried to rise up in the name of restoration but instead he died for it.

"Those who live in the margins, who travel by the rivers and the lakes, took me in."

Boklao limped around the counter. "Heaven & Earth Society..."

"Heaven & Earth was later, boy," her father said. "The Societies back then were forged from the internecine feuds that had so long plagued our people. They drew on farmers' cooperatives, money-pooling unions, bandit groups, and only a very few took up the cause of anti- Ch'ing rebellion. The Iron Rulers I belonged to, well, they took up no more cause than their own survival."

He coughed and, when he pulled his hand away, dark red flecks glistened in the lamp-light.

"Father...?"

"I'm fine."

"Master Fong..."

He glared at Boklao. "Fong is dead, a ghost as I told you and as you shall hear soon enough."

Wingchun went to the kettle. "Take some tea at least?"

"Not that one." Her father pointed back through the curtain. "My old pot, the one in the kitchen. It's a... a special blend."

She retuned with it quickly, the liquid black and the steam almost caustic.

"Whoa..." Boklao's nostrils flared. "Is that... wild ginseng?"

Her father glared again, took a sip, and continued. "We stuck together, the Iron Rulers, to protect ourselves from those who were stronger and to prey on those who were weaker. We fought, first for fun, soon enough for coin...

"Eventually we graduated to the real thing—the traditional raised platform. My first match boasted an ample purse and buoyed by my victories in countless back alley brawls, I bet everything I had on it. I thought my opponent would be one of those itinerant boxers who made his living taking challenges from town to town..." He shook his head. "How young I was, how stupid...

"My opponent was the lieutenant of the local detachment of the Constabulary Army of the Green Standard. He'd heard about the fights and had chosen that night to prove his superiority over the local men.

"He probably would have beaten me anyway, not that it mattered. Win or lose, it meant my death..."

Boklao leant in. "What did you do?"

Her father shrugged. "I ran. I dove off the platform, grabbed the purse, and took off into the woods as fast as my legs would carry me. Either way, my life in the village was over, and so if I had to start anew, better to do it with coins in my pocket.

"They chased me, of course. I heard the lieutenant screaming for his men. I kept going. My friends shouted and ran off in different directions. They hoped to draw some of the constables off, but there were too many...

Their footsteps grew louder. I darted from path to path. Then, after a particularly sharp bend…"

Wingchun's eyes widened. "They caught you?"

"Someone did. Someone caught me and dragged me through the woods, faster and farther than I could imagine, and then just as suddenly stopped and dumped me off into a clearing.

"I was sure whoever it was would kill me right then and there but, when I looked up, instead of a constable I saw a man cowled beneath shiny black robes split open on both sides, a long string of beads dangling from his left hand.

"I scrambled to my feet, the purse clutched tight to my heart. 'Who are you?'

"He offered no reply. He simply stood, his fingers tolling the beads. I lunged at him, swung my fist hard as I could. But I hit nothing and once more my face met the dirt.

" 'What do you want?'

"Again there was no reply, so again I lunged, and again I fell.

" 'Say something!'

"He lifted a purse—the purse I'd stolen—and scattered the coins to the wind.

" 'That was my future!' I yelled and lunged a final time.

"His arm barely grazed mine but its subtle turning swallowed every ounce of my force. I stumbled forward and his other hand spat out.

"At first I thought he would spear right through me—he seemed perfectly capable of doing so—but then, just as I was certain I was at my end, his hand folded and his palm stamped into me. I felt myself lifted up and hurled back, my flight arrested only by a tree over a dozen feet distant."

Boklao huffed. "Know that feeling…"

"I dragged myself up," her father said, "my arm was numb where he'd touched it and my chest felt as though it was on fire. I tried to move, tried to make a fist, tried to draw a full breath. I failed. My legs buckled and I crumpled to my knees.

"He stood in front of me for what seemed an eternity, not a word, just the toll of those damn beads.

"I continued to struggle, to fight, to resist, until I could struggle no more. I… I gave up. And only then did he approach.

"He placed one hand on my head and the other on my belly. Lightning surged through my marrow and thunder shook my organs, and when it passed I could breathe again, I could stand…

" 'I would have for you a different future,' he said, his voice both hiss and snarl.

"And then he was gone.

"I stayed there, on that very spot, spent in both mind and body. I did not rest, however, could not sleep. Yet the next thing I knew the sun was rising before me and he with it.

"His hood was down and I saw his head was unshaven and his hair unbound. Long and full, it was piled atop a face old yet vibrant, set with eyes piercing and profound...

"He appeared still at first but then I noticed one of his arms was moving forward. It was slow like the rising of the tides, imperceptible yet undeniable. He brought it back and then extended the other. I watched him until the sun sank again and he stopped and turned to me.

" 'What did you learn?', he said.

" 'I... I'm not certain.'

" 'Then perhaps doing will succeed where watching has failed.'

"I tried to mimic what I'd seen but I had no way of knowing... I looked to him for assurance but he was gone. So I kept at it through the night and into the next morning. I stopped only when I had to, slept briefly, foraged for what food I could, and then tried some more. It was days before he returned again.

" 'Bend your knees but keep you spine straight,' he said. 'Sink through your outer leg and float through your inner. Let your body find its tranquility and your breath return to its source.'

" 'Yes, master.'

" 'I am not your master, Fong Dak. Not yet.'

"It continued like that, for how long I'm not certain. He would appear and give me corrections—sink more, twist more, relax more. Always relax more. Then he would disappear again for weeks at a time. The seasons changed around me and changed again. And I changed as well. Physically, I grew stronger. My skin tightened and my muscles thickened. My bones felt dense and the marrow within them charged. My breath became deep and smooth and it sunk down to the very center of my being. I grew calm yet alert. Each repetition became easier than the one before, each movement better than the last.

"One day, perhaps as much as a year later, I felt his presence again. Without looking, I knew he was behind me. I continued through the movements, I wanted him to see, to be as proud of me as I was of myself. When I was done, I turned and basked in anticipation...

" 'What did you learn?' he said.

" 'I… ' I fumbled to answer the most obvious question I'd completely failed to expect. 'I have learned to be one," I said. "I have learned to connect my whole body, my shoulders and hips, my elbows and knees, my hands and feet. When I move it is like the river and when I stand it is as the sea.'

" 'And?'

"I was crushed. I'd expected some measure of acknowledgement for all I had achieved and I was sure my face betrayed that.

" 'You have realized yourself, Fong Dak, but have you realized nothing beyond that?

" 'Beyond myself?'

" 'What of the ground, what of the earth beneath your feet?'

"It hit me like a physical blow.

" 'I'm connected to the earth as well… I'm… I'm braced by it!'

" 'Your weight sinks through the bubbling-spring point," he said, "and the earth returns it to you in support.'

" 'I have substance…'

" 'And?'

"I stared at him, helplessness welled in my eyes.

" 'What of the sky, of the heavens above?'

" 'I'm connected to them as well?'

" 'If it remains a question then you need more doing.'

" 'But I've been doing for so long already. Look.' I pointed to where my months of training had worn the ground bare. 'See?'

"He shook his head. 'It is you who looks without seeing. Was the ground like that when you began?'

" 'No…'

" 'Yet I trained in this same spot for years.'

" 'Impossible!'

"He said nothing.

"I sighed. 'More doing…'

"The seasons changed again but this time I felt no improvement. My failure frustrated me and that in turn led to even greater failure. Each repetition became more difficult than the last, each movement harder than the one before. I despaired. Then, one day, my frustration reached its peak. I could take no more, not a another second. I cried out. And of course, that is exactly when it happened…"

Her father stopped and took a long, slow sip of tea.

"What happened?" Boklao said.

He turned the cup in his hand.

"Father," Wingchun said. "What happened?"

"I let go… My mind flew while my body moved on. I learned to use my intent to move my breath and release my spirit. I felt weightless yet filled with joy. A heat manifested in my limbs and then settled down to my center. I was truly one—with myself, with the world, and with the beyond. I awakened. I *became*.

"He returned later that day.

" 'I understand,' I told him.

" 'You understand little, only the first training…'

" 'First?'

" 'If you are strong enough, my disciple, there will be more.'

"I fell to my knees and knocked my head to the ground.

" 'I am strong enough, master.'

" 'We will see.' He turned to go but this time—'Follow…'

"He was taking you there, wasn't he?" Boklao said. "Taking you to the temple…"

Wingchun angled a brow. "Temple?"

Her father took a final sip of tea and then set his cup down. "Yes."

"What temple?"

"*The* temple," Boklao said. "Shaolin…"

8
The Shaolin Temple

"Shaolin," Wingchun's father said. "That is what some called it later—Southern Shaolin in the legends that followed—but it was not the seat of Damo proper, high atop the Song Mountains of far off Honan Province. Back then, to us, it was simply the Nine Little Lotus Temple, and I have never before nor have I ever since beheld anything to compare..."

"What was it like?" Boklao said.

"I... I cannot describe it. I lack the words... or perhaps it is the words themselves that lack... First was the climb, step after step, thousands on end, and when at last I laid eyes upon it, it seemed formed from the mountain peak itself.

"We passed through the ancient gates and into the courtyard. Monks were there of every age, from initiates who were no more than children to masters who looked every bit as old as the temple. Some of them trained boxing, stamped out their sets in perfect harmony atop stone worn the deep of generations, the others meditated nearby, their bodies contorted into a variety of arduous postures.

"Beyond them were the main halls of the temple, gleaming white walls beneath bright red shingles. Paths connected them, dotted with pagodas and small, covered bridges. I was led to the main hall, and—"

"And you became a monk!" Wingchun said. "I can't believe it, my father was—!"

"Too old..."

Her nose crinkled. "What?"

"At least that's what they said. I was too old to begin the eighteen years of study and training that a monk's life demanded."

"Eighteen years...?" Boklao said.

"Boxing, weapons, and internal work, along with constant spiritual study. You can't imagine the patience, can you? Well neither could I, not then. I'd already wasted more of my life than that..."

"But if you couldn't be a monk," Wingchun said, "why did your master even bring you there?"

"I could still be his disciple and an unshaven disciple of the temple."

"Unshaven?"

"When a novice takes his first vows, his head is shaved to symbolize his new life. Mine was not."

"I've heard of that," Boklao said. "Of the unshaven..."

"Later, in the dark days, it became far more common. Back then it was all but unheard of. But it was my master's will, and few there were would even attempt to hinder the will of Miu Sun."

"Master of the Snake Shape Fist," Boklao said.

Her father bowed his head. "And abbot of the Green Snake Temple that was lost during dynastic succession, though I knew none of that at the time. All I knew was that my life became very simple—

"I arose each day before dawn to train the Tendon Change Classic and the Warrior Attendant Fist, the breathing and fighting systems passed down from Damo himself. A breakfast of rice followed, eaten in the same arduous postures I'd seen upon my arrival. After morning study—supervised by seniors with lashes ever-eager to compel our absolute attention—we trained the Three Star Arms and other two-man sets. We also strove to develop the Iron Sand Palm and the Golden Bell Cover that allowed an adept to both deliver and absorb devastating amounts of force. Then came more study and dinner, same as breakfast.

"We trained weapons as well, pole first and foremost, but later anything that lacked a blade."

"No blades?" Wingchun said. "What difference does a blade make?"

"All the difference in the world to a temple of the Chan School that does not eat meat, does not drink wine, and does everything possible not to kill.

"Poles can kill as well as any blade," Boklao said.

"But they do not have to," her father said. "Blades are life-taking weapons, that is their only purpose, and all life is sacred. These and other virtues were drilled into us until we were beyond exhausted, until the day would end and the disciples were permitted a few hours of rest. All of them but me...

"My master, it seemed, had specialties of his own still to teach me—the Twelve Postures descended from the Golden Summit of Szechwan's O-Mei Mountains and the Snake Shape Fist of Shaolin for which he'd developed a particular affinity.

"It was more work than I could ever have imagined but I persevered. I wanted to prove to them that I could finish their training, that my master's faith in me had not been misplaced. And in the end I did. I have no idea how long it took—a decade, perhaps two, and I am certain I missed many of the details, martial and especially religious—but one day my master told me I was ready for the test."

He turned to Wingchun. "To graduate, you see, a novice had to pass a test, one of spirit as much as reason and skill. The knowledge and power of the temple was considered far too dangerous to entrust to anyone but the most righteous. Better a hundred should die, they felt, than a single apostate be allowed out into the world.

"There was a special place—the Hall of the Wooden Man—lined with one-hundred-and-eight traps. If the novice survived them all he came at last to a cauldron filled with burning embers.

"In homage of the true Shaolin, it stood waist high to a man and blocked the exit completely. If he would leave, as a show of faith and strength, of discipline and mastery, the novice had to wrap his arms around it, move it from his path, and return it to its proper dais. And as he did, the patterns raised on either side were branded onto his forearms..."

Her father unbuttoned his cuffs and the sleeves of his slate-gray robes fell open.

Wingchun gasped.

And the dragon and tiger coiled and snarled bright across his arms.

"How could I never have seen," she said, "not in all these years...?"

"Because he hid them," Boklao said. "Because they became marks of death."

"Yes," her father said. "Though I did not know it at the time, something was happening at the temple—at all the temples. We began to get more visitors and to accept more unshaven disciples until their numbers surpassed those of the true monks. There was great hardship in the land and rumors of Ch'ing brutality abounded. I assumed that had much to do with it but it was not my place to ask.

"Then one day our abbot, Chi Sim, called my master to the center of the temple—to the Wingchun Hall—"

"Wingchun..." she said.

"Like you," Boklao said.

"Other elders joined them," her father continued, "monks and priests... even a nun. They gathered in the hall and did not emerge again for a day and a night.

"My master sent for me immediately—

" 'Shaolin,' he said, 'the temple of Damo itself, has been destroyed.'

" 'No...' I couldn't imagine much less comprehend...

" 'You have trained hard,' he said, 'mastered the Twelve Postures of O-Mei and the Snake Shape Fist of Shaolin. You have mastered all I had to teach you—until now.

"I don't understand?"

" 'The core of Shaolin, the Warrior Attendant Fist, has been leaked to the Ch'ing and is now being used against us. The elders have met on this, we have come together to share our knowledge and experience in order to create a new method that can be used to undo the damage of the old, that can restore the harmony. We have created something... revolutionary.

"And he taught it to you," Boklao said. "He taught you the rebel fist, the Fist of the Elders..."

"No."

"But—"

"He taught me only a Little First Training. They never had time to finish it, you see—

" 'Master, the Ch'ing are at our gates!'

"His composure, his absolute serenity of being, never wavered.

" 'We are surrounded,' he said. 'The invaders stand ready to lay siege...' His eyes closed. 'They will succeed.'

"My body went numb.

" 'But this... this cannot be!'

" 'It is.'

" 'We can hold the gate!'

" 'The gate is already broken. "

" 'How?'

" 'Someone—one of our own—has set fire to the temple from within.'

"My heart tore open but my master was already up and across the room and in front of me.

" 'I must go meet with the other elders but first I would ask something of you.'

" 'Anything...'

" 'Flee the temple. Do it now while there is still time.'

" 'No!' How could he? 'I will fight at your side. I will die at your side if that is my future!'

" 'There is a saying among my people, an ancient saying—lose all battles but the last. Our battles with the Ch'ing are not yet done and we will lose many more before the last one comes.' He looked at me, his eyes like the rays of the setting sun. 'Here, now, your death would be meaningless.'

" 'Master...!'

" 'You will go down into the tunnels beneath the temple and there you will find my daughter—'

" 'Daughter?' I had never heard him mention a daughter.

" 'As you are my son.'

" 'But—'

" 'She has been under the care and tutelage of my sister, Wumei, Nun of the White Crane Temple. When my sister joined us here so did my daughter. You must protect her and see her to safety.'

" 'Master, I—'

" 'That is why I chose you all those years ago, Fong Dak, why I trained you, why I told you I would have another future for you, one I would entrust to no one but you.' He turned towards the hall. "In your hands I place my legacy.'

"Then he passed into the smoke and was gone."

"And the temple fell," Boklao said.

"And the temple fell."

"I knew the story, of course, but never the details..."

"You still do not know them, but you know now what I knew then, and—"

"Wait." Wingchun tucked her hair back beneath her scarf. "What about the girl? Did you... did you find her? Was she...?"

Her father's face warmed and, for a moment, the years slipped away. "She was Choyfa and she wanted nothing to do with me... at least at first. But she could not deny the wishes of our master any more than I could."

"But, I mean, was she—?"

"Graceful and beautiful, powerful and passionate." He gazed at Wingchun. "So very much like her daughter has become..."

"Mother..." Tears welled up inside Wingchun. "My mother!"

"Not yet, of course," her father said. "The road from the temple was long and fraught with peril. We had to dodge the constables and bannermen who dogged our every step. And we argued constantly—I wanted to travel back to our master's house in Kwangsi, beneath which we sit and speak here and now. She wanted to stay in Fukien. We compromised—we stayed in Fukien and settled in Wingchun County. We couldn't resist the name, you see." He smiled, wide but thin. "Our marriage was a cover at first, a way to hide from the Ch'ing, but eventually the illusion became reality and we were husband and wife...

"It was only then that I began to consider my master's words, that either of us began to suspect their true meaning..."

"Where I come from..." Wingchun shook her head. "All this time I thought I was nothing, nothing but a skinny little girl, in a tiny little town..." She laughed and cried. "Daughter of Fong Dak and Miu Choyfa! I always wondered but I could never have imagined, not all this!"

"Child..."

"Not this..."

"Child...! The next part will be... will be difficult for you to hear," he said. "It will be almost unbearable for me to tell...

"We built a home in a remote part of the county, your mother and I, high in the mountains. We farmed by day but by night we joined with others who had sworn to rise up against the Ch'ing." He looked at Boklao. "We met another survivor of the Nine Little Lotus Temple, a disciple of Chi Sim named Leung Hong. We swore a blood oath and together we formed the Red Pole Sect.

"At first your mother took an active role, fighting by my side." He smiled again. "She could make the double knives dance like a butterfly caught in a spring breeze...

"Knives?" Wingchun said. "But knives would have been—?"

"Life-taking weapons, yes, and forbidden to the Chan School. But your mother's skills were from Wumei, and Wumei came from a very different school…"

"But she fought—Mother fought! Everything you said about 'fracturing and separating'…"

"Would come true soon enough," he said. "But we felt powerful then, we… we felt as though we were doing something, striking back somehow…

"Then your eldest sister was born, and your mother decided to lay down her knives and to devote herself entirely to our children."

"I… I had a sister?"

"You had three of them, sisters and brothers both."

"What were their names?"

"After Nimming came Seiyuk, and then Yumming, Haoyuk, Meiyuk, Chuming, and, finally, our seventh, our last…"

"Me…"

"You."

"Three sisters and three brothers—a family. I had a family! Why didn't you tell me? Why didn't you—" A chill bit her to the bone. "Wait… What happened? What happened to them?"

"The Red Poles intercepted a letter meant to inform Viceroy Yude that additional arms were being sent to help suppress the rebels," her father said. "The caravan was to pass nearby. It was too good an opportunity… The ambush was flawless, the Ch'ing humiliated, the weapons ours. I was so happy, so proud. We raced back to tell our families…

"The village was burning when we arrived."

"No…"

"We hid in hopes our presence would remain undetected and the villagers might somehow be spared, but the Ch'ing started killing them and Leung… he would not have it. He rose up to stop them and he could not do it alone… We stood together, fought side-by-side, then Leung saw constables up the mountain—he saw them moving on my home…

"I did not want to leave Leung but I had no choice. I flew, too late—the constables were not moving on my home, they were moving *from* it!

"I-I took care of them and rushed inside."

Wingchun crossed over to him.

"My children lay there butchered. My wife was stabbed through and left to die in the fire…

" 'My husband…' she said.

"I cradled her head and tried to comfort her.

" 'Everything will be fine,' I said. 'Don't waste your strength on words.'

" 'They came for us...'

"Even with her dying breath, she sought to protect me—she hadn't been active, not in years... The Ch'ing had not come for *us*, they had come for me! For *me*! And my family had paid the price!

" 'I tried to stop them,' she said. 'But there were too many...'

"Though the bodies had been taken, the dark pools of blood at the door showed just how well she'd tried.

"'A Lama led them,' she said, 'a devil in bone-colored robes. I have never felt such emptiness, such rage... I told them you'd gone north, tried to lead them away from the village...'

"I did not have the heart to tell her...

" 'Most of them went off in search of you but some yet remain...'

" 'No more, my wife,' I said, hollow comfort.

" 'They killed our children. I could not save them—' Red tears streaked her face.

" 'Don't, I—'

" 'Listen to me.'

" 'I'm listening.'

" 'I could not save them *all*.'

" 'All...?'

" 'They did not get our seventh daughter, our youngest. We... we hid her...'

"I followed her gaze to where broken, burning furniture covered the cellar door.

" 'Fetch her,' she said. " 'Bring her to me.' "

"I threw aside the debris, ripped away the heavy rug, and wrenched the door open." Her father reached out to her. "You were there, right where she said you'd be."

Wingchun's eyes broke wide. "My nightmares..."

"Your memories."

"They were real... They *are* real!"

" 'Take her,' your mother said to me.

" 'What?'

" 'I came to your home, now you must go to mine and take the last part of me with you.'

"I felt sick, I felt dead.

" 'For our daughter's sake, our last daughter—our legacy. Promise me. Vow to me you will protect her.'

" 'I will. I swear it on my life and on the spirits of my ancestors.'

"She smiled and… and was gone.

"I did not want to leave," he father said. "If it had been just me, I would have lain down in the fire and gone with my family to the next life. But she'd placed you in my hands and… and I had to protect you…

"We fled west, hid by day and traveled by night. And when we arrived at last in Lanchow, Fong Dak and his seventh daughter were dead and buried with the rest of their family. I gave us the name Yim in strict adherence to the promise I'd made, the vow I'd sworn to keep. I called myself Yee for it was my second life, and I called you Wingchun so that not a day would go by that I did not remember…"

Wingchun sobbed and Boklao moved to support her.

"Now you know." Her father withered back towards the window. "Now you know where you came from."

9
The Buddha's Skull

The strings of paper lanterns suspended between the huge Market Gates singed the moon-white square red about its edges.

"They look like spring rolls," Mrs. Law said.

Master Law smiled. "They look fine."

"Spring rolls split down the middle, their fillings burst out..."

"They're perfect. Why must you always worry so much?"

"Because *you* always seem to worry so little." She fussed with the silver clasp at the shoulder of her best gown, where the rich turquoise silk gave way to thick, peony-flowered brocade. "Or have you forgotten last year?"

"If you're referring to the firecracker incident, Butcher Ngao has sworn to keep his grandmother away from the lizard wine until well after—"

"I'm referring to all of it."

"Come," he said, "give me another cake and let's watch the moon reach its fullness and our first son dance the lion!"

She handed him the pastry, its golden-brown crust pressed with the character for 'luck' framed by the Dragon & Phoenix. "You're impossible, do you know that?"

"Of course I am, that's why you married me."

"I married you because you were the last scrap left at the matchmaker's. If only there'd been just one spare beggar or actor…"

"You told me that I looked particularly auspicious," he said, "that you had a good feeling about me!"

"My parents told me to tell you that," she said. "Unfortunately for you I get to speak my own mind now."

"And I would have it no other way."

She shook her head and smiled back. "Smart boy."

Then the double doors of the Azure Mountain Hall cracked open.

"Look," he said. "It begins…"

The fruit and vegetable stands, fish and barbecue counters, soup and noodle stalls, geomancy and astrology booths, lute and zither players, jugglers and acrobats, and even the gamblers and beggars paused, and a slow, steady tapping echoed down the steps. The tempo increased. The taps grew louder and faster. Gongs and cymbals clanged, the doors burst open, and the drums boomed to life.

"A boy created it, you know," Master Law said.

"Hush," Mrs. Law said. "I know the story."

"A thousand years ago, a terrible beast with a curved horn, a roar like the wail of ghosts, and steps like the crash of thunder preyed on the local villages…"

The Big Headed Buddha tiptoed out, his fan still closed. Behind him a body of layered cloth shifted, fringed eyes fluttered open, and a paper mouth yawned. The sleeping lion stirred.

"The beast returned every year," Master Law said. "It always had and it always would, and that was just the way things were. Only one day, one boy—did you know he was a furniture maker?"

Mrs. Law rolled her eyes. "Goddess of mercy, you've told me a hundred times!"

Lady dancers in vivid blue swirled red streamers in front of the Jade Garden Teahouse, and the indigo- and brown-coated market crowd raised white banners.

"This one boy," Master Law said, "got his brothers together and from bamboo and paper they made a beast far more terrible, its roar, its steps—"

The crash of cymbals and the pounding of drums echoed through the square.

"And when the real beast returned again it took one look, turned tail, and fled. And every year since, the lion dance keeps the beast at bay. It keeps us all safe."

"Your point," Mrs. Law said. "If you ever had one?"

"That everything will be fine," Master Law said. "Go and put on the water and by the time it boils we'll all be back at the shop, sharing a pot of silver-needle tea, its aroma like the first sweet breeze of morning, laughing and counting the greens as a family."

"Promise?"

A gong clanged and the lion leapt up.

"It's Autumn Moon. What could possibly go wrong?"

詠 春 傳 說

Birds squawked and took flight, beasts yelped and fled, reptiles and insects slithered and skittered for deeper cover.

Dust billowed, the earth shook.

And steel-shod hooves tore up the thinly etched path.

詠 春 傳 說

Old Yee wasn't stooped so much anymore as broken over, his hair white like sackcloth and his face lined as though by decades of tears.

"I was right," he said, his voice all but ground away. "Sharing this did nothing to decrease the depth, only to spread the breadth… You did not need this burden, child."

"She did," Boklao said.

"No, this was you. You forced this."

"She needed to know. We both did."

Wingchun stared at them. "I can answer for myself. Why are you talking about me like—?"

"You are everything I was," Old Yee said to Boklao, "everything I have tried so hard to leave behind."

"I am." Boklao took Old Yee's cup, fell to his knees, and thrust it up. "Master!"

Old Yee scoffed. "You would have me teach you? Ever since you came here you have turned our lives upside down. You have single-mindedly pursued your own selfish agenda without any thought as to what effect it may have on my town, on my family. Now, after hearing my story—our story—you still have the temerity to make such a request?"

"Now more than ever."

"Why? Tell me why I should even consider teaching you?"

"Because of my single-mindeness, because of my temerity." Boklao thrust the cup up again. "Because I am everything you once were and more."

"Those are not reasons. None of those are reasons."

"They're the only reasons." Boklao glanced from Wingchun to the strongest, bitterest tea and back. "The same reasons your master chose you—to care for his daughter when he was gone."

"What...?" Wingchun said. "What are you—?"

"I'm not going anywhere," Old Yee said. "Not yet. And while I draw breath my daughter won't ever need anyone to take care of her, not anyone but me."

"I can take care of myself," she said.

"No you can't."

"You just watch me!"

"Child—!"

Boklao thrust the cup up a third and final time. "Master!"

"Damn you boy!" Old Yee's hand blurred, the cup shattered, and Boklao flew back through the tables and across the floor. "I'm not your master and I never will be!"

"I... I don't understand, I—"

"No, you don't. You've traveled across the south and back again, wasted what precious life was spared you, all for something that no longer exists, for a dream—a fool's dream—and all you need to understand is that my daughter is..."

Old Yee stopped and frowned and scoured the room.

"Gone..."

And then he was up and after her, out the door and into the night.

詠 春 傳 說

The heavens faded, the bamboo shrank back, and the twin columns of the Constabulary Army split up the fork in the road.

"First and Fourth Squadrons west to seal all egress," Eagle-Shadow said. "Second and Third north to secure the town!"

詠 春 傳 說

Wingchun watched from the narrow alley beside the Jade Garden Teahouse as the Fai children jumped and flipped and spun from one end of the market to the other while, behind them, Fire-blower Fo's cheeks ballooned, he lifted a torch to his lips, sprayed the wine, and spat flame past the tumbling Fai and across the heavens.

Lady dancers twirled their streamers, the crowd raised their banners, and children threw strings of firecrackers at the lion's feet.

Five-Metal Yang leapt over them, thrust the lion's head up, and manipulated the controls that made its big eyes blink and its huge, bamboo-framed mouth open. Big Kung kept pace behind him and undulated the layers of red and gold scales that covered the lion's indigo back. Then Butcher Ngao spread the Big Headed Buddha's fan open, the drums beat faster, and the Seven Stars Steps became the Three.

The lion circled around to the teahouse, stared down any would-be challengers, and then turned towards the green cabbage leaves that dangled from the second floor balcony. It riled itself up for the Crossing of the Bridge and riled the crowd up with it.

The Big Headed Buddha took position directly beneath the greens and waved the lion on. The drums softened and the crowd fell silent. The lion approached.

Big Kung crouched, grabbed Yang by the legs, and hefted him up on his shoulders.

The lion reared double tall, its mouth opened, the lion roared, the greens tore free, and the leaves drifted down over the crowd.

Chao Jeet pounded the drums, Lai Bang crashed the cymbals, and Little Kung clanged the gong. Yang jumped down off Big Kung's shoulders and the crowd burst into cheers.

Wingchun cheered with them. Then she was grabbed from behind and yanked back into the alley.

詠 春 傳 說

Eagle-Shadow pulled his ebon steed up behind the Lama's pale mare. "Master?"

"Find the Shaolin. Find him and drive him to me."

詠 春 傳 說

Boklao glared at her. "What in the hell do you think you're doing?"

Wingchun pulled away. "Where's my father?"

"He's looking for you, just like me. Probably checking every face in the market...I just figured I'd start with the alley closest to the noise..."

"Well then don't you just win the prize."

"This isn't a game!"

"Isn't it?"

"A girl out here alone and unescorted? Do you have any idea how dangerous this is, how many men are just waiting to take advantage of you?"

"You mean besides you?"

"I—What... what are you talking about? I'm—"

"Who? The young martial hero who swept me off my feet two weeks ago or the scheming opportunist who just slammed me back into the ground tonight?" She crossed her arms. "Back at the river you saved me, me and Mrs. Law and Little Kung all brave and true enough, but then you wanted nothing to do with me. You tried to send me away."

"It wasn't safe..."

"Until you heard my name and realized that it could mean something, that it could lead you to what you really wanted, and then it was all so suddenly safe?"

Boklao's face fell.

"You talked to me," she said, "you were... you were nice to me just in case you might need to use me, just in case I was the key to unlocking my father's secrets—"

"No, I—"

"—but then you realized that you didn't need a key at all, you could just peek through the lock to get what you wanted. So you discarded me again, cast me away like so much trash, until you were discovered and had to revert back to your first plan."

"That's not true! I—we..." He let out a breath. "We all wear many faces and sometimes we forget which one we have on. There's no time now but the moment I have you home safe again I'll explain everything to you if you let me. I'll make things right if you just give me the chance."

Her body stiffened. "No..."

Boklao stumbled back. "No...?"

But she wasn't looking at him. She was looking past him...

Boklao spun around.

Old Yee stood at the far end of the alley, white as a ghost.

"The heavens are gone," he said, "but for a few stars that scorch their way across the night, a constellation that should not yet be…"

"Father…"

She began towards him but he was already in front of her.

"The Buddha's Skull Trailing Smoke," he said. "The Devil."

"I don't understand," Wingchun said. "What—?"

"Child…"

"Father, what is it?"

"They're here."

詠 春 傳 說

Eagle-Shadow crashed down from his horse in salute.

"It was abandoned, master."

The Lama's voice rumbled. "What?"

"Abandoned and set ablaze, but only moments ago. He's still here, still close. I'll find him, master."

"Pray that you do."

詠 春 傳 說

Wingchun stared over the somber-shingled roofs at the oily black smoke that billowed up from the Yim Family Tofu Shop…

"Go." Boklao circled around, hands out and eyes slashed narrow. "I'll delay them as long as I can. I'll delay them or die trying."

"No," her father said.

"Damn you, old man, would you please trust me!"

"This enemy is beyond you, boy. You *will* die trying and your death will not delay him, not enough…"

"There's nothing else!"

"There is… and now I am forced to risk everything upon it. I am forced to have another future for you—"

"What are you doing?" Wingchun said.

"—a future I can trust to no one but you."

"No…" Wingchun tried to back away but her father held her. "I won't let you do this!"

"Forgive me, child." Her father whispered a prayer and shoved her to Boklao. "Take her, head for the mountains and go until leg or land fail you. Take her and protect her."

"I swear it," Boklao said. "I swear it on my life and on the spirits of my ancestors."

"Let me go!" Wingchun thrashed. "I'm not leaving you!"

"You have to, child." Her father turned down a side street. "You have no choice."

And then he passed into the darkness and was gone.

詠 春 傳 說

The lion head, its horn broken and its eyes put out, blew abandoned across the square. It sparked and flamed, and the fire devoured the paper skin from its bamboo bones. Then the ground shook and steel-shod hooves crushed it fully into oblivion.

詠 春 傳 說

Wingchun's tears caught the moonlight. They weren't the kind that flowed down and disappeared but the kind that welled up and stayed.

"Stop shoving me," she said.

Boklao didn't. "We have to keep moving."

"I told you, I'm not leaving without my father!"

He shoved her again but this time she was around him, behind him, and then she raced back up the alley.

"Wingchun!"

The square was in chaos. The huge arches of the North and South Market Gates were on fire, her friends and neighbors were screaming, and the constables—

Ghosts swarmed outside the walls, their horns polished silver.

She couldn't run...

The screams were drowned out by the thunder of horsemen. They tore past her—

Demons breached the gates, their hides scaled ebon.

Couldn't move...

And then she was slammed through the refuse and into the rough brick wall of the teahouse. Her heart pounded. No... not hers...

"Forbidden Bannermen," Boklao whispered in her ear. "They're sweeping the town, driving everyone into the square and onto the spears of the Army of the Green Standard."

"I have to find him," she said.

"Hold still! If they see us—!"

"MASTER!"

The voice tore at her from the center of the market.

A monster reared up, its body shadow, its fangs dripping with familiar blood.

"The scarface..." Boklao pressed her tighter against that wall. "The damn scarface from the river, but how—!"

"Master, we have him!"

The devil turned, its robes bone, its face ash, its eyes the inferno—

"Lama!" Boklao snarled. "Your father was right, I can't protect you, not from that." He pulled her back. "We have to go, now!"

"You go!"

Two bannermen dragged a body into the square.

Boklao stopped pulling.

Wingchun's stopped breathing.

"Father..."

詠 春 傳 說

Eagle-Shadow reached down, grabbed him by the braid, and hoisted him up. "I told you he would not escape, master. Not again."

Withered and broken, his head shook and his eyes rolled around. "I-I am Tofu Vender Yee," he said. "Old Yee..."

"You are Fong Dak, Shaolin heretic and rebel traitor who, thirteen years, six months, and four days ago, we tracked to Wingchun County and the Red Pole insurgents, who threw a burning spearhead at me, who left me this..." Eagle-Shadow scratched his finger down the jagged hook-shaped scar that ruined his face. "How long I suffered with that disgrace, how often I thought of ending it... Do you know what allowed me to live? Do you? The certainty that *you* still lived, that you were out there, that if I could just hold on, if I could just find you, I could have my revenge—that I could send you to hell to join the rest of your family!"

Old Yee looked up and spat full in his face.

"*Lehele!*" A bannermen raised his fist.

"No." Eagle-Shadow grabbed it. "Not when he's expecting it. You would only break your hand."

The bannerman stared at Old Yee and stepped back.

"You were supposed to drive him to me, my once and former disciple," the Lama said. "If he is truly what you claim, how could you have subdued him so easily?"

"We found him skulking through the side streets, master. We moved to surround him, to drive him to you, but he collapsed on his own, coughing, seizing…"

"Yes, I see it now." The Lama's eyes burned into Old Yee's chest. "Consumed…"

"Master, he—"

Eagle-Shadow stopped, his eyes raked across the square, and he locked on the alley beside the teahouse. "The boy," he said. "The boy from the river!"

詠 春 傳 說

Boklao cursed.

"He's seen me! Wingchun, he—Wingchun?"

詠 春 傳 說

Her eyes met her father's and the distance between them evaporated. They were together again as they'd always been. As they always would—

"Wingchun!" Boklao yanked her back. "We go now or so help me I knock you out and carry you!"

Scarface barked and bannerman advanced towards the alley.

Wingchun looked to her father again but this time he looked away and the wind seemed to ripple through his robes.

"No, not the wind…"

詠 春 傳 說

The two bannermen holding Old Yee hurtled head over heels through the air, smashed into the ones advancing on the alley, and knocked them to the ground.

Close… too close… Old Yee glanced at his daughter. Why was she still here? Why hadn't that damn boy gotten her out of town? He needed to give them more time… and a distraction…

The constables attacked.

Old Yee breathed out and everything seemed to slow. Spears slipped past his turning body and constables snapped between his twisting arms.

It felt like the old days.

They fanned out to surround him. So predictable... He flowed through them like the river, wove them together, and then angled out between. And the only bodies caught on the ends of their red-tasseled spears were their own.

A dozen fell.

The bannermen bore down, their thick-bladed, two-handed choppers high. The two behind him lunged in first. Old Yee let them draw close and then he stepped back. The choppers sliced past him on either side and he reached out, grabbed their wrists, added to their momentum, unbalanced them, and then twisted and turned under and around.

Cracks echoed through the square but Old Yee was already coiling into two more—

It *was* the old days.

詠 春 傳 說

Alone and unarmed, one, two, three at a time, Boklao watched Old Yee cut down constables and bannermen both like so much chaff...

The old man was gone and in his place was the disciple of Shaolin, the hero of the rebellion—

The legend.

詠 春 傳 說

He soared beyond Wingchun's most distant memory, straight and proud and stronger than she'd ever known. His hair, no longer cotton or sackcloth, was a white now somewhere between silver and pearl, and the way he moved—it was beyond even her dreams...

But it wasn't the tofu-maker or even the warrior monk. Just him— Just her father.

詠 春 傳 說

Old Yee ducked more spears, dodged more choppers, turned and— His lungs seared and the weight slammed back down on his chest.

Blades ripped across him.

And the old days fled.

"No, not yet..."

詠 春 傳 說

The surviving Ch'ing closed in on her father, but then Scarface barked again and they backed away and formed a circle around the square.

"You made a mistake, old man," Scarface said. "You should have made sure I was dead back in Fukien, when you were still young and strong, and I was just a child playing at being a commander. Now I'm the one who's strong and you—you've grown soft and weak."

Scarface charged, his chopper sparked across the earth and struck amid slate-blue robes that swirled with the smoke...

"You are strong," her father said, "hard and rigid as the company of death—" He clapped his hands and the heavens splashed bright. "—as the blade that breaks under its own force."

Scarface's chopper shattered, the shards a steel rain.

"I... I don't need a weapon, old man." He clenched his fists. "Your death is the only company my vengeance needs, and I will claim it. I will claim it with my bare hands!"

Her father's arms extended out just like the movement in the old exercises...

"Then come and claim it."

Scarface screeched and struck, a long, looping punch.

Her father didn't even move, he just reached out, his arm a snake parting the water...

Scarface tried to pull back but he was stuck. His face twisted, he yanked and yanked, and then kicked out and wrenched back at the same time.

Cloth tore, wet and red.

Her father smiled.

And Scarface gaped. "Poison bridge..."

His sleeve was shredded and beneath it, where her father had touched him, his skin was gone.

"You should have killed me, old man!" Scarface swung both arms. "You should have killed me when you had the chance!"

Wingchun's world spun. Her father met the attack. One hand swallowed in while the other spat out. And between blinks, Wingchun saw his palm graze Scarface's chest. Then they were past each other.

Scarface wheeled back around. His mouth opened but blood was the only thing that came out. He reached up and tore open his tattered black jacket. A palm-print was stamped on his chest, blistered red as cinnabar. He glanced back at her father, his legs already giving out beneath him.

"You—"

"Corrected a past mistake," her father said. "Nothing more."

Then he turned.

The wind boomed. The air sizzled.

Slate-gray snapped against the white of bone and gleaming eyes locked on burning flame.

Wingchun's blood ran cold.

And her father faced the Lama.

10

The Sixty-Fourth Trigram

Master Law slid the false wall aside, ripped the trapdoor open, and shoved his people down—as many and as fast as he could.

"Come on!"

"Not without you!" Mrs. Law clutched on to him. "I'm not going until my family goes with me!"

The walls groaned, shelves came crashing down around them, drawers broke, jars shattered, and medicine scattered across the flow.

"Last," Master Law said. "I get in last, when there's no one else who needs getting in. It's my duty—" He glanced at Big Kung. "—and the duty of my first son!"

"You have *two* sons!" Mrs. Law said. "Where's the second, where's Little Kung?"

"Inside!"

Master Law shoved her through.

"What are you talking about?" Big Kung said. "Little Kung isn't down there!"

"I wasn't answering," Master Law said. "I was ordering."

The beams creaked, the ceiling shifted, and more shelves came crashing down. Wine spilled out and fire raced across the floor.

"Why didn't Fok warn us?" Piebald Chan shuffled towards them. "That's what the Inner Gate is for!"

"I don't know." Master Law shoved him down and then turned back to Big Kung. "A few more minutes and then no matter who's left behind, we seal the entrance and let everything fall down on top of us. Do you understand?"

"But this is our home, our medicine, our life!"

"Not if the Ch'ing find a way into the tunnels, Yatkung. If that happens the only thing this will be is our tomb!"

詠 春 傳 說

The fire flickered low, the wind held its breath, and her father settled, a dreadful calm before the Lama.

"We have to help him," Wingchun said.

"Too late," Boklao said. "They're already committed."

"What are you talking about?"

"Look at them, they're wound like springs, their eyes measuring every ounce of skill and spirit… They're locked on each other, on the instant between winning and losing, between life and death. Everything is set. One will move first and one last."

"I don't believe you! There has to be something we can do!"

"We can get you out of here. That's what we can do!"

"No! You… you want his system, right? His super secret fist? That's what all this is all about, isn't it, why you came here? Well there it is, out there in the square. But you're going to have to help him to get it!"

Boklao shook his head. "It's not about that damn system, it never was. You heard me—I'd be out there right now if it meant keeping you safe. But the only way to do that is to get you gone, otherwise—"

"What, I'll die? I don't care!"

"Then you're crazy."

"And you're a coward!"

詠 春 傳 說

The flaming shadow of the South Market Gate rose behind Old Yee and the North burned above the Lama. This close, Old Yee could see that the Lama's robes weren't bone-colored at all but white as snow, embroidered with hundreds of esoteric spirits, their faces bestial, their bodies strewn like corpses across the silk...

"Your skills have atrophied, *Shaolin*."

Old Yee glanced down at the deep red stains that crisscrossed the slate gray of his robes, and then out over the Ch'ing that littered the square.

"Yet still they suffice, *Lama*."

The Lama's eyes flared and his hand twitched.

"So like a disease," he said, "infecting everything you touch, killing everything you claim to hold dear. You are a scourge, a plague, contained only by the inferno, cleansed only when all that remains is a stinking pile of blackened bone..."

Old Yee's eyes gleamed and his foot inched forward.

"From you who scorches the earth and chokes out the heavens, killing only yourself... From you I bear such condemnation like the sweet dew of morning. Drinking it in, I renounce all." He smiled, dark and bright. "At last, too late, I understand the inconceivable—you may reduce my flesh to char and my bones to fragment, but I am beyond birth, beyond death..."

The Lama's hand went to his falchion.

"You may be beyond birth in this life, Shaolin, but death inescapable comes now to claim you for the next, and all that is left is for you to pray that your next incarnation brings you closer to the Pure Land of the West."

Old Yee's fingers joined like the head of a snake.

"Delusion. The Pure Land is not in the West—it is in the mind. Once you realize the essential nature, whatever land you call home is pure." He looked to the heavens one last time. "Even now, as it grows so dim around me, I can still glimpse my own Pure Land—the South."

"The South is not pure," the Lama said. "It is infected and it begs to have the source of its infection burned from it before the whole grows sick and dies. It begs for it, just like your family begged all those years ago in Fukien..."

"My family..."

"Gone. Forgotten. You have nothing left—"

"No, not yet..."

"Not even your life."

詠 春 傳 説

Wingchun caught her father's gaze again. It was so certain, so resolute—it terrified her...

Lightning flashed above the clouds.

"Go," he said.

The word shot straight through her.

The Lama's head cocked to the side. "Go?"

Thunder crashed beyond the mountains.

"Go!"

The force knocked Wingchun back.

"Who are you—?" The Lama turned, his burning eyes blazed, and in them Wingchun saw her death.

"Now!"

And her father moved first.

The sights, the sounds... they blurred together, colorless and toneless. Her father's hands lashed out. The Lama's blade cleft down.

The heavens tore open, the dragons set loose.

And Wingchun screamed.

詠 春 傳 說

The bright gilded, dark nielloed sign clacked against the brown brick of the Vast Beneficence Apothecary Shop. Then the wind surged, tore it fully loose, and sent it hurtling through the rolling curtains of rain.

Little Kung's eyes bulged, he ducked, and the sign sliced past his head and broke against the remnants of the North Market Gate. Then Little Kung clutched the ragged cloth bundle to his chest, and slipped past the toppled Dragon & Phoenix Poles, through the broken double doors, and into the wreckage of his home.

The flames were out but dark, oily smoke clung to what was left of the ceiling. Little Kung dropped low and crawled over the thick sludge of charred roots and herbs, burned liniments and pastes, singed bits of wood and brick, and blackened shards of glass and porcelain to the stairs in the corner.

Through the false wall, along the hidden passage, he knocked three times atop of the secret cellar, waited, knocked three more, and—

The trapdoor flew up and a hand thrust out. It grabbed him by the scruff and yanked him down.

"Hey!"

"Quiet!"

Little Kung balled up to protect the ragged cloth bundle, and thumped down onto the rough stone floor. It was inky black all around him. Rain beat the floorboards above, trickled through the cracks, and dripped down over everything.

"Of all the stupid, noisy—!" Big Kung snatched him back to his feet. "Do you have any idea how—!"

The trapdoor creaked and began to fall closed.

Big Kung cursed and scrambled for it, but their father was already there. He caught it, eased it down, and slid the iron-bound locking bar back into place.

"Even in the monsoon sound travels and echoes linger for those intent enough to hear them," Master Law whispered. "Silence is now our most desperate ally."

Little Kung blinked. Shapes struggled to form from the shadows. People were crammed against the walls and huddled across the floor, their sobs just beneath the rain.

Then his mother grabbed him by the ear. "You went back to the market, didn't you?"

"Ow! I was—"

"I know what you were doing, idiot boy!" Mrs. Law looked down at the ragged cloth, and the dented brass gong that peeked out from within. "You were risking all of our lives for some worthless hunk of metal!"

"It's not worthless! It was grandfather's and I... Well, I couldn't let the Ch'ing have it!"

"But you could let them have us, couldn't you?" Big Kung said. "You know we'd never leave without you, so you kept us here waiting. You know the Ch'ing are everywhere, so you led them straight back to us!"

"I didn't lead anyone anywhere! I didn't even make a sound until *you* went and—"

"And nothing," Mrs. Law said. "That it was your footsteps above us, Mankung, that it was your knock upon the trapdoor and not the butt of some constable's spear..." She looked at Master Law. "You're his father, you tell him!"

"Later," Master Law said.

"But—"

"We've wasted too much time already." He turned away. "Brother Chan, you were saying?"

Piebald Chan cleared his throat. "I was saying that we take the tunnels to the outskirts and follow the old river bed to the Lan. Then we cross

the bridge, slip back into the bamboo, and make for the caves above the
foothills of the Eight Immortals, yes?"

"Very well," Master Law said. "I have the lead, Five-Metal Yang and
Big Kung will bring up the rear. Make it so."

Yang bowed, Big Kung grumbled, and Little Kung hugged his gong as
lightning flashed through the cracks above and gleamed off steel tinted
the bright red of blood.

詠 春 傳 說

Boklao skidded around the bend, put his body between Wingchun and
the impact of the bamboo, and then pushed her on through the monsoon,
faster and farther from the murdered town.

"Is this the old riverbed?" he said.

She retched.

"Answer me! Is this the shortcut you told me about, the way to the
Western Road?"

"What does it matter?"

Boklao growled and pushed her on until they passed an outcropping
of rocks and broke onto the thinly etched path.

"About damn time," he said. "Now if we can just make it to—"

Sooty red torches flared up ahead.

He cursed. "Whatever happens, "you keep running, understand?
Run until you find the deepest, darkest pit in the backwater and hide
there until I come get you. Promise me, Wingchun. Promise me for your
father's sake."

She glared at him, her eyes accused...

He held her as long as he dared and then gave her a final shove and
charged past.

" CH'ING!"

The lead constable attacked but Boklao slid beneath his spear and tack-
led his legs out from under him. The sooty red torch tumbled across the
night and Boklao jumped up, spun around, and kicked it right at the other
constables. The rain sizzled and the constables scattered, and Wingchun
raced through them and into the smoke and mist.

Boklao slammed back down in a crouch, hands clawed, braid loose,
hair wet and free across his face.

The constables spread out around him, almost a dozen of them and
maybe twice as many more not far behind...

Boklao reached down, claimed the first constable's spear, buried the silvery blade in the second constable's chest, and smashed the dark, wooden butt into the third's head. Then he swung the spear in a vast, horizontal arc to keep the forth, fifth, and sixth back, and pitched it at the seventh.

詠 春 傳 說

Spears crisscrossed through the air. They were fast... and yet so slow they stretched out forever... It was almost like Wingchun could just move past them, around them... maybe even through them...? It was like her body knew exactly what and she only had to let it...

The bamboo streamed by, the howls of the constables dropped away, and the slosh of mud became the creak of old wood...

"The bridge... I made it to the bridge..."

Then she glanced back...

詠 春 傳 說

Bamboo faded and smoke spread, a grim shroud over a rotting corpse. The sky was ashen, but wreathed in the flames was a thin silhouette that rose from the bridge like a lily... a lily caught in the middle of the damn inferno!

"What are you doing?" Boklao roared. "Run, you crazy—!"

詠 春 傳 說

He leapt from the bamboo, blurred by mist so thick it choked out the heavens. But constables swarmed all around him, their spears glinted...

"Boklao!" She took a step towards him. "Behind you!"

He looked up at her.

Flame splattered across her arm. She flinched.

His leg buckled...

Fire flared and water flooded. The roof collapsed over her, shingles fell like blades.

詠 春 傳 說

"Wingchun!" Boklao dragged himself up. "Get out of here!"

She looked down at him.

Cold sliced across his back. Boklao clenched his teeth.

Her arms shot up...

Wood thrust. Steel slashed. Spears bit into him, blood leapt like red tassel...

詠 春 傳 說

"Boklao!"

Smoke billowed. The constables piled up over him.

Everything became silent.

And he was gone.

詠 春 傳 說

"Wingchun!"

Mist swirled. The river swept up over her.

Everything became still.

And she was gone.

11

Heaven & Earth

The Lama glared up from the heart of the inferno, empty, enraged… chanting his ritual to the abyss. Then, his chanting ended, he flexed his frame and stepped over the Shaolin's head.

"Fetch—"

He paused, his burning eyes raked the chaos, and he reached out, grabbed the closest constable by the throat, and hefted him up off the ground.

"My disciple?"

The constable kicked the air, scratched at the Lama's adamantine arm, and strained to look back over his shoulder. Eagle-Shadow was splayed out amid the ruin of the market square, his scarred face drained white and his chest blistered cinnabar.

The constable crashed back down and the Lama's bone robes flared at Eagle-Shadow's side. He broke the seal on his nostrum, poured it down Eagle-Shadow's throat, and began to chant again—a very different ritual.

The bannermen paled. The constables shrank back.

And Eagle-Shadow's eyes burst open.

The Lama rose.

"Fetch the Emperor his trophy."

詠 春 傳 説

Boklao's nostrils flared. He smelled blood.

Steel hummed towards him.

He tasted death.

He relished it.

Then the hum became a buzz, a blade thudded into flesh, and mud splattered all around him...

No—just behind him...

The hum returned, louder. Sharp metal shimmered straight at him. Boklao ducked and the hum split and buzzed past both ears.

More thuds, more splashes, this time beside. He glanced down and three constables squirmed in the mud at his feet, flying daggers embedded in their faces and necks...

Lightning burst the heavens.

Townsfolk, maybe fifty of them, fled from the bamboo out over the steaming skeleton of the bridge. The constables wheeled around to intercept, but a dozen townsfolk turned back to stop them, their sashes red as blood.

"Rebels..."

A shaggy headed knot of a man rushed in first. Brave and blunt, his octagonal-headed hammers battered down spears and crunched into bone.

A lean lash of a man glowered behind. Sly and sharp, his scholar sword twanged against sabers and pierced through vital points.

Others fanned out around them, old and young, big and small, armed with crescent spears, and three-section staves, and broken tools...

Lightning burst again.

More constables charged at Boklao. He grabbed a saber from one of the bodies at his feet and twirled it back into a reverse-grip, put its spine against the strong bone of his forearm.

Mud churned, the saber screeched and sparked off the spears. Boklao saw an opening and cut the first constable across the side. He began to twirl the saber straight again to increase the range so he could follow-up and finish, but the second constable kicked him and the saber slipped from his hand just as the third constable stabbed.

A chill sizzled across Boklao's thigh even as the taste of salt and smell of iron filled the reddening air.

The second constable lunged again but Boklao growled and spun past his spear, slammed one claw-hand after the other into his face, rammed an elbow back into his sternum, a fist into his groin, and then another elbow up into his jaw.

The first and third constables stabbed. Boklao snapped back. Their spears crossed just inches in front of his face. Boklao wrapped their red tassels around his hands, and yanked. They jerked forward, their heads cracked together, and Boklao snarled and shot in. He smashed the first one in the temple with his palm and then his elbow, grabbed the third and head-butted him in the nose, turned and side-kicked the first, his leg a tiger's tail, kept turning and uppercut the third, his fist a tiger's head.

Then Boklao stood back to back to back with the two rebel leaders, Shaggy-head in a wide, square stance with hammers high, Glower-face angled, sword straight out in front of him, and Boklao in-between, claws low.

The remaining constables looked at them and then broke ranks and fled back up the Western Road.

"Big Kung," Shaggy-head said. "We're—"

"Clear," Glower-face said. "Yes, Yang, thank you I can see that. Now help me get everyone across the bridge before—"

"The bridge..." Boklao's eyes fell on it and then he fell on the banks beside its scorched foundations.

The wind screamed, the rain pounded, and the water raged by. Boklao strained for any sign, any trace... Then, off to the side, caught on the rocks... a scarf, a beige scarf—her scarf...

He reached out and caught it with his finger tips. It was dark now and, when he clutched it, blood seeped out over his hands—her blood...

"Wingchun!"

"What are you doing?"

Boklao leant further out, slipped in the mud, caught himself, and leant further still. "Wingchun!"

He was grabbed and pulled away. "Are you out of your mind?"

Boklao roared, his fist swung, and impact reverberated up his arm. "Let me go!"

"You...!" Big Kung's sword twanged free.

Then the ground shook.

"Bannermen!"

And Boklao was being dragged away, across the bridge and up into the mountains.

詠 春 傳 說

Eagle-Shadow turned his knife. Blood and rain rippled down the blade. "A daughter, master—a single daughter."

"The one who watched," the Lama said. "The one who screamed..."

Eagle-Shadow jerked his head back to where nearly a dozen townsfolk lay bound and butchered. "I can inquire after her, if she has not already been sent to join her family. If she has not—"

A horse snorted and skidded across the muck, and a bannerman leapt from its saddle and crashed down in Manchu salute.

"Rebels," he said. "They ambushed and murdered the constables sealing the western egress, and now flee towards the mountains. Four of us pursue."

The Lama glanced up at the spear, at the Emperor's trophy mounted high atop it. "Rebels do not concern me."

The bannerman bowed.

"And what of the single daughter, master?" Eagle-Shadow said.

"A single daughter is nothing," the Lama said. "The Shaolin presence here is no more."

詠 春 傳 說

Whipped by wind and pelted by rain they zigzagged through bamboo, circled around and around, climbed higher and then dove back down... Boklao didn't know where they were going. Didn't care. Didn't even realize it when they finally stopped...

"About damn time!"

"Quiet!"

"We're not being followed any more, Shaggy. Those pesky little banner-boys broke off hours ago."

"Well why the hell didn't you say so, Kwai?"

"Guess I was too busy overestimating your competence again."

"Or maybe you were too busy helping them let us off just so that they could snare us!"

Boklao collapsed back against the bamboo and stared at the scarf—her scarf...

Then lean fingers poked at his wrist and a sly, sharp face glowered down at him. "Where do you come from?"

"Here and there…"

"Not here," Big Kung said, "that's for damn sure."

"Just there, then." Boklao yanked his arm away and stood back up. "I have to go…"

"You're not in any condition to go anywhere. Do you have any idea how much blood you've lost?"

"It's not mine." Boklao clutched the scarf tighter. "It's just on my hands…"

"What are you—?"

Boklao shoved past him, stumbled a few steps, and then the ground fell away beneath him. "A cliff…"

The bamboo spread out below, dark green torn white by the monsoon, bleeding oily, black smoke.

"What have I done…?"

"Stay where you are!"

Boklao turned back.

Rebels closed in around him, their weapons up.

"I don't want any trouble," Boklao said.

"Trouble?" The voice was gratingly familiar… "There's eight bushels of them, boy, and only the one little sad speck of you. Don't expect it'll be much trouble…"

"Shut up, Kwai." Yang poked in Boklao's direction with one octagonal-headed hammer, winced, and then poked with the other. "He's no Ch'ing."

"Well, he's sure as hell not one of you…"

"He just fought with us! He's—"

"A stranger, an unknown—a threat."

"That's right," Boklao said. "That's why I have to go."

"And that's why you can't let him." Kwai circled around, his coarsely woven, conical hat low, and his strangely mottled robes blending with the bamboo. "You have no idea what he really is but he knows just exactly what you are now, doesn't he. More to the point—he knows exactly *where* you are. When the Ch'ing catch him, he'll talk. Maybe willingly, maybe at the end of a saber. But he'll talk…"

"We're wasting time." Big Kung tore a long swathe from his sash and pressed it into the blood-soaked shoulder of an old, crow-faced man. "Time some of our people don't have!"

"Listen to Number-One-Son, Shaggy. This has to be ended now..."

"Only way this ends," Boklao said, "is with me leaving."

"You're not going anywhere," Yang said. "Not until we sort this out."

"I'd rather go past you—" Boklao's hands clawed open. "—but I'll go through you if I have to."

"He's bluffing," Kwai said, "a fox ready to bolt for its hole. Rush him before it's too late. I'll supervise."

Boklao dug his right foot into the mud for stability and then emptied the weight off his left for speed. His breath rose hot and high.

Yang cursed. The rebels advanced and—

"Stand down!"

The voice cracked like thunder across the cliff.

Kwai scoffed. "Yes, stand down. Sit down. Why not just bend over and—"

"And what?" The rebels parted and a broad, bold man strolled out from between them.

"Master Law." Yang rushed over and bowed. "They fought well, all of them—your first son especially. He made you proud."

Master Law turned. "Big Kung?"

"We lost four defending the crossing and that many more will not last the night..." Big Kung pressed his fingers into the wrist of the mousy guest-house owner, Tsui. "Twelve need blood-clotting and eight bone-setting, including Five-Metal Yang."

Yang huffed. "I'm fine."

"Your arm is broken."

"Yes, but just in the one place..."

"Then our next great task falls to you, my son," Master Law said. "Take whomever is still able and secure us a perimeter. No engagement—you find out if the Ch'ing are following us and you report back, that's all. Do you understand?"

"I need to stay with the wounded, father," Big Kung said. "They—"

"Will be seen to by Brother Chan and the others."

"But I—"

"Must focus on the greater duty now, my son. Your people cannot suffer any more surprises tonight."

Master Law turned back to Yang. "Everyone else goes to the shelter."

"Everyone?" Kwai glared at Boklao. "He's given no sign, no signal."

"Want me to point to the earth and tell you I come from the water?" Boklao said. "Want me to take your tea with three fingers and tell you the path is clear? I know the signs, vagabond, the signals... they just don't have any meaning for me anymore."

"With a hundred mouths anyone could cough up a few words, boy, use them to save his own skin..."

"And you would be the expert in that," Yang said. "Wouldn't you?"

"Which is why you should listen to me, stumpy, and gut this bastard—"

Boklao growled. "Before this bastard guts you?"

"Kwai," Master Law said. "Go with Big Kung. Use your knowledge of the mountains to help him."

"Even my knowledge has limits..."

"Test them."

"Fine..." He kept his eyes on Boklao. "We'll finish this later..."

"Hell of a fighter," Yang said to Master Law. "I didn't recognize the system though... The legs were embroidered a little but the fists were short as the South..."

Master Law glanced at Boklao's clawed hands. "From Honan to Fukien to here, those traits are... rather specific..."

"From here to somewhere else," Boklao said. "Whatever traits you think I have are rather specifically getting the hell away from you and yours."

Master Law smiled and then his hand shot out, his first knuckle extended like the eye of a phoenix.

Boklao tried to block but too late—the phoenix eye pressed into his stomach and his hands fell limp to his sides. Then it measured its way up his chest, sealed point after point. Boklao tried to pull away but his legs were already stuck. His waist, his shoulders, one after the other they went as cold and dead as he felt inside. Couldn't see, couldn't even smell...

"Forgive me." Master Law's voice faded. "But that we cannot allow."

詠 春 傳 說

Smoke twisted up, bow shaped and high as a tower, high as the world...

Fire fell, but water rose up and engulfed her. It wiped away the pain and the grief... It wiped away everything...

She surged down the river.

Flashes of light and dark streaked by.

Ten Palaces loomed silent.

Silent but for the voices...
The voices whispered...
She smashed across the rocks.
The dark laughed. "Death comes for you."
The light wailed. "But it comes in degrees."
And tumbled out over the mud.
Vast wings strummed the wind and an ancient grace descended.
She couldn't move.
The light faded. The dark flew.
Couldn't even breathe.
And mercy claimed her.

詠 春 傳 說

Water dripped dark, numbing... Then fire flared bright, searing... Boklao roared, exploded into it, and slammed it against the jagged wall.

"What the—!"

A lantern splashed down and sputtered out. Pain shot through Boklao. He clenched his teeth and strained his eyes to focus through it. Cave... He was in a cave surrounded by corpses... No, not corpses... In the flickering light, they writhed and moaned and coughed and cried out—corpses that didn't know it yet...

"How remarkable," the old, piebald man said. "It looks like the Ch'ing actually managed to pierce every spot on you but the ones that really matter..."

Boklao held him pinned to the wet limestone. "Out..."

"Careful, if you move around too much you'll dislodge the poultices and start bleeding all over again, and then it really won't matter how many spots they missed, yes?"

"Have to get out..."

He dropped the piebald and stumbled past his curses. The tunnel was crammed with women and children, groaning, sobbing... Boklao pushed through them towards the faint glow and muted din of the monsoon.

Outside, men scrambled to carry bags and cart barrels, but when they saw him, the rebels dropped what they were doing and reached for their weapons.

Boklao wanted to fight, wanted to get away, but he couldn't raise a hand, couldn't take even one more step. He collapsed down on the far side of the clearing.

"Wingchun…"

Then he tore open what was left of his indigo jacket and bound her scarf and her blood around his hand.

Their eyes met.

Fire flared. Water flooded.

She called out his name.

She accused him.

And she was gone.

詠 春 傳 說

Their eyes met.

Wood stabbed and steel slashed.

He called out her name.

He reached for her.

And he was gone.

"Boklao…"

The raw edge of an earthenware cup pressed against Wingchun's lips and strong, bitter tea swirled into her mouth. "Drink."

The smooth hardness of a porcelain spoon pushed past her teeth and spicy, sour broth poured down her throat. "Eat."

But she felt no warmth, no substance.

"Where… where am I?"

"Safe, girl."

"Girl…?" her nose crinkled. "Who…?"

A face descended over her, elusive yet full, warm yet serene, kind yet certain. A face she'd known all her life—

"Auntie…"

12

In Panther's Eye

Dawn broke pale and thin behind the wall of clouds, and the wind drove the rain across Boklao in sheets layered like brocade. But it did nothing to wash away the stench, the ash and blood and—

"Tepid rice porridge...?"

A boy hunkered in front of him, maybe a dozen years old, already bold if not yet broad. "I'm Little Kung."

Boklao nodded. "Law's son..."

"Second son, not that most people seem to notice the resemblance..." Little Kung shrugged open his blanket and held out a covered bowl. "Butcher Ngao swears it's supposed to smell like that, but then he spends his life nose-deep in pig guts..."

"Not just the resemblance...." Boklao tilted his head. "I've seen you before..."

"Seen me? You saved me! Me and my mother and chopstick girl too!"

"Chopstick girl?"

"You know, Yim—"

"Wingchun..."

"That's what I said! You saved all of us, like something right out of the Three Kingdoms! Like a... a martial hero!"

"Don't say that."

"What, why? It's true, isn't it?"

"Go." Boklao turned away. "Get back to the caves."

"But I'm—"

"Not safe out here."

"You think I'm afraid of a little monsoon?"

"He's not talking about the monsoon—"

Boklao's nostrils flared. "Vagabond..."

Kwai seeped from the bamboo. "—he's talking about me."

"What are you doing here?" Little Kung said. "You're supposed to be helping Big Kung with—!"

Kwai lifted his ragged slipper and kicked Little Kung towards the caves. "Time to scurry on back to your mother."

"Pig headed, ox balled—!" Little Kung's face bunched up and he stomped off. "I'm telling!"

"Do." Kwai turned back to Boklao. "Look at that, both your feet so conveniently out of town... "

A smile cut across Boklao's face. "I know your kind, vagabond—bully, extortionist... You prey on others because you're terrified of being preyed on yourself."

"Brilliant insight, boy. Makes me feel so brave and true that I wasted three perfectly good flying daggers on saving your worthless hide... Of course, if I'd known it was *your* worthless hide—"

"You'd have wasted them in me?" Boklao stood. "I could have dealt with those constables all by myself, vagabond, just as easily as I'm about to deal with you."

"I don't have to refrain this time, not like I did back at the guest-house..."

"But you don't have that pack of rebels to do your killing for you either, not like back at the cliff..."

"If I wanted you killed, boy, you'd know it by the shamed reception of your ancestors in the next life."

"Only shot you had, vagabond, was with those flying daggers thrown from hiding."

Kwai looked up. Water streamed off the coarse rim of his hat and down past his sneer. "My signature."

Boklao's hands clawed open. "Here's mine."

詠 春 傳 說

Smoke hissed. Flame snarled.
And the voices whispered.

Wingchun's eyes flew open. She lay in a rickety hovel, wrapped in strong, bitter bandages and cocooned in thick, woven blankets. Rain dripped down from the cobbled mass of wood and metal above. It made the muddy pools next to her ripple and jump and her reflection in them all but unrecognizable...

"You cannot drown life out with emptiness, girl," Auntie said. "Not any more than you will be able to consume it with rage."

"I'm not drowning anything out," Wingchun said. "I don't have anything left to drown. Everything I ever had is gone."

"Not everything." Auntie pushed more tea at her. "Much remains within you."

"You don't know that, you weren't there. You... you left...?"

"Girl..."

"Did you know what was going to happen, is that why? Did you warn my father? Did you even try?"

"Not nearly hard enough..." Auntie sighed. "What happened was always a possibility, but we—but I—felt my presence would only increase the risk. So I stayed nearby, kept watch until..."

"Until you saw the Ch'ing coming?"

"Until I allowed myself to be distracted, to be led astray. It all happened so fast. I returned as soon as I realized but it was too late. Lanchow was burning and your father... Your father was..."

"Gone."

"And you all but with him, so far down the river that, at first, I thought you no more than an illusion. I was not sure if I could bring you back but you are strong... Something within you would not give up, would not yield."

"Or maybe it really was an illusion..."

"Is that how you feel?"

"I don't know." The steam from the teacup rushed up over Wingchun's face. "I don't feel anything, not really." She took a sip. "Even this tea seems so cold, so bland..." And set it back down. "You say much remains within me but I feel nothing, nothing at all..."

"Like trying to escape the inferno by leaping into the flood..." Coins clinked in Auntie's hand. "Heaven and earth mingle now within you, girl, and you are trapped apart from your essential nature. Yin & Yang are confused, bright without and dark within. The Tao is faint and by fire, through water, your essence is disturbed and your life shaken."

"Maybe... maybe my life was shaken but not by fire or water. It was shaken long before that."

詠 春 傳 說

Lightning flashed, thunder boomed, and Master Law was between them. "What do you think you're doing?"

"Business," Kwai said. "As in ours."

"Your only business," Master Law said, "is to help my first son secure the perimeter."

"I'm working my way out..."

"Work faster, unless, that is, you've decided to dissolve our arrangement and return what it is I gave you?"

"What...? No!"

"Then leave my sight before I make that decision for you."

Kwai spat and seethed and seeped back into the bamboo.

Master Law turned to Boklao. "I wanted you to rest, to give your considerable injuries a chance to heal. Now I don't know whether I should paralyze you again or just put your stubbornness to work for us."

"Don't know what your deal is with the vagabond, old man, but I don't do servant. I didn't ask to be here and—"

"And you think any of us did?" Master Law swept his arms wide. "Look around you, boy. We're scattered like geese across the field, do you really think any of us asked to be here?"

"Then I'll just be one less to worry about." Boklao glanced at the rebels. "Soon as you call off your dogs..."

"Answer a question for me first."

"What?"

"My second son managed to delay our departure from Lanchow. He claims that while doing so he saw Old Yee. He claims... Well, he claims he saw things that cannot easily be explained unless Old Yee was..."

"Shaolin."

詠 春 傳 說

"He told you," Auntie said. "He finally told you..."

"You… you knew?" Wingchun's face crumbled. "Of course you knew… Everyone else knew but me…"

"No one else knew *because* of you. Your father felt it necessary for your protection."

"I didn't need that protection. I didn't need to be his burden."

"Your father needed it."

"And what about you? You could have said something. You could have told me."

"It was not my place," Auntie said. "All I could do was trust that your father would tell you in a time of his own choosing."

"Well then your trust was misplaced," Wingchun said. "He didn't tell me in a time of his own choosing at all. He told me only in a time when he no longer had a choice. He told me only when Boklao forced him to, when Boklao offered to take up the burden of my protection, to suffer me as his wife, if only my father would teach him his secrets…"

詠 春 傳 說

"I asked to learn from him," Boklao said, "so I could protect her…"

Master Law nodded. "When Old Yee was gone."

Boklao tilted his head. "How did you—?"

"He came to me for medicine."

詠 春 傳 說

"The lungs are governed by the metal element," Auntie said. "They hold all the grief, all the pain. If they hold it too long, too deep—"

"How long?" Wingchun said.

"Since that night, the night your family died."

"No, I mean, if that devil hadn't come?"

詠 春 傳 說

"A few years," Master Law said.

"Years?"

"Perhaps less. Such deaths come in degrees."

"But Old Yee still had time…"

詠 春 傳 說

"Time enough for Boklao to get his secrets."
"You truly think secrets are what he sought?"

詠 春 傳 說

"Doesn't matter."
"How could it not?"

詠 春 傳 說

"Because Boklao died as well," Wingchun said. "He died without ever getting what he really wanted or wanting what he really got."

詠 春 傳 說

"Because Wingchun died too," Boklao said. "Died without ever knowing what I really wanted or what I really got…"

詠 春 傳 說

Little Kung tiptoed around the bamboo. Boklao and his father were still talking at the edge of the clearing but the wind and rain blotted out their words. He needed to get closer but he had to be very, very—

"You're supposed to be with mother in the caves."

—careful.

Little Kung rolled his eyes. "Isn't anybody actually *on* patrol?"

Big Kung glowered. "When mother learns you've snuck out…"

"She won't.

"She will when I tell her."

"When you tell her what, that my eavesdropping interrupted your own?"

"She won't care about that."

"Father will."

"And you think that matters to me?"

Little Kung turned away. "I think it's supposed to."

Big Kung grabbed him. "Kwai might be an insufferable ass, but he was right about one thing—that man with father—"

"His name is Boklao!"

"—is a threat."

"What are you talking about? He—"

"Saved your life, yes, and then just two weeks later the Ch'ing follow and very nearly end all of ours."

"That wasn't his fault!"

"You don't know that, you don't know anything." Big Kung stared back at the clearing. "And don't ever let me catch you outside the caves again."

詠 春 傳 說

"I'm sorry," Master Law said. "I truly am."

"Don't want your sorrow," Boklao said. "Just your distance."

"Where will you go? Where have you to go?"

"I answered your one question."

Master Law glanced at the rebels. "Humor the hand that holds the leash."

Boklao shook his head. "Anywhere."

"And do what, find another disciple of Shaolin?"

"That door is closed."

"Yet another can open…"

"Not here. Not with you."

"I made a mistake with Old Yee," Master Law said. "I had my suspicions but I never acted on them. I won't make the same mistake with you."

"No," Boklao. "You'll make a whole new one."

"You lack purpose—I can give it to you."

"I don't want it."

"Why? Why fight so hard to leave when you have nowhere to go?"

"Because I won't let anyone else carry me across the river!"

"You think yourself a scorpion, do you?" Master Law smiled. "You think that if I pick you up, I'll be stung?"

"Nature of the thing, even the novice knows that."

"I am no novice and when I pick up a scorpion it's not to carry it."

"Then…?"

"It's to hurl it into the face of my enemy."

Boklao blinked. "Well, that's plain enough…"

"My people are in desperate need, boy. My rebels are righteous and they are trained, but that training has never been tested, not really, and I fear even now so much remains to test them still…"

"Like me?"

"You have skill and experience that can help them. You have proven yourself a brave man and true—a martial hero."

"What some call heroes are just those unlucky enough to survive what destroys everything else around them. When that happens time and again, they learn not to tempt fate any more. They let it go."

"Only if they lack the strength to wield it." Master Law's bronze cloak billowed, red silk fell away, and a cutlass leapt up into the night.

Its brass handle shone gold in the lightning and the nine-rings bound across its spine jangled louder even than the thunder.

Boklao gaped. "Ming Dynasty..."

"This was given to me many years ago by a grand-disciple of Abbot Chi Sim in thanks for saving his life." Master Law bowed and held it out with both hands. "I offer it to you now in thanks for saving the lives of my wife and second son, and for fighting by my people's side."

Two characters gleamed along the blade. "One man, one cutlass," Boklao read. "All you need to be a warrior is a weapon."

Master Law turned it over. "One family, one heart," he read. "A weapon is nothing if not wielded in righteousness."

"And a warrior is nothing if he does not fight for the good of his people. My father told me the same thing once..."

"This is the blade of a martial hero," Master Law extended it to Boklao. "Take it."

"Can't, I'm not worthy."

"Perhaps, perhaps not. Take it and how you wield it will show us both."

詠 春 傳 說

Wingchun peeked out past the tattered curtain of the hovel. Long, thin drawers etched with tiny characters squatted on a lopsided counter beside chipped bottles and crusted jars.

"Kwang will find it, great lady."

"I have asked you not to call me that," Auntie said.

A wizened old man with a gap-toothed grin hopped around and rummaged through a set of crates. "You are a crane among the chickens, great lady. What else could Kwang call you?"

"Hopeful—that when I return with the final ingredient you will have everything in place."

"Kwang would have phoenix feathers and unicorn horns in place if you'd but ask it, great lady! You can bet your Buddha he would!"

Auntie sighed and pattered out into the gray-hued drizzle.

Wingchun waited for Kwang to hop back around and then slipped out after her.

There were stalls everywhere, a maze filled with sizzling oil, roasting meat, and bodies too many and too close. People haggled and coins clinked back and forth, hot and loud...

"Nice pendant?"

A man shoved a handful of necklaces at her. His hair was piled unshaven and unkempt atop his head. "Pretty pendant? Pure jade. You like? You buy?"

"No..."

Another man barged between them. "Tribesman," he whispered. "You're wise to avoid them—not well suited to retail. One of my paper blessings would ensure—"

Wingchun pushed past him, past the blanket-weavers and dressmakers, the noodle and soup stands... She pushed until she came to a small counter at the edge of the market and then she stopped dead.

"Tofu..."

A ragged customer waited, mouth open, hand thrust out... A shiny white square plopped into a dull black bowl... Wingchun almost reached out to serve it...

Metal buckled. Wood splintered.

And the voices cried out.

"—Miss...? Hello, miss!"

Wingchun blinked.

A stubby, pot-sticker of a man stared back at her. "Your order?"

"My...? Where—? I'm sorry, I... Where am I?"

"Mr. Tao's Tofu, of course, only—and therefore best—in all of Donglai Market!"

"Donglai...?"

"Now," Mr. Tao said. "Can I get you a firm square or perhaps some silken pudding?"

"Nothing, I—"

"No need to be polite! Skinny as you are, you should take both before the wind picks up too much!"

Wingchun shook her head and backed away. "Please..."

"What's the matter, you don't like tofu?"

"It's not the tofu..."

"Then—" Mr. Tao stiffened. "No, it's too early, it's not yet time!"

Wingchun turned and saw one of the far-off mountains move... But it wasn't a mountain—just a man who loomed every bit as large, a mass of muscle and bone clad in black pants and an open vest, with beady eyes and a braid thick as rope.

As she watched he lumbered over to the winemaker and snatched something from his hand. Then he swatted the old man aside and plucked two full jugs from his stores.

Mr. Tao poked his head through the curtained doorway and into the hovel behind his counter. "Stay still. Not a move, not a sound, understand?"

He spun back around and yanked the curtain closed, but not before Wingchun glimpsed a young girl inside. "What's happening?"

"Are you joking?" Mr. Tao fumbled to fill a red envelope with all the coin he had.

"No, I—Who is that?"

"Not who, what! Panther-King, leader of the mountain bandits. He comes to Donglai once a season. We have to pay him tribute, half of everything we make, and he still takes more—our food, our supplies, our *daughters*..."

"He takes...?"

"Whatever he wants!" Mr. Tao stopped and stared at her. "You... you shouldn't be out here, a girl alone and unescorted! What were you thinking? Hurry, hide before—"

The gray sky went black as Panther-King reached over Wingchun, scooped up an entire cake of tofu into his maw, belched, then scooped up another.

"Still edible, Boy Sao..."

"T-Tao, Honored Panther. My name is—"

Panther-King stared at him.

"Sao is fine..."

"And where's that daughter of yours?" Panther-King said. "She must be just about edible now as well..."

"She's not here. She... she died over the summer. You know, what with the d-drought and..." His face shattered. "Please, she's all I have!"

"You have your life, tofu-maker, at least for a few moments more." Panther-King tore the curtain off the hovel. "Come out, little blossom."

"Honored Panther, I beg you," Mr. Tao said.

"Quickly, or you may not have sufficient time to see to your father's burial rites before we leave…"

Mr. Tao put himself between his daughter and Panther-King. "Please!"

Wingchun shook. She should do something…

Panther-King knocked Mr. Tao aside.

She had to!

"Leave them alone!"

"Who…?" Panther-King's massive head swung down and around. "What's this, another daughter? Have you been holding out on me, Sao?"

"N-no!" Mr. Tao scrambled back to his feet. "She… she's just a customer Honored Panther. Nothing—!"

"Nothing?" Panther-King grabbed Wingchun and pulled her close. "Riper than the little blossom, if not as lush… More bone than meat really, but still—something to gnaw on through the winter…"

Wingchun thrashed. "Let go of me!"

"Spirited, I like that. Spirited tastes good."

"I said let go!"

Her hips twisted and her arm shot out.

Panther-King's head cracked to the side. He stayed there a moment, his huge brow folded and his eyes beaded dark. Then his palm lashed back.

Fire raged outside the walls. Ghosts swarmed past her window. They couldn't get out, couldn't run…

She could hear their whispers.

Wingchun's eyes blurred, her ears rang, but there was no pain. Shouldn't there be pain? "Is that… is that all you've got?"

Panther-King bellowed and struck again.

The door burst open. Demons drove into their home. Hands covered her, she couldn't cry out…

But they could.

Her face was thick and her legs light, but still no pain. "That… that it?"

Panther-King howled and his hand clamped around her throat.

The monster reared up. Blood fell like rain. They passed her from one to the other, so tight she could barely breathe.

But they could scream...

Then she was floating high above her body. Her limbs dangled like over-cooked noodles and her face was pale beyond porcelain. Life was leaving her... or was she leaving it?

She could. She knew it. All she had to do was give up and let the emptiness drown her. She could leave this life and hope for some small mercy in the next.

She could be with her family again...

13
House of the Green Snake

Boklao crouched, his nostril's flared, he rolled the broken end of a bamboo shoot between his fingers, and his eyes scanned from east to west…

"Well?"

The forest spun, stalk and leaf blurred by. Then—

"Nothing."

Big Kung bent over him. "Nothing?"

"In this monsoon?" Boklao stood. "A whole damn division could march through here and it'd be washed clean within the hour."

"If that's the height of your skill then I don't know what use my father thought you'd be to me."

"Me neither, but he did seem real anxious about leaving you out here all by your lonesome. Anxious enough to send me *and* the vagabond out after you…"

"You talk of anxiety but can't even manage the expression on your own face, and you question me when I'm here serving my father while your's is… where exactly?"

"Dead."

Big Kung's eyes flickered. "And you're supposed to be his rites?"

Boklao growled. "What did you—?"

A cry, half-chitter, half-caw zipped through the bamboo.

"Kwai's signal," Big Kung said.

"That was a signal?"

Big Kung glanced east. "A warning... I'll pass it on to Lai Bang and Chao Jeet. Wait here and—"

"You wait."

Boklao plunged through the dense foliage, over a rise and down a ravine, and Kwai was there, at the edge of a river, bodies at his feet—a man, a woman, a boy and... and a girl...

"A family," Boklao whispered. "Slaughtered and left to rot..."

Their eyes empty, they gazed off to the heavens... all except the girl. She gazed right at Boklao. She accused...

"Not slaughtered," Kwai whispered back. "Not hardly..."

Boklao tilted his head.

"Don't you turn your back on me," Big Kung yelled as he caught up. "Don't you ever—!"

Then he saw the family and his face drained.

"They yours?" Boklao said.

"They're all ours."

"This is the Baksoy River," Kwai said. "Used to be no more than trickle, one of the smallest tributaries of the Lan, but now all the damn mulberry fields have turned to seas..."

"We need to tell my father," Big Kung said. "He needs to—"

The bamboo stirred.

Big Kung spun.

Boklao's hand went to his cutlass.

Kwai snorted, dashed around, and plucked Little Kung out from the underbrush.

Big Kung's eyes puckered and bulged. "What did I tell—!"

"You weren't the one who caught me!" Little Kung said.

"This isn't a game! Do you have any idea how dangerous it is in these mountains? You could have gotten yourself killed!"

"Forget him," Kwai said. "He could have gotten *me* killed."

"Hey!" Little Kung said. "You didn't even know I was following you until—"

Kwai's face curdled and he wiped his hands off on Little Kung's robes. "Until your utter lack of experience came spewing up all over us?"

Little Kung flushed. "I only lack experience because no one will give me any!"

"You want experience?" Big Kung said. "Prepare to experience being dragged back to mother by your ear! If you're lucky, you're beating will last only as long as it takes me to tell father that the bandits are making their move, and—"

"Bandits?" Boklao said.

"Panther's Head." Big Kung glanced at Kwai. "We had an understanding but, now that our house burns, they obviously see their chance to loot."

Kwai chuckled.

"You have something to add?"

"I don't cast pearls."

"Wasn't bandits," Boklao said. "That's what he has to add."

Big Kung scoffed. "Look at the bodies, ransacked, slaughtered..."

"You look at them." Boklao crouched down. "Look at the wounds, small, precise—uniform. Ransacked maybe but not slaughtered. This family was—"

"Executed...!"

Boklao reached down to close the daughter's eyes, but then he snapped back up and his cutlass jangled out. "Still warm..."

"Run." Big Kung shoved Little Kung. "Now!"

Kwai tilted his head. "Footsteps... maybe a dozen..."

"Fading?" Big Kung said.

"Getting louder... Circling back around!"

"Not for long..." Boklao hefted his cutlass.

"No," Big Kung said. "We're not supposed to engage, just scout and report back. There's a good chance they don't even know we're here."

"They know."

"Even if they do, we can still leave, disappear back into the bamboo before they ever finish circling. We can leave them to—"

"To stumble over another family? I don't think so."

"You don't think at all! You—Wait, what are you doing?"

Big Kung grabbed for him, but Boklao was already up the ravine, off the ridge, and into the Constabulary Army.

詠 春 傳 說

The screams grew louder.
They beckoned...

All Wingchun had to do was give up…

Then something gleamed bright and cold.

"Release the girl."

Panther-King grunted. "Be gone, Little Grandmother. You are far too fermented for even my tastes."

"She is under my charge," Auntie said.

"No more—I have claimed her."

"She is not yours to claim."

"Why? Is… is there another? Is there another who dares claim what is mine by right? If so I challenge him to come forward! I challenge him to face me!"

"Your challenge is accepted."

"Then bring him on! Bring him on so that I may tear the arms from his body and beat him to death with his own fists!"

"Such things must be handled properly."

"My hands, his mangled corpse, what could be more proper?"

"There are traditions…"

"Traditions…? You propose a formal match?"

"I have heard you favor Donglai with your presence once a season," Auntie said. "I will make the arrangements for winter's end and—"

"No, Little Grandmother," Panther-King said. "The unseasonable weather has made me… feverish. I doubt my current kennel will last out the month, much less the winter. We will do this now."

"Tradition cannot be rushed. Two months."

"After I have just so perfectly tenderized this morsel? Two months is far too long."

"One month then. Time enough for word to spread and crowds to gather, for Panther-King to once again prove his power."

"You're as cured as thousand-year egg, Little Grandmother, but spirited… I give you your month, no more."

The floating stopped and the falling began.

"But know this," Panther-King said. "Know that if by some chance my challenger fails to appear, or if somehow my morsel loses its way back to me, I will make horrors here such as even the Ch'ing themselves have yet to conceive. I will make horrors here, Little Grandmother, and then I will come and visit worse upon *you*…"

詠 春 傳 説

The world flashed black and red in time with the pounding of Boklao's heart. Between each flash faces broke from enraged to panicked, cries shatter into screams, and hot, acrid blood filled the air.

He brought his cutlass down again and again and again and—

"You really are out of your mind!"

Boklao swung his cutlass around but a sword twanged up against it.

"You inglorious bastard," Big Kung said. "I should cut your throat and leave you to rot with the Ch'ing!" He glanced at the cutlass. "A weapon for a weapon... you got yours so that my father would get his and inevitable as nature, it turns against all of us!"

Boklao's chest rose and fell.

"Are you listening?" Big Kung said. "Do you even hear me?"

His ears rang and the red drained gray.

"He hears you." Kwai reached down and plucked two flying daggers from a constable's arm and one from the side of his head. "I reckon they'll be hearing this all the way back to the damn capitol..."

詠 春 傳 說

They flew up the mountain from Donglai, past rough-hewn crags and jagged spires etched through by water wound into streams and stretched into falls. They ascended narrow ridges and sheer cliffs, up and up, into a sea of clouds.

"Where—" Wingchun coughed. "Where are we going?"

"To the summit," Auntie said. "To the temple... or what remains of it. The way is very old. There are few who remember it anymore and fewer still who can follow."

"Temple...?"

Colors faded in the mist and the sounds grew long and deep. They crossed an overgrown bridge and passed beneath a crumbled arch and a scorched pagoda.

"The House of the Green Snake."

"—*Our master's house... beneath which we sit and speak here and now...*"

It soared above her in splendor and ruin, its outer wall broken, its gate breached... The wind picked up and debris swirled from their path. The courtyard was desolate and the plum trees that lined it were barren.

"The house of my brother..."

詠 春 傳 說

The barest light of day flickered through the rain and the bamboo.

"Let me guess," Boklao said. "You want your cutlass back?"

Master Law folded his arms. "It would be a grave mistake for you to underestimate the seriousness of this situation."

"For the both of us."

"Damn you, boy, do you think I don't know what burns inside you now—rage like the race down the mountain, each step faster and less controllable than the one before, each moment that much closer to the stumble, to the fall? Do you think I don't feel it too, that part of me would not have wanted to do the very same thing?"

Boklao tilted his head.

"The other part, however," Master Law said, "the responsible part, would have stepped up immediately to remind me just how utterly short-sighted actually doing it would be."

"You knew," Boklao said. "You knew what I was when you picked me up."

"I still know, even as you try everything you can to prove me wrong."

"I did what I had to do. Now you have to do the same."

"What, send you away?"

"The Ch'ing are savage in avenging the deaths of their own..."

"Those constables were left behind, cut off," Master Law said. "Their loss will not draw any attention. And even if it does, we disposed of the bodies. There's no way for them to be traced back to you."

"You can't know that," Boklao said, "and if they are, the wrath of the Ch'ing will be brought down on you and everyone around you, including your family. Just like... like..."

"Just like Lanchow." Master Law nodded. "That's it, isn't it? You don't want to be away, you want to draw *them* away."

"I'm not unskilled..."

"That's what makes you so valuable."

"So costly."

"Tonight we will be holding the initiations, formally swearing in those townsfolk who survived and will now join our brotherhood. I would very much like for you to be there as well."

Boklao turned away. "I told you, I've forgotten all that."

Master Law turned him back. "Then it's long passed time for you to remember."

詠 春 傳 說

The whispers grew louder.
She floated towards them.
Then the world went dark.
And the screams became deafening...
Wingchun bolted up but something soft as cotton yet unyielding as steel eased her back down.

"Relax, girl."

She was surrounded by walls, smooth and slippery, and steam rushed up over her, so strong, so bitter...

"Your wounds run deep, girl. The medicinal bath will help."

The face above her flickered in the lantern light and then blurred and split, one part old and familiar, the other timeless and transcendent...

"Auntie...?"

"So you have always called me."

"Another lie..."

"Another life."

"Whatever that means..."

"You know."

"I don't! I don't even know who I am anymore. I thought I did once. I mean, I thought that even if I didn't know where I came from at least I knew who I was. And then my father finally told me, I finally found out where I came from, but I've lost who I am..."

"No, girl, all you lost was delusion."

"Really? Then you tell me, am I Yim Wingchun, daughter of Old Yee the tofu vendor, or am I the seventh daughter of Fong Dak, rebel of Shaolin?"

"There is no duality. Names can be known but not true names, not any more than true Tao. They change as we change—as we are born, as we study, as we take the vows or the stage or the field of battle, even as we die and are born again. Names change but essential essence remains—we are as we have always been, as we will always be."

"And you, who have you always been?"

"Who you've always known."

"A stranger."

"Girl…"

"My father's master's sister, my mother's teacher… The nun of the White Crane Temple…"

Auntie nodded.

"Wumei."

14
Origins & Initiations

Eagle-Shadow crashed down the Seven Star Crags, his eyes locked on the glistening river that tore through the provincial capitol of Kwailam while his finger scratched along the scar that tore through his own face—gone now in every way that mattered...

"The most magnificent place in the entire world," the old priest said, his voice a writhing whisper. "Here, behind the Old Palace Gates, over hills of brocade, caves of Buddhas and dragons, and twin lakes like silver eyes above their Banyan sentinel, and what is it you see? Certainly not what generations have eulogized..."

"Lamented, old priest, in the utter degradation of their exile... And as to what I see..." Eagle-Shadow gazed north. "I see endless plains thrust from the Long White Mountains down into the Yellow Sea... I see seasons, real seasons that scorch the earth and freeze the heavens to their marrow. I see Manchu, old priest, the home of my ancestors whose magnificence reduces this festering Southern quagmire to dust... I see it and I lament."

"Because exile too comes in gradations."

詠 春 傳 說

"The Ming Dynasty was a golden age for the Han people," Auntie said. "My father was a general and I grew up at court—"

"The Ming court?" Wingchun's nose crinkled. "But the Ch'ing have been in power for more than two hundred years already..."

"Should I fetch you an abacus, girl, or would you prefer I continue?"

"Sorry..."

"Back then there were no Ch'ing, only the scattered Jurchen tribes of dynasties past, and they paid tribute to the Ming..."

詠 春 傳 說

"The Aisin Gioro united the Jurchen clans," the old priest said, "forged the Manchu, and hammered out the Eight Banners. It was a second Jin Dynasty and with the great seal of the Mongol Khans, you claimed succession to the Yuan as well."

"I know the rise of my own people, old priest," Eagle-Shadow said. "Of my own empire..."

詠 春 傳 說

"But I understood so little of the politics at the time," Auntie said. "While my elder brothers followed in father's footsteps, and my elder sisters married men just the same, I was..."

"Different?"

"Mother called me 'lively', father preferred 'disgraceful'. This, of course, led to disharmony and to settle things for the good of the Lui clan, father decided I would be sent away.

"Mother was powerless to prevent it but not to effect it... Instead of the cloister father had picked out she sent me to an ancient temple high in the Wutang Mountains of Hopei.

"I doubt the old masters had ever seen anything like me but their patience was inexhaustible. Through their grace, I became the best of the novices—or one of the best at least. Li Bashan, my brother disciple and my dearest friend, was also my greatest rival.

"At the temple we received martial instruction alongside our scholarly pursuit for the Tao is to be found in all things. The masters preserved an ancient set of Eight Palms from the Song Dynasty, and Li Bashan and I practiced them constantly. He was especially adept at the Fire Palm and I the Water.

"The temple became our world and we knew nothing of what was transpiring beyond its gates…"

詠 春 傳 說

"The Ming were corrupt," Eagle-Shadow said. "Trade faltered, harvests fell short, and time and again they failed to respond."

"So the bandit lords grew bolder," the old priest said, "and finally they marched their hordes into the northern capitol of Peking itself. Most of his councilors dead or deserted, the last Ming emperor committed suicide, and the satrap—"

"Turned to *us* for help."

"The bandits were defeated but Peking was still lost."

"It wasn't lost, old priest—it was reclaimed. Our emperor ascended the Dragon Throne and took his rightful place beneath the heavens."

詠 春 傳 說

"I still remember the moment I heard," Auntie said, "the instant I found out my family was dead. I remember it down to the smallest of details…"

"How… how did you…?"

"Cope? I didn't, not at all."

"But your training—"

"Deserted me. Or rather I deserted it. I allowed myself to be consumed by emptiness and filled by rage. I wanted vengeance. I went home, stormed the Forbidden City, and ended up in a duel with one of the imperial princes…"

"And?"

Auntie's face fell. "I killed him… But there were others. There are always others… I would have died there or worse, I would have betrayed my masters, my family…"

"What happened?"

"Fahai happened. The Abbot of Shaolin himself appeared—how and from where I still do not know—and he pulled me back."

詠 春 傳 說

"You proclaimed the Ch'ing," the old priest said, "but dynastic succession took time."

"The South was problematic," Eagle-Shadow said, "but—"

"Before the South."

"You mean the Outer Mongols? A minor—"

"I mean the Tibetans."

"The Western Barbarians were nothing."

"Really? You consider your master nothing?"

Eagle-Shadow glanced back at the palace. "No... of course not!"

"Then do you really believe pacifying a nation of Lama would be nothing?"

"What are you talking about, old priest?"

"You've never seen their land, have you?"

"Have you?"

The old priest's eyes glinted. "I have seen mountains so vast they divide the earth in two," he said, "so high they press against the foundations of the heavens... Perhaps that is why everyone, from the smallest boy to the Diamond Master himself, is so devout in their search for the Buddha mind."

"The Buddha mind...?"

"Of course, did you really think that when the Indian Prince crossed over from the edge of world, his footsteps would not leave their trace?

"But the Lama—!"

"Were founded by him, by Ordator as they called him, long before the first of *your* people had heard even the briefest utterance of sutra.

"He climbed to the very top of their mountains, touched one finger to the earth and the other to the heavens themselves, and then opened his mouth and let loose the Lion's Roar—a sound so thunderous it shook the world...

"Before he left to continue his journey from the West, it was with that spirit, the spirit of the Lion's Roar, that he taught his first disciples the movements of the Bodhisattva so that they would have the strength to cultivate their enlightenment and to protect the purity of their faith.

"And they did, they took the Lion's Roar and embraced within it the grace of the crane and the power of the ape, the fists of the meteor and the body of adamant. They embraced within it all that and more..."

詠 春 傳 說

"Fahai brought me to Shaolin," Auntie said, "to the very seat of the Indian Prince, Damo..."

"Damo?" Wingchun said. "My father mentioned him..."

"He came to the Song Mountains millennia ago, found a cave and meditated without sleep or food for decades. As he sat, follower after follower gathered around him and when his meditation finally ended, he passed on to them the Buddha mind.

"He taught his disciples the Diamond Sutra to free their spirits, the Tendon Change Classic to deepen their breath, and the Warrior Attendant Fist to defend them from bandits and beasts. Then, when he was done, he placed the temple that had grown around him under the care of Kuo Yuan, the first abbot of the Young Forest—of Shaolin.

"Kuo Yuan developed the Warrior Attendant Fist into the Seventy-Two Postures and from him it was passed down and elaborated upon by succeeding generations until it reached the harmony of One-Hundred-and-Eight Postures in the Five Shape Fist—the strength of the tiger, the agility of the leopard, the speed of the snake, the precision of the crane, and the elusiveness of the dragon."

詠 春 傳 說

"Now there are many different sects of Lama," the old priest said. "Most, like the Diamond Master's, are numerous and known to all but there are others... even some who dress in crimson robes, paint their faces with ash, and carry blades to protect their people from raiders."

"Sounds like—"

"Your master but for the color of his robe and the purpose of his blade? Back then your master had no blade and his only purpose was the good of his sect, one of barely a handful and all but unknown..."

"Yet you know of it?"

"As I know the origin of all things..." The old priest shifted. "They learned both the scholar and the warrior arts, you see, but they favored peace and the sanctity of life above all. And for that, I am sure they considered themselves far superior in their faith to the others, which no doubt contributed to all the rumors..."

"Rumors?"

"That they still practiced elements of the forbidden Bon arts, that they were witches, sorcerers..."

"Were they?"

Laughter echoed all around, and a terrible presence surged over Eagle-Shadow.

"What is a sorcerer?"

詠 春 傳 説

"The Shaolin spread," Auntie said, "and their teachings flowed from temple to temple, from Shantung to Fukien to Kiangsi to Kwangtung, but there was never anything to rival Song Mountain, and never anyone to match Fahai.

"He became my mentor. He called me... he called me his Wumei, short for his Five-Petal Plum Flower in your dialect. It does not yield in the face of winter, you see, and so he somehow felt that it captured my essential nature." She smiled. "A reflection...

"We debated the sutras and I developed an affinity for his Crane Shape Fist as well..."

詠 春 傳 説

"Your master's people welcomed the coming of your Ch'ing Dynasty," the old priest said. "Did you know that? They considered you cousins, the fellow children of the great Khans of old, and thought peace, at last, might be on their borders. But you treated them like dogs, no better than any of the others you conquered.

"They were no better."

"So arrogant, so proud—so much like them. They could not stomach such a loss of face and so demanded that your emperor recognize them as brethren and allies, and when he would not, they rose up against you."

"And we put down their pathetic rebellion."

"You did no such thing."

"Careful, old priest, you speak to a captain of the banner..."

"A once and former captain, but yes, banner born and bred... And what is it they say about you again, about your prowess in combat?"

"That one of us, alone and unarmed, is the match of a hundred constables."

"And about your master?"

"That he could match a hundred bannermen..."

"Then consider dozens like your master, scores even... And with so many bannermen already committed to the campaign in the south, they were matchless. No Ch'ing could stand against them."

詠 春 傳 說

"Outside Shaolin, conditions continued to worsen," Auntie said. "The remnants of the Ming resistance were still waging their struggle in the South and word even reached us of an uprising in the northwest...

"There was a meeting of the elders, of the monks and priests of Shaolin, Wutang, O-Mei—of all the temples. The more militant among us wanted to get involved, some to join the fight against the Ch'ing, others to ally with them in hopes of currying favor.

"Fahai counseled that we should remain apart from worldly matters and take no action."

詠 春 傳 說

"The Lama had been feuding with the monks of Shaolin for centuries," the old priest said. "They felt the Shaolin had betrayed the teachings, had let their hereditary beliefs in the Tao, in Confucius—in all their petty ancestors and gods—destroy the purity of their faith. They considered the Shaolin heretics, worse than unbelievers. And, of course, the Shaolin held the Lama in the very same contempt.

"Debate settled some disputes, combat others. Your master's order preferred the former to the latter but, in either case, the Lama won more than they lost. Perhaps that is why the Shaolin chose the time of the uprising to attack..."

詠 春 傳 說

"Though many disagreed," Auntie said, "including my brother, Li Bashan, none would go against the will of the abbot of Shaolin."

詠 春 傳 說

"Some say it was as few as thirteen monks," the old priest said, "others a hundred-and-eight. Few know for certain..."

"But you do, don't you, old priest?" Eagle-Shadow said. "As you know the origin of all things?"

"That... is another story. For now all I will say is that those Shaolin who went did so to kill and to kill in such numbers that the snow was stained red with the blood of a generation.

"They broke the revolt and more—they laid whole villages, whole towns to waste...

"Your master was only a boy at the time, but not even children were to be spared. One of the Shaolin—pale as death and with eyes like the inferno—breeched the gates of his temple...

"Your master's master placed himself before the Shaolin and begged him in the name of the Goddess of Mercy to leave, to go back to wherever he'd come from, to find his own peace..."

Eagle-Shadow inched forward. "And...?"

"The monk killed him, of course."

"And then?"

"And then your master took the falchion from the monk's hands and, breaking every vow he'd ever made, every virtue he'd ever held, he took the head from the monk's shoulders."

15
Thirty Spokes

Boklao watched as the initiates' eyes were unbound and they were turned towards a small pavilion. Five-Metal Yang stood on one side of it, his right arm splinted but his left with flag held high—"the gate is open". Big Kung stood on the other—"the path is clear."

Piebald Chan carried a small incense burner down the steps between them. "Hereby, knowing full well the depth and breadth of our commitment, we join in this Society of Heaven & Earth, in communion and harmony."

The initiates repeated after him. "In honor and memory of the House of Ming we make this joining and adopt these principles of family. We bind ourselves together forever, beneath the heavens, upon the earth, beyond father, beyond brother, beyond son.

"May we be united against malice and deceit, and walk together as heroes under the brightness of the sun and moon, the fortunes of our family never to wane."

Water was poured over them to wash away the past. Their hair, shaved and bound in oppression, was cut loose and left to hang free down their shoulders. Their clothing, sullied by their oppressors, was stripped away and they were draped in cloth white as dawn, bound in sashes red as blood. Then they stepped out of their slippers and walked on, new men.

詠 春 傳 說

Wingchun gazed into the lantern. "Shaolin versus Lama... but my father told me that the Shaolin didn't kill, that they used bludgeons instead of blades?"

"Because with the bludgeon, the chance is less," Auntie said, "but there is always the chance."

"You're talking about intent but these Shaolin, they weren't taking any chances—they intended to kill. And the Lama, if they're also Buddhist, then—"

"Then how could it have ever happened?" Auntie sighed. "Words are easy, girl, and what else are vows or even virtues until put to the test?"

詠 春 傳 說

"My master killed the monk," Eagle-Shadow said.

"He killed many," the old priest said. "He gave his people a chance. They rallied around him, they fought back, and when there were no Shaolin left in his land, he buried his master by air and watched as the raptors carried him away. Then he vanished."

"Vanished?"

"His master dead, his sect no more, his faith shattered, and even his enemies slain or fled, it is not hard to imagine what happened. Such emptiness, such rage—

"It can be transcendent."

詠 春 傳 說

"When Fahai learned that some had gone against him," Auntie said, "that some had so utterly lost their way, he grew distant, distracted, and when I went to him, he ordered me to go."

"To go?" Wingchun said. "How could he do that to you?"

"I demanded the very same thing..."

"And what did he say?"

"That I had no choice."

"Of course you did! We all have the choice, even when they try to tell us otherwise. We have the choice and so did he!"

"He was Fahai, girl, and it was his will."

"So you just left..."

"I journeyed to Szechwan, to O-Mei. It was the last of the three great mountains and the only one I had yet to experience.

"I began my own meditation and my own training, and eventually others came to join me. The White Crane Temple was founded."

"The...?"

She has been under the care and tutelage of my sister, Wumei, Nun of the White Crane Temple.

Auntie nodded. "It was years later when Miu Sun appeared at my gates, a small girl cradled in his arms. They were injured and I hurried them inside. His temple—this very temple—had been destroyed by the Ch'ing and your mother's village wiped out along with it. Miu Sun found her, starving and alone in the mountains, and brought her to me."

"Why you? I mean—?"

"Why not care for her himself?" Auntie said. "His home was gone while mine was still safe, still secure, and... and I think he also felt we would share an affinity... We did, of course, and she became my seventh disciple."

"Tell me about her," Wingchun said, "what was she like?"

"You don't remember?"

"Only fragments, not enough..."

"She was alone but not abandoned, scared but still strong. She was just exactly like you."

詠 春 傳 說

Boklao stepped back into the shadows of the bamboo as Master Law came down from the pavilion and Piebald Chan, Five-Metal Yang, and even Big Kung formed up behind him.

"It began the first time under the harshness of Ch'ing rule," Master Law said to the initiates, "when the people banded together in family, then in extended clan, and then in societies. They swore to a common name and purpose, to share resources like the One Coins, or community services like the Fathers & Mothers, to feud like the Iron Rulers against the Children of the Dragon, and the bravest and the truest to support the anti-Ch'ing resistance. That was before..."

詠 春 傳 說

"I contented myself to teach and train your mother and my other disciples," Auntie said, "and to see to the education of the various novices until, one day, I felt... I felt ill...

"Other temples had fallen but there had been no survivors and so the true breadth of the Ch'ing plan had never been revealed, never even been imagined until... until Song Mountain Shaolin was destroyed and for the second time, my family was dead."

"That's... that's why he sent you away, wasn't it?" Wingchun said. "He knew, didn't he?"

"Of course he knew, he was Fahai."

"He didn't want you to die with him, he just didn't realize what it would be like to have to live without him, without any of them..."

"But *for* all of them."

"Sorry?"

"A message came, you see. It was from Chi Sim, greatest of Fahai's disciples and abbot of the Nine Little Lotus Temple in Fukien. It asked that I join him there and I could no more refuse him than I could his master.

"I dismissed the novices and sent most of my disciples back out into the world, to hide them and to keep them safe. I took only your mother with me and that only because of Miu Sun's request which accompanied Chi Sim's.

"Still, I left her in the tunnels where she would not risk the attentions of the unshaven disciples, and went up into the temple. Along with Chi Sim and Miu Sun, Miu Hin and Fung Dodak were there, and Yinian and Yichen, and others... even my oldest friend, Li Bashan, master of the Dragon Shape Fist, who many had come to call White-Eyebrow.

"Chi Sim told us what he knew—that one of our own had betrayed us and taught the Ch'ing the most ancient of the Shaolin arts, the Warrior Attendant Fist of Damo, and that they were using that knowledge to wipe us out.

"We went together to the heart of the temple, to the Wingchun Hall, and began to work on a new system, a system that combined the secrets of the three great temples—the shapes of Shaolin amplified by the changes of Wutang and bound by the power of O-Mei. We felt it was the only way to counter the combination of Mongol wrestling and traitor-taught Shaolin we would face.

"It took eighteen years to fully train a traditional warrior monk, after all, and we did not think we had eighteen months...

"Still, we were slowed by discord. Miu Sun wanted us to finish as fast as possible so that we could teach all the rebels who had flocked to our gates and joined our cause. Li Bashan, however, thought it better that we keep it to ourselves so that it would not also be betrayed to the Ch'ing and used against us."

"What did you decide?"

"Nothing. We came to no decision. We never had the chance..."

詠 春 傳 說

"It began again with the destruction of Southern Shaolin," Master Law said. "One of their novices, Ma Ningyee, had seduced a young lady and her daughter in a nearby village and killed them to cover his sins. But Abbot Chi Sim had seen through his deception and ejected him.

"In shame and anger, Ma went to the Ch'ing and offered to show them the secret path that led to the temple gates..."

詠 春 傳 說

"But Ma was not the only traitor," Auntie said. "While he led the Ch'ing armies from without, one of our own set fire to the temple from within."

詠 春 傳 說

"That idiot Ma ruined everything," the old priest said. "His spite coupled with your emperor's growing paranoia led them to move too soon..."

詠 春 傳 說

"I emerged from my meditation chamber in search of the others," Auntie said. "Smoke filled the corridors... I was intent on seeing your mother safely from the temple but Miu Sun convinced me to leave her care to another..."

"My father..."

"It seems even I had failed to fully appreciate the Old Snake's wisdom." Auntie's cheeks rounded but only briefly. "Then alongside my brothers and the monks and rebels all, we made our stand."

詠 春 傳 說

"Chi Sim himself," Boklao found himself saying, "met Ma the Apostate on the field of battle."

Master Law nodded. "Sent him to the next life in hopes of redemption."

詠 春 傳 說

"What does it matter, old priest?" Eagle-Shadow said. "What does it matter if they finished their little system or not, so long as they are dead and their system died with them?"

The presence surged stronger and more terrible.

"But they are not all dead, are they? They fled and the seeds of their system were scattered with them!"

詠 春 傳 說

"So many died..." Auntie shook her head. "We agreed that we would split up and meet again at my temple...

"I waited so long, so very long, but no one ever came."

"What happened?" Wingchun said. "Were they... I mean, they couldn't all be...?"

"Miu Sun fell at Fukien, Miu Hin and Fung Dodak were murdered later. Others—" Her eyes grew distant. "Others are still out there, somewhere...."

詠 春 傳 說

"Chi Sim fled to Kwangtung Province," Master Law said, "to the Vast Flower Pavilion. There he met with the descendants of the surviving Ming Generals and the leaders of the most powerful lineages.

"We are told they walked together until they came to a pool of surpassing beauty where they found a stone carved into the shape of a plum blossom. They picked it up only to discover that it was broken in half and yet each piece bore an inscription—'overthrow the Ch'ing' on one, 'restore the Ming' on the other.

"They took the halves, placed them upon the pavilion's altar, and offered up an oath sealed in blood in hopes the heavens would give them a sign. And though there was not a cloud in the sky, thunder crashed and, when they looked again, the stone was unbroken and the inscription was made whole. They had been given their sign.

"On that day—at that very moment—the Heaven & Earth Society was born.

"Together the founders trained the First Ancestors and sent them out to find the scattered Shaolin survivors and Ming loyalists, to spread the movement, and to train heroes brave and true enough to one day rise up and reclaim our land."

詠 春 傳 說

"Shaolin fell," the old priest said, "but like a phoenix the rebellion rose from its embers. You Ch'ing tried to stop it but you could not even find it.

"Your emperor could have come to me—he should have! Was I not the one who helped him before, who arranged *everything*? But his advisors had begun to fear me, to poison him against me. So, instead, he turned to the Lama. He knew—for I had told him—that the Lama had driven the Shaolin from their land, and he hoped they could do the same to the survivors in his. In return he offered them the one thing they wanted most in this life…"

"The pact," Eagle-Shadow said.

"Yes—the pact. He would recognize their people as cousins, equal to the Mongols and second only to the Manchu themselves. Few accepted, but enough…"

"My master…"

"There is a saying, a very old saying—'to walk through the fires of hell and emerge a demon'… But what do you call something that walks into those fires and takes its place in their very heart?"

"A devil…"

"So it was that he came before your emperor, painted in the ash of death, clad in robes the color of bone, and wielding the very falchion that had both killed and avenged his own master.

"And no one held their ground at his coming."

詠 春 傳 說

"As we were taught to speak of Heaven & Earth," Master Law said, "so we now teach you."

Five-Metal Yang stepped up, lifted his good left hand, and extended three shaggy fingers. "By this sign may you follow the path."

Big Kung stepped next to him, extended his right hand, and pointed his index finger up. "And by this sign may you gain entry."

Red lanterns flared and steel sparked. The initiates gasped and the rebels crossed blades above them.

"In accordance with Heaven & Earth," Master Law said, "in respect for the Founders and the Ancestors, and in honor of the House of Ming, we make this oath—"

The initiates knelt in a circle around a large bowl. Each in turn slid a knife across his palm and let his blood join the wine.

"You will not speak carelessly the affairs of Heaven & Earth or reveal them to others in any way," Piebald Chan said. "You will protect the weak and the helpless. Your strength will be their strength.

"If your rebel brother is in need, you will support him. If he is in trouble, you will defend him."

"And if we fail to do so," the initiates said, "may we be drowned by river and by lake."

"If you have a home, you will offer shelter. If you have a wagon, you will offer transport. If you have a junk, you will offer passage."

"And if we turn our rebel brother away, may we be immolated by thunder and lightning."

"If your rebel brother dies, you will help care for his wife. If your rebel brother's children are left orphaned, you will help raise them."

"And if we refuse this responsibility, may we be impaled beneath sun and moon."

"If your brother by birth asks one thing, and your brother by oath asks another…"

"If we do not follow the dictates of our brother by oath, may we be broken into thirty-six parts and thrown into the four seas."

"If your brother by birth turns against your brother by oath…"

"If we do not side with our brother by oath, may we be cut into thirty-six pieces and scattered to the four winds."

"You are bound by the oaths of Heaven & Earth," Chan said. "Now and forever, we are as one. The friends of Heaven & Earth are our friends, the enemies of Heaven & Earth are our enemies. Where the gates stand, we shall pass, and where the elders lead, we shall follow."

Master Law strode from the pavilion. "Then follow."

And Boklao watched them go.

詠 春 傳 說

Auntie poured more dark, boiling liquid into the bath, and strong, bitter steam billowed through the chamber.

"Your father took you and fled west," Auntie said. "I knew where he was headed... Miu Sun had told him of the small town below his temple, of how far away it was, how isolated and inaccessible. Your father only hoped it would prove far enough away from his past to keep you safe."

"Safe..." Wingchun closed her eyes. "Another lie..."

"Another life."

"One I don't need anymore, not now that I know."

"You know, but you do not yet understand. Still, I pray it will be enough."

"Enough for what?"

"For what comes next."

詠 春 傳 說

"Since then," the old priest said, "your master has hunted down and killed Shaolin after Shaolin..."

"It's almost as though he can feel them," Eagle-Shadow said.

"He can, though not precisely enough for his own good."

The laughter returned and, for an instant, Eagle-Shadow glimpsed something beneath the old priest's indigo cowl—

"White-Eyebrow!" Eagle-Shadow recoiled. "You're... you're him, the fallen emissary—the exile!"

"Like you," the old priest said.

"I have been redeemed!"

"Have you, when you see all this—" The old priest swept a talon-like hand across Kwailam. "—and you lament...?"

"That exile too comes in gradations..."

"And so can redemption."

"It—?" Eagle-Shadow paused and his scarred face stiffened. "Why should I listen to you, old priest? Why should I believe anything you have to say any more?"

"Because I am the connection that led you down this path, the fate that made your way clear. I am the one who brought you this far, who granted you this small enlightenment, and I and I alone can grant you one far greater still."

"But at what price, old priest? At what price comes your enlightenment?"

"Enlightenment, dear boy, is ever and always its own price."

16
Little First Training

Eighth month, seventeenth day. The calendar hung yellowed and scorched against the charred brick of the temple's main hall, between massive columns, chipped and cracked, that leapt up to the vaulted ceiling where equal parts drizzle and dawn leaked past the broken shingles.

Wingchun stood robed in layers of gray and stared down through the blackened windows at the sea of clouds far below.

"Less than a month," she said, "before Panther-King returns."

"To face his challenger," Auntie said, perched cross-legged on the dais behind her.

"To face me…"

His palm lashed out, his hand clamped around her throat…

"You, girl? Why?"

"Because I have to."

"You could run."

"If I do I abandon Donglai to his terror."

"You could ask me to face him for you."

"And if you do the Ch'ing will come and I'll have abandoned Donglai to far worse..."

"Perhaps," Auntie said. "Yet still I feel all but compelled to intervene, to protect you..."

"You can't. No one can. Not anymore."

"Girl..."

"Do you want to hear something funny? I asked my father if I could learn how to fight and he wouldn't hear of it. I asked—I was such a fool—if Boklao could teach me. I didn't... All those years and I had no idea..."

"But you do now?"

"Yes."

"The old breathing exercises... The ones you—"

"Taught your daughter the boxing—"

"—when I was little..."

"They're building something inside me..."

Her father didn't even move. He just reached out, his arm a—

"Snake Parts the Water... Dispersing..."

"—She's still got the movements inside her..."

It was like her body knew exactly what to do—

Her hips twisted and her arm shot out...

—she only had to let it...

"A little one..."

詠 春 傳 說

From between char-black shingle and flame-gold railing, the Lama gazed down at the Kwailam Palace square. Forbidden Bannermen moved across it in the ancient patterns of Imperial Fist. They kicked and punched in perfect synchronicity, their red crests like blood splattered across tile white as snow...

Eagle-Shadow lurched down in salute. "Master..."

The Lama's voice rumbled.

"You, once my disciple, allowed yourself to fall to a Shaolin."

"But you pulled me back, master... at least part of the way..."

"I granted the Shaolin his final failure, nothing more. Now I grant you something as well—your final chance."

Eagle-Shadow knocked his head to the floor.

"Long ago," the Lama said, "you abandoned your foundation of Mongol wrestling and heretic boxing to learn the Lion's Roar, the speed and precision of the mountain crane. But now what life remains within you is too thin, too broken for such grace. Now you must begin again, you must embrace the cunning and brutality of the *yeti*."

詠 春 傳 說

Master Law gathered the rebels, new and old, in the deepest part of the caves, and Boklao and Kwai along with them.

"What is it?" Five-Metal Yang scratched at the splint on his right arm. "Master?"

"The Constabulary Army of the Green Standard has received orders," Master Law said. "Orders to close the Northwestern Road."

"How do you know?" Piebald Chan said. "Did... did Fok—?"

"Later..."

Big Kung fussed with the needles in his small acupuncture case. "Why close a road that goes nowhere?"

"It goes here, my son," Law said. "The constables you encountered yesterday were stragglers, true enough, but they were stragglers with a purpose. They were surveying the waterways and sending dispatches back to Kwailam. It seems the Kwangsi governor does not share the Imperial Emissary's—"

"Lama," Boklao said. "Call it what it is."

"—lack of concern for the rebel threat."

Yang puffed up. "The governor himself considers us a threat!"

"Enchang considers everyone a threat, Shaggy," Kwai said, "even impotent backwater riff-raff like you. That's how he stays governor."

"Really, and just what does Enchang plan on doing about us riff-raff?"

"Bannermen," Boklao said. "He plans on sending in bannermen, doesn't he?"

Master Law nodded. "Territorial bannermen."

"There's more than one kind?" Big Kung said.

"Three kinds" Kwai said. "Eight Manchu Banners in and around the Forbidden City, eight Mongol Banners deployed throughout the central plains, and eight Northern Han Banners which the emperor never fully trusted and so exiled here, to the southern territories to train what became the Army of the Green Standard."

"That's quite a lot for somebody to know about Ch'ing military organization," Yang said. "For somebody who's not a collaborator..."

Kwai shrugged. "Price of a youth misspent studying for the licentiate exams."

"How long?" Boklao said.

"Few years, until my parents got fed up and sold me to the opera—"

Boklao growled and turned fully towards Master Law. "How long before they get here?"

"The Territorial Banners are not what they once were, when they poured down from the north and slaughtered the Ch'ing into empire. They have become sedentary, their function now more administrative than military..."

"But they're still bannermen," Boklao said. "Still sharp."

"Sharp but rusty," Master Law said. "Normally it would take months to muster and deploy fully supplied banner columns this far into the backwater but, as their scouts no doubt discovered, the monsoon has awakened many a slumbering dragon..."

"The Baksoy River," Big Kung said. "It'll deliver them right to us..."

"Four weeks," Boklao said. "Five at the most."

"What do we do?" Chan said. "What can we do?"

"We run."

The rebels turned and Master Law half-stood.

"My wife..."

Mrs. Law circled around to him, the silver clasp of her best gown gone, the once-turquoise silk tattered, and the peony-flowered brocade torn. "We run as fast and as far as we can," she said. "If our problem is with the Kwangsi governor then we leave Kwangsi, we go north to Kwaichow or west to Yunnan, we go... we go anywhere we have to—" She glanced at Big Kung. "—for our children to have some chance at life..."

"Our ancestors tried that before," Master Law said, "when they fled from Fukien after the Ch'ing betrayed us in the skirmishes with the Hokkien. They came here, to Lanchow. They thought it would be far enough but now... now I wonder if anywhere will ever really be far enough..."

"What else can we do?" Chan said. "If we try to hide they'll hunt us down. They'll hunt us down and grind us up into the mountain side!"

"No they won't," Boklao said. "Not if we grind them first."

"Grind them...?" Yang's shaggy face knotted. "You mean attack... attack first and seize the initiative! Brilliant!"

"It is," Big Kung said. "If by that you mean utterly insane."

"Now wait one—"

"Attack the Ch'ing first, just like that?"

"How else for brave men and true? We'll have righteousness on our side and surprise to our advantage!"

"Good! We'll need it, because all they'll have is massive overwhelming superiority of force!"

"The more, the better!"

"The more of *us*, you idiot! Did you break your head along with your arm? It's supposed to be the more of us, the better!"

"Yang is your senior, my son," Master Law said. "You will speak to him with respect."

"With all due."

"Big Kung—!"

"He's right," Boklao said to Master Law.

"I don't need your support!" Big Kung said.

"I don't care. And I don't think we have to care about the so-called superiority of Ch'ing force either, not if we do this right..."

詠 春 傳 說

Eighth month, twenty-second day. Wingchun stamped her hand into the yellowed calendar. The wall shook and mortar crumbled down.

"Your power is improving," Auntie said from the dais.

"Thank you."

"But not enough."

"I—What?"

"Don't stamp and then hit. Hit and then stamp. Touch the page and express the power. It's simple."

Wingchun angled a brow and then placed her palm flat on the page, tensed, pushed, and promptly stumbled back.

She tucked her hair back and looked at Auntie. "Simple?"

"But not easy. The wall behind the calendar is so much bigger than you, girl. If you use only your arm, then you are broken and segmented like Yin, and whatever power you send will be divided and rebounded back into you. If, however, you brace yourself and stand like Yang..."

"Then I align my meridians and connect my body. I provide direction and the ground returns stability. I make my power whole... It's how my father taught me to stand at the tofu grinder..."

"And in his Little First Training."

"I... I never realized they were the same..."

"Form comes from function, girl. There is no duality."

詠 春 傳 說

"You are broken, segmented," the Lama said. "Be broken."

The crimson glow of the braziers flickered across the vast mandala charred onto the stone tiles. Eagle-Shadow staggered towards it.

"Give no direction that your enemy can perceive," the Lama said. "Require no stability but what your enemy provides. Do not bind yourself to the earth, crash through it like a meteor from the heavens."

詠 春 傳 說

The ox bellowed, the cart lurched, the ramp rattled, chunks of limestone crashed into the shallows of the Baksoy River, and mud splattered across the banks.

"Careful." Stonecutter Sek lowered his slab-like arms. "This may be just be the craziest fool plan I've ever heard, but you get too close and you'll save the Ch'ing some trouble."

Boklao held his ground. "Not until I've caused them plenty first."

Big Kung glowered and turned back to the bamboo. "Go!"

Rebels burst out and rushed the heavy, rock-laden bags slung across the make-shift benches that lined the banks. Then, for the ten-thousandth time that day, half of them prodded with whatever blades or bludgeons they had while the rest ducked behind, grabbed the bags, and dragged them to the ground.

Five-Metal Yang adjusted his splint. "Not bad."

"Stop that," Big Kung said. "The faster you heal, the faster you can resume your duties, and the faster I can be left to mine."

"Come now, you're doing an excellent job! And they'll be all but invisible when they have the greens. That is, if Mrs. Pang and the other ladies ever finish stitching them..."

"Dressing up like forest demons doesn't turn away Ch'ing spears, and bags of rock don't fight back."

"Tell that to Broomstick-head." Boklao said. "That bag of rock has him pinned down pretty good..."

"Chao Jeet? Where...?"

"Third from left," Yang said. "That's his leg sticking out there... twitching..."

Big Kung cursed. "Not again! Lai Bang, don't help him! If you leave position you'll expose the flank!"

"Lai knows that," Boklao said. "Just like he knows the others will cover for him."

"He's right," Yang said. "They trust each other, Big Kung. You need to learn to trust them as well."

"The way you and my father do?"

"Yes, exactly."

"Trust them to follow you straight into calamity..."

詠 春 傳 說

Wingchun slipped and fell. Her arms shot out and she caught herself, stretched out on fingers and toes, shaking between the three narrow Plum Blossom Posts in the small chamber at the back of the temple, suspended above the darkness and emptiness that plummeted away just below...

"Does it frighten you?" Auntie said.

The whispers of her sisters and brothers grew louder...

Wingchun pushed herself back up and began the Little First Training again. "No."

詠 春 傳 說

"Fear is delusion," the Lama said. "There is no fear. There is no pain."

The braziers were empty, their contents raked along the outermost circle of the mandala, the Purifying Flame of Wisdom. Still red, still flickering, Eagle-Shadow walked again and again over the smoldering coals.

"There is nothing in all the universe, nothing but power I now grant you."

詠 春 傳 說

Boklao widened and squared his posture, pushed his long, bold arms down, then to the sides, and then straight out in front. Waking Tiger Stretches his Claws. He bent his elbows and then swung his palms out. Rising Tiger Reaches for—

"Soggy noodles?"

Boklao's nostrils flared. "That what that stench is?"

"So Butcher Ngao would have us believe." Little Kung scampered up onto a rock weathered in the shape of an elephant's head. "Doesn't seem to be fatal, though—I made sure to watch his boy scoff down at least two helpings before I took any..."

"Smart."

"Was that... Was that Old Yee's system you were doing?"

"What...?"

"The boxing you were just training, it was Old Yee's system, wasn't it? An ancient, righteous system like in the epics?"

Boklao slurped down one of the cold, congealed noodles. "I don't do Old Yee's system."

"If it's a secret or something, you don't have to worry, my family is really good with secrets. Our own system is so secret I can't even tell you its real name! I can't tell anyone who isn't Hakka, who isn't part of the family."

"No?"

"All I can say is 'Southern Mantis' or 'Southern Shaolin'—"

"You hide behind legends..."

"—Not that I can actually *learn* much either, of course... not the master set, not for the *second* son..." Little Kung rolled his eyes. "You wouldn't understand..."

"Being a second son? I understand that plenty..."

"Really? Then that boxing you were doing, that...?"

"Tiger Shape Fist."

"Your father taught you?"

"A student of my father's. The scraps I know, anyway..."

Little Kung's face bunched up. "Your father's student and he only taught you scraps? Why?"

Boklao slurped down another noodle. "Turned out I wasn't part of his family either."

17

The Mind Ground

Ninth month, first day. Wingchun flew past the calendar, banged off the column, and crashed down to the tiles.

"Snake Parts the Water," Auntie said. "Or more plainly—"

"The Dispersing Arm..." Wingchun scrambled back up, the layers of her gray robes torn to reveal the yellowish-purple bruises that lurked beneath. "I know what it is, I've done it since I was child, I even saw my father fight with it. 'One Dispersing Arm to...' "

"To what, girl?"

"I don't know, he... he never finished. All he said was, 'one dispersing arm to—' "

" 'Defeat all under heaven,' " Auntie said. "It was the essence of Miu Sun's system. It opens and uproots, spreads power away from your center like a pointed roof sheds rain."

Auntie assumed a posture very similar to the Yang Clamping, but with one leg a half-step forward. Then she spiraled her arm out to join Wingchun's at the wrist, but instead of her elbow down and palm up, her elbow was up and her palm twisted out.

"This is the Wing Arm," Auntie said. "It redirects and repels, twines power from inside out or outside in like a reel does silk. It is the essence of *my* system."

Wingchun's nose crinkled. "There's more than one essence?"

"Many."

Then Auntie's palm shot out and once more Wingchun flew across the hall, banged off a column, and crashed to the ground.

"What did you feel?" Auntie said.

Wingchun pushed her hair back out of her face.

"The wind, the stone, the ground..."

"On the inside, girl."

The world went dark...

"Nothing."

Auntie extended her Wing Arm. "Then we go again."

詠 春 傳 說

"You must harden yourself," the Lama said.

Eagle-Shadow's head bounced off the stone tile and blood bounced with it. An iron rod smashed over his back and another slammed into his ribs. He skidded out across the mandala.

"Harden yourself beyond flesh, beyond even steel, beyond anything in nature."

Eagle-Shadow rolled up—just as a third bannerman spun around and swung at his face...

詠 春 傳 說

Boklao clawed one hand down and the other out, and then stepped again and switched. Hungry Tiger Bounds from the Cave. He squared up and drove both claws out to the sides and then to the front. Wild Tiger Seizes the Goat. He clawed up and down, and then twisted around and—

Master Law stood beside the elephant-head rock. "By rights," he said, "you should be trussed up in the caves, half of what grows and crawls smeared over the wounds you seem so continually to suffer. Yet here you are training every day with my rebels and, by the looks of it, every night with Chi Sim's boxing as well."

"You spoke to Little Kung," Boklao said.

"My second son spoke to me, asked me to consider teaching you."

"Teaching me?" Boklao shook his head. "He doesn't understand..."

"He has grown a great deal in the last few weeks but he is still a child and, you're right, he doesn't understand. The only thing I could teach you—"

"An outsider."

"—is what we call Monk's Palm."

"An outsider's set."

"Oh, it's useful enough, but not to someone who already knows the Tiger Shape Fist."

"Not all of it. Not enough."

"But alongside Old Yee's system..."

"You spoke to Little Kung so he must have told you that—"

"That you don't do that system."

"Yes."

"But not that you don't know it..."

Boklao turned away. "Only know what I saw..."

Master Law circled around. "What you saw of Old Yee when he fought the Ch'ing, or did you perhaps see more...?"

"I saw him teach Wingchun."

"He let you watch that?"

"Until he found out..."

"You spied on him? You spied on him and he didn't kill you?"

"Gave me a hell of a beating—narrated it and everything—but no, he really didn't..."

"Then why not do it, why not use his system?"

"Weren't you paying attention?"

"The disciple of Miu Shun allowed you to see his methods, to hear his principles, and to feel his application... to do all that and to *live*, and I'm the one not paying attention?"

"I made a promise." Boklao clenched the scarf still bound around his hand. "I failed to keep my end so there's no way I'm keeping his."

詠 春 傳 說

Ninth month, fifth day. Wingchun stepped off the Plumb Blossom Posts, lowered her hands, and breathed out.

"Done. One set, no me slipping or tripping or otherwise suffering hideous injury at the bottom of your little torture pit..."

"Do not mistake the journey for the destination, girl," Auntie said. "The goal of a pattern is not to perfect the pattern but, simply, to come to understand the concepts and forms that compose it so that you can, when needed, make patterns of your own."

Wingchun sighed. "Which chamber am I following you to now?"

Auntie turned. "No chamber."

They crossed the desolate courtyard, passed the barren plum trees, and descended long stone steps to a small island afloat in the sea of clouds. More Plum Blossom Posts rose from it but not like the flat and even ones back in the temple. These were as jagged as the mountain itself, their tops slick with morning dew, and their bases lost to oblivion...

"The delusion of pattern will not serve you here," Auntie said. "To survive this, you must be able to flow in accordance with the moment, change in accordance with your feeling."

"Are you joking?" Wingchun said.

Auntie glanced up at her. "Frightened yet?"

The world went dark and a terrible claw fell...

Wingchun stepped out.

"No..."

詠 春 傳 說

"Stay to the pattern," the Lama said. "Never vary, never change. The pattern is everything. It was ancient before you were born and will be eternal long after you are gone."

Eagle-Shadow walked the diamond, the Indestructible Clarity of Mind burned into the middle of the circles. Eight knees, eight kicks, eight steps, eight punches, eight elbows, again and again...

"The moment will confuse you, feeling will betray you. Only the pattern will remain—its purity, its truth..."

詠 春 傳 說

Butcher Ngao burst out of the Baksoy River and thrashed his way to the rocks.

Boklao burst out after him and thrashed his way through every curse he knew.

"My foot felt like it was caught on the anchor line," Ngao said. "I swear, I—"

"You foot's supposed to be caught on the anchor line," Boklao said. "That's what the anchor line is for, that's why it's called a damn anchor line!"

"I know, I know, but—!"

"First!" Woodcutter Mok clambered up over the wall of lashed bamboo, let go of the tow line, and punched his axe to the heavens. "Take that!"

"—I can't breathe through these things. I swear, I don't even think mine's hollow!" Butcher Ngao held up the long reed and gawked through one end.

Kwai sneered back through the other. "Hollow as that head of yours, Tubby…"

"Where have you been, vagabond?" Boklao looked at the gray-brown mud splattered across Kwai's strangely mottled robes. "Up mountain again?"

"Up your—"

"Strutting and sniping," Woodcutter Mok said. "That's where he's been. Where else?"

"Here else," Boklao said. "Training."

"Under you?" Kwai scoffed. "Boy, I was pre-salvaging junks when you still reeked of milk…"

"Pre-salvaging…? You mean pirating, don't you?" Boklao chuckled. "You're a damn pirate!"

"A damn good one, among many other things."

"I don't understand," Butcher Ngao said. "If you're a—I mean, if you know—I mean… Why aren't you helping us?"

"Because we're nothing but fire on the far bank to him," Boklao said. "He doesn't give a damn about us or our cause…"

Kwai crouched down. " 'Our'? Did somebody learn a new word?"

"I'm getting real tired of you, vagabond!"

"Then by all means, boy, take a nap."

"I'll take my foot, kick it up into your mouth, and walk around with your head as a shoe!"

"You think that will shut me up, stop me from asking why you, who wanted nothing more than to run away, now so suddenly wants to stay and do his bit for Heaven & Earth?" Kwai leant in close. "I know who you really are…"

"He's a brave man and true," Woodcutter Mok said. "Something you wouldn't know anything about, you putrid piece of—"

"Go ahead," Boklao said to Kwai. "Tell them."

"Tell them what?" Kwai stood and strutted off. "This is suicide and I only do that by proxy..."

詠 春 傳 說

Ninth month, eighteenth day. In the desolate courtyard Wingchun extended one arm to join Auntie's... and then extended the other. They began to circle at the elbow.

Auntie pushed.

Wingchun turned and dispersed. "Keep what comes."

Auntie withdrew.

Wingchun stepped and stamped. "Send off what goes."

Auntie skidded back to a stop. "Good."

Wingchun angled a brow. "Your mouth says 'good', but your face says 'wait until she sees the upside down Plum Posts...' "

Auntie arched one back. "Sticking Arms can show you the way, girl, but it's not fighting. To fight, you need Free Arms as well."

"We're at the part where I go flying again, aren't we?"

Auntie raised her hands like the wings of the crane. "To stick, you must first bridge."

Wingchun raised her own, twin snakes. "Then I'll bridge."

They closed, the courtyard spun around them, their wrists touched... And Wingchun was off the ground, into a tree, and out over the tiles.

"Stop doing that!"

"Bridges go both ways," Auntie said. "What lets you cross lets your opponent cross as well."

Wingchun pushed her hair back. "And you couldn't have mentioned that before?"

"You should already know, girl. You should know how to—"

"Flow according to moment..."

"Change according to feeling."

"I've told you ten-thousand times now, I don't feel anything."

"You have to. In the instant of contact your feeling will divine your opponent's intent and let you control their action. Then you will be like the Goddess of Mercy and nothing will escape you."

詠 春 傳 說

"Never let your enemy touch you. Their bridge is poison."

Eagle-Shadow walked the lotus blossom scorched inside the diamond. Eight gods and goddesses marked its petals and, from each one, banner-men swung their choppers.

"If they try to divine your intent, break their limbs."

Eagle-Shadow's leg cracked like a steel whip. Their weapons splintered.

"If they seek to control you, destroy their being."

His fists streaked like meteors. Their armor shattered.

"Then, like the Adamantine Bodhisattva, nothing will withstand you."

詠 春 傳 說

Boklao circled his hands high overhead. Fierce Tiger Claws the Heavens. He swung down and in and then thrust out to the side, switched, and... stopped.

"To think I picked this spot for its solitude..."

Big Kung folded his arms and leant against the elephant-head rock. "Interesting, that must be Tiger Shape Fist because you don't do Old Yee's boxing, do you?"

"Been eavesdropping?"

"Sorry, I know you prefer spying."

Boklao clenched his fist. "What did you—?"

Big Kung glanced at it. "That scarf you bound there, that's the one soaked in not your blood, isn't it? That's what you said back at the cliff—that the blood wasn't yours, it was just on your hands... And when you sucker-punched me back at the bridge, what was it you said then?"

Boklao spun around. "I'm warning you...!"

"I'm scared."

"You should be."

Big Kung laughed. "Please, I've seen you fight. Your so-called skill—the skill my father believes we so desperately need—is a joke. You can punch and kick and you know which end of a blade is sharp, but that's it. That's as far as it goes. You never got the deeper levels. You never learned a complete system." He held up his hand, first knuckle extended like the eye of a phoenix. "I did."

"That why your father's so desperate to keep my unskilled self around, because you give him all the food a dog could eat?"

"I revere my father and I will take up his burden if I have to!"

"Long as he's here to watch. But the minute he withdraws, that light goes out, doesn't it, and you beat a path right back to your real home..."

"This *is* my home, the only one left since you got the real one destroyed! But that wasn't enough for you, was it, just like that cutlass isn't enough... You want more and *that's* what scares me.

"You want words that will be put into action, listen very carefully—kill all the Ch'ing you like, kill every damn one of them if you can, but if anything goes wrong, if you put my family in the slightest danger again—if even one drop of their blood gets spilled because of you—then the Ch'ing will become the least of your problems. Do to my family what you did to the Yims and, I swear, I'll kill you myself."

詠 春 傳 說

Ninth month, fourteenth day. But all that remained to tell it was the charred outline of where the calendar had once hung before all its pages were stamped into dust.

Outside, at the edge of the Plum Blossom Posts, Wingchun stared down through the silvered clouds that swirled, billowed, and faded away... Like mirrors transparent and yet utterly impenetrable...

And the screams became deafening...

"I have prepared your medicinal bath," Auntie said. "You should get ready."

"I am." Wingchun turned back towards the temple. "I'm ready to face Panther-King."

"No, girl," Auntie said. "Not if you still think Panther-King is who you must face."

18

The Rebels Strike Back

Torches flared, sooty red eyes in the smoke-white mist. It was the only sign of the coming transport junk. The only one they needed.

Boklao clenched the anchor line and plunged down beneath the Baksoy. Cold and quiet, he soaked it in as long as he could, until the junk was almost on top of him. Then he balled himself up and covered his ears...

Water surged past him. He let go of the anchor and grabbed the tow, and then he surged along with it, pulled by the junk until the wooden hull smashed into the limestone and the river itself screamed.

Boklao began to climb even as the bow crumpled and the stern drove on. Then the junk crashed back, the river flooded over the sides, lanterns toppled, oil spilled, water took flame, and Boklao slammed down on the deck.

A cerulean-jacketed sailor raced at him, pole held like a cudgel. Boklao bent at the waist, let the sailor fold over him, then stood back up and dumped him, kicking and wailing, into the river.

Woodcutter Mok and two dozen other brown-cloaked rebels scrambled up over the rail behind him, Butcher Ngao last of all.

"Made it," he said. "I swear... I made it onto the boat!"

Boklao broke the string that secured the cutlass to his back and the nine-rings roared free. Boklao roared louder.

And a clang reverberated up and down the banks.

詠 春 傳 説

Big Kung peered through the bamboo and the rain. Thirty horses mounted by blue-bordered bannermen... Bannermen who dug in their heels and yanked on their reins in a desperate attempt to turn the panicked animals around and drive them into the shallows after their runaground junk...

"That's it." Five-Metal Yang said. "That's our opening!"

"Not yet," Big Kung said. "I want them hip-deep before I risk any of my people."

"If we wait too long they'll turn back and we'll lose the flank!"

Big Kung's eyes stayed on the horses but his hand slid down to his waist.

"Listen, boy," Yang said. "I'm just trying to give you the benefit of my experience. This is no time for—!"

Then Big Kung's scholar sword hummed loose and his voice cracked like thunder. "Go!"

Three dozen rebels shrouded the dark green of forest demons streamed past Yang and burst out onto the banks.

And the clang reverberated again.

詠 春 傳 説

The air groaned, birds burst into flight, and towering stalks of bamboo came crashing down behind the junk.

"Watch out..."

Stonemason Sek clutched his barrel-wide chest and glared up from the mud. "*Before*, you damn vagabond! I told you to warn me before you cut the bamboo loose!"

Kwai slipped the dagger back beneath his strangely mottled robes. "Funnier this way."

"Funnier? We'll see how funny any of this turns out..." He gazed at the junk trapped in place on the river. "Sticks and stones... We engage the Ch'ing army and all we bring are sticks and stones..."

And the clang reverberated a third time.

詠 春 傳 說

Little Kung lowered his beater and set down his gong. "Now aren't you glad I went back for it?"

Mrs. Law grabbed for her slipper.

"That's it, then," Piebald Chan said. "Everyone is engaged."

"Not everyone-" Master Law said.

"What?" Mrs. Law gaped at him. "What are you doing?"

Red silk fell away and Master Law's enormous Kwan halberd flashed like lightning. "Not yet."

Little Kung beamed, snatched his gong back up, and brought his beater down one last time.

詠 春 傳 說

From the sea of clouds, past the sheer cliffs and narrow ridges, and water stretched into falls and wound into streams, Wingchun followed Auntie down into Donglai.

The centermost tables were gone and in their place was a stage a dozen feet wide, double that long, and high as Wingchun herself.

"The raised platform," Auntie said. "Victory can only come through knock-out or knock-off. That is the tradition."

Then the market crowd shrank away and Panther-King loomed up, and all of a sudden the platform hardly seemed raised at all. Men circled out behind him, sneering, leering, covered in dirt and rags, mismatched weapons itching in their hands...

"Bandits," Wingchun said.

"Eyes forward, girl. Focus your intent. The time has come for you to choose."

"I made my choice," Wingchun said, "when I stepped out in front of the beast."

"You chose to leap from the confines of your nest, now you must choose whether you will spread your wings and soar higher even than the heavens themselves, or whether you will close them and allow yourself to crash and fall back down to the earth."

Panther-King launched himself up on the platform. The wooden frame rattled and the taut canvas boomed. "I see you have brought my concubine, Little Grandmother." His lips smacked. "But where is my appetizer? Where is her so-called champion?"

Wingchun took a slow breath, tucked in her layered gray robes, and then kicked her legs up and wheeled through the air. She alighted on the platform, slung her hair back, and rose to face him. "Before you."

"It speaks, how rare! Come, grovel at my feet while you still have a tongue!"

"It's not my tongue you should be worried about." She extended her arm, a snake parting the water...

"What?" His huge face curdled. "A girl? You think I would fight a *girl*?"

"You don't have to fight me, beast, just survive me."

"Survive you? I am the butcher of Zhou Village, scourge of the Eight Immortals! Survive *you*? You need to learn your proper place, little morsel, and I will show you, right here, right now, right on this very stage."

Wingchun's eyes kindled.

"Show me."

詠 春 傳 說

The sun flickered through the clouds of northeast Kwangsi, water frothed and churned, and steel-shod hooves tore up rice terraces coiled as a dragon's spine.

"The rebels," Eagle-Shadow said, "they hide among the Jong and Yao, master, in the villages near the Kwaichow border."

"Test them," the Lama said. "Slaughter those who fail and drive the Shaolin to me."

詠 春 傳 說

The sailors grabbed for spears and sabers and formed up in a crescent around the main cabin, set to repel boarders.

Boklao's nostrils flared. "Ready?"

"Of course we're ready," Woodcutter Mok said.

Butcher Ngao's eyes widened. "I... I don't think he was talking to us..."

The spearmen lashed out. Boklao sidestepped one, spun past a saberman, and cross-parried another. Then he uncrossed, angled and sliced, lunged and stabbed. Nine-rings jangled, blood sprayed hot and numbing, the rain took on the flavor of the sea, and Boklao hacked into three more.

詠 春 傳 說

The bannerman skipped his horse around the rocks, reared up, and slashed down with his saber. Lai Bang clacked his three-section staff open, blocked with one end, and whipped the other at the bannerman's head.

Big Kung circled behind, waited for the bannerman to parry, and then jumped up and stabbed him in the armpit.

The bannerman gasped and slumped in his saddle. Lai Bang dragged him down to the mud and then reached for the reins. But Big Kung held them fast.

"You're our leader," Lai Bang said. "We need you here!"

Big Kung placed Pang Keung's body over the back of the horse. "I know where I'm needed."

詠 春 傳 說

Drizzle bounced off the long canvas platform stretched out between them. Wingchun stared across at Panther-King. Rage beaded in his eyes, but not enough, not yet…

"I will show you!" Panther-King bellowed. "Here, in front of everyone, I will make you mine!"

He leapt at her, the distance between them vanished in a single, bestial stride, and as Wingchun had imagined every moment of the last month, she angled out of his path, aligned her meridians, and stamped her palm into his floating ribs.

The impact shot down her legs but like a spring she absorbed it, harmonized it, and rebounded it all into him.

Panther-King staggered back.

Wingchun drove straight in and her palms struck one after the other like links in a chain. She kept him off balance, kept him hurtling back… right up to the very edge of the platform…

詠 春 傳 說

Eagle-Shadow's chopper culled the farmers like blight through a herd, all but three…

His chopper screeched off an old man's antler knife, clanged off a wild man's iron crutches, and sparked against a fat man's wind-and-fire wheels.

Eagle-Shadow yanked back on the reins of his horse and crashed down from the saddle.

"Come!"

The old man cross-stepped in front, his antler knife's axe-like outer crescent and the two dagger-sharp tips of its inner crescent thrust up.

The wild man slanted to the left, spun one iron crutch back by its short handle and extended the other out, hook-like, by its long.

The fat man stole a step to the right and flared the seven rippled teeth that ringed each of his wind-and-fire wheels.

And then they leapt at Eagle-Shadow, one drew, one attacked, and one covered, each in turn.

Eagle-Shadow walked the circle. The wild man mistimed. Eagle-Shadow smashed through. He walked the diamond. The old man over-committed. Eagle-Shadow cut. Then he walked the lotus. But the fat man matched him stroke for stroke.

They spun apart.

Eagle-Shadow's hands tensed, his body trembled, his scar twisted... But he forced himself back and down, and then he bowed to the Lama.

"Shaolin..."

詠 春 傳 說

Butcher Ngao wilted against the railing, his meat-cleaver slapping away like a leaf caught in a gale.

"—Made it on the junk... I made it on the junk..."

Woodcutter Mok chopped his axe into a sailor's gut and then kicked him clear.

"More bannermen are coming up from below deck, don't let them flank us!"

"Let them? You think they're asking *my* permission?"

"Just stay with me!"

Boklao ducked behind the mast. Three sabers bit into it right in front of his face. He faked left, pulled the first bannerman in, and then spun back around and slashed...

"Boklao!"

He parried the third bannerman, swept down and—

"BOKLAO!"

"What?"

Master Law raced across the rocks. "They're trying to lever themselves free!"

Boklao glanced astern and saw poles and spears bent against the bamboo...

"If they succeed," Master Law said, "the current will pull you back downriver! It will be too fast...!"

"Too fast?" Butcher Ngao's head whipped side to side. "Too fast for what?"

"For the other rebels to follow," Woodcutter Mok said. "We'll be cut off, first from our support and then, very likely, from our heads..."

"What do we do? I swear, I—We'll never be able to take the stern, not the way these sailors keep throwing themselves at us!"

"Well then maybe we should throw ourselves back—starting with you!"

"No," Boklao said. "With me."

Woodcutter Mok blinked. "Joking... I was—Wait!"

But Boklao was already up, off a barrel, and over the rail.

詠 春 傳 說

Big Kung zigzagged through the bamboo, circled, back-tracked, checked a final time, and then broke into the clearing. "Chan!"

"Little Kung." Piebald Chan said. "Little Kung!"

Boy Ngao ambled over and took the horse's reins. "I've got it!"

Little Kung stared out through the bamboo. "They're out there fighting for us, dying for us... while I'm stuck here with the old men and the children!"

"Where's the weapon?" Chan said to Big Kung.

"There was no time," Big Kung said. "Pang needed blood clotting, other's as well. I'll start treatment and—"

Chan's face splotched red. "What's the matter with you two? Little Kung, despite all the evidence to the contrary, your father somehow believes you're old enough now to do your part. So either you do it and help us bind the horses in the corral or I'll have you bound like one just to keep you out of trouble. And you—" He turned on Big Kung. "You are your family's successor and that means you lead the charge, not the clean up. Now go, the both of you, and do your duty!"

詠 春 傳 說

Chao Jeet's double-crescent spear twirled through the rain and splashed down into the mud, and Chao splashed down after it, a thin, bloody gash on his forehead in the shape of a horseshoe.

The bannerman spun back around to finish him but Five-Metal Yang was there, single octagonal-headed hammer high in his one good hand. He knocked the saber aside and then knocked the bannerman from his saddle.

"Lai Bang, Chao's down!"

"Lai's down too!" Master Law scanned from east to west. "Where's Big Kung?"

"I... I don't—"

"Here!" Big Kung grabbed the horse and handed its reins to Yang. "Get Chao and Lai some help, and get some for yourself too while you're at it."

"I need to hold the line," Yang said.

"I'll hold the damn line!"

"But—!"

"You heard my first son." Master Law swept his halberd in a vast arc and slammed its butt down into the rocks. "The Law family will hold the line!"

詠 春 傳 說

The sailors pried away another stalk of bamboo and the junk began to sway.

Kwai shrugged. "Easy come, easy go..."

" 'Easy go'—?" Stonemason Sek's block of a face cracked. "This... this is crazy, all of this, and I'm even crazier to be here! And you, vagabond, you—" He ground his head around. "Vagabond...?"

詠 春 傳 說

Panther-King's legs strained, his arms paddled the air, his massive frame teetered over the edge of the platform, and his eyes beaded but still not enough, not yet...

"Butcher of Zhou Village, scourge of the Eight Immortals," Wingchun whispered. "You really showed me, didn't you? Beaten and humiliated in front of everyone—" She glanced at the crowd. "—by a girl."

"No!" Panther-King crunched down and his body seemed to swell even more massive. "Not by you!"

He howled and sprang back at her, and his eyes beaded murderous at last.

"You are nothing!"

His palm lashed out. Her head snapped to the side.

"Nobody!"

He bellowed and struck again. She doubled over.

"An empty shell, a hollow vessel! You are not worthy to be my concubine—to be my dog!"

His hand clamped around her throat. The world went white. *Her family beckoned…*

"Only to die," Panther-King said. "To die and to take the shame of your death with you into the next life!"

19
Nature of the Weapon

Flames danced in Butcher Ngao's eyes and, in their center, Boklao's reflection hung over the edge of the junk. "I swear…"

Then Boklao's foot hooked the railing and he catapulted himself back up and around, over the Ch'ing, and onto the roof of the cabin.

"Stupid son of a—!" Woodcutter Mok glared up. "We can't follow that way!"

Boklao dropped down onto the stern. "Good."

The junk heaved. Boklao advanced on the polers, nine-rings jangling with each step. All he had to do was cut a couple of them down and the junk would stay stuck. He raised his cutlass and—

"DOG!"

One of the sailors broke away from the pack, gangly tall and draped in silk and gold.

No… Boklao's pulse quickened. Not just a sailor—

"Captain…"

Bamboo whimpered. Rock groaned.

Boklao shook his head, clenched his cutlass, and advanced again on the polers.

The captain tore a two-handed sword from his scabbard and held it up. "You ambush and murder righteous men, *my* men, but when called out into the open all your skill turns to shadow and you run like the dog you truly are!"

Boklao glanced back, his eyes red. "Want to see what I truly am?"

The nine-ring cutlass ripped across the deck. The two-handed sword wailed through the air. The cutlass rose. The sword fell. Steel sparked and shattered.

Boklao dropped to one knee against the railing, hand clutched to his side, blood oozing from between his fingers.

The captain just dropped, blood gushing out all around him.

A smile cut across Boklao's face. Then he saw the nine-ring cutlass— the blade of a martial hero—broken at his feet. "No..."

Bamboo snapped. Rock cracked.

The polers cheered.

Boklao staggered back up. "What... what have I done?"

And the junk broke free.

詠 春 傳 說

Master Law flew over the horse, through the pieces of bannerman, and slammed down on the other side of the banks, iron-black braid whipped around his neck, Kwan halberd gleaming beneath the heavens, and his eyes locked on his first son.

Like the scholar sword—the only weapon he deigned to use—Big Kung lacked the full boldness of Southern power, and yet his skill was undeniable. He parried, feinted, and then pierced straight into the most vital of points. He applied his sword as he did his acupuncture needles and it made him all the more deadly.

The Law family stood with their backs to the river but they held the line!

"My father to me and me to you," Master Law said, "generation to generation, stronger each time. I always knew you had it in you, the martial as much as the medical. My first son, my only successor, you—"

"Can never be what you want me to be," Big Kung said.

"—Proud that I—What...?"

"Your father to me but not through you—grandfather was an apothecary first!"

"I… I don't understand?"

"No, you don't, so please, father, just listen. I revere you as Confucius taught, and I will provide you your food and take up your burden, but only the healing. You told me to lead this… this calamity and I complied, but when it's done, I'm done too.

"If any of us survive this day, the only thing I'm ever going to lead for you again is the recovery. From now on, that's the only home I will know and the only rites I will ever practice."

"You… you don't know what you're saying!"

"I do, I finally do."

"You couldn't possibly. You—!"

"Father, I—"

Big Kung's face went white.

"Look out!"

詠 春 傳 說

Boklao drove into the closest sailor, knocked him overboard, and ripped the pole from his hands as he fell, screaming, into the rocks. The other sailors turned on Boklao but he swung the pole around, scattered them back across the deck, and then jammed it through the railing, into the river, and between the rocks.

The pole bent, the junk turned… but not nearly enough.

Boklao wrenched again, wide and bold. His muscles burned and his tendons popped, but still not enough! He wrenched and wrenched until his body felt like it was about to burst and then, suddenly, his legs rotated in and adducted…

The pole creaked and the junk began to turn.

Boklao dropped his elbows, closed them on his center, gathered everything he had left, and wrenched a final time.

The pole snapped, water broke white against the dark wood, the junk heaved back around.

Boklao reeled across the deck and slammed into the railing. The banks spun, rebels and bannermen blurred by. And then he saw them…

詠 春 傳 說

A horse leapt at Master Law—a white colt at the crevice. The man atop it bore a gold chest-plate of the raging bear, of a major of the banner, and his huge tiger-fork shot down at Master Law's back.

But Big Kung was there. He shoved Master Law, the full boldness of his Southern power obvious for the very first time.

Master Law tumbled back across the rocks but rolled immediately to his feet and dove for Big Kung. But the horses were stampeding. They rammed into Master Law, one after the other, and sent him hurtling farther and farther from his first son.

He cursed and flung himself to the side, skidded through the mud, and then zigzagged back through the chaos. The banner major lay trampled by the horses, a scholar sword pierced through his heart...

"You did it," Master Law said. "You cut off the millipede's head! You killed their leader! Big Kung, you—!"

Then he saw his first son against the banks, three savages gashes torn through him. "No..."

And then the sky went black, eclipsed by the junk...

詠 春 傳 說

The voices whispered to Wingchun...

The voices of her sisters and brothers.

Fire raged outside and constables swarmed past the windows. They couldn't get out.

Their whispers grew louder.

The door burst open and bannermen drove in...

But her family spread out around her, stretched back and forth across the generations...

Her eldest sister snatched her up.

A bannerman reared over them, scarred but not yet. Steel fell and with it, blood like rain.

Her sister screamed and stumbled and passed Wingchun to their eldest brother. From one to the next they handed her down.

Then the Lama turned, his bone robes flared...

And he mother was there, eyes gleaming bright, and cold, steel hands like the wings of a butterfly caught in a spring breeze.

The bannermen fell back and the constables fled.

The whispers returned, her youngest sister beckoned....

Wingchun floated towards her, and then wood creaked and iron clacked shut. The world went dark but for a tiny crack of light that captured her mother's face, beautiful and dreadful...

And then the light flickered, a single, terrible falchion cleft down, ash choked the air, and gleaming eyes were replaced by ones that burned with the inferno—

That burned with her death.

The screams became deafening.

But they weren't beckoning anymore.

They were calling out.

They were demanding...

詠 春 傳 說

"Lama!"

The fat man whipped around and hurled one of his wing-and-fire wheels. It wailed across the rice terraces and buzzed straight at the Lama's head.

But the Lama's bone robes parted, his falchion split the mist, and the wheel was shorn in two and left to sputter and splash out into the water.

"Pathetic." The Lama's robes settled closed. "You are a ripple, a murmur... barely anything of Shaolin."

"I am Wan Yok, once novice of the Kiangsi Temple, now leader of the Younger Brothers of Heaven!"

"You are the dispossessed scion of a forgotten heresy, bereft of consequence or karma, hurtling towards extinction inevitable."

"The only extinction here, Lama, is yours!"

Wan Yok whipped back, brought his last iron crutch up, and launched himself at the Lama.

The Lama remained still.

Wan Yok spun the iron crutch down under his arm, up behind his head, around his stomach, and then back out to strike.

The Lama remained still.

Wan Yok's eyes glimmered and set.

The Lama remained until the iron crutch was all but at his skull, and then his bone-robes parted once again.

Wan Yok finished his charge, his body flopping into the water, his head spinning through the mist.

Eagle-Shadow tore the spear from a constable, lurched around, and caught the head on the red-tasseled blade. Then he crashed back down in salute. "The Emperor's trophy, my master."

詠 春 傳 說

The junk leapt the banks, so high it seemed as if it might take flight... Rock burst like fireworks and shards of wood fell like daggers. But Boklao fell faster. He hit the ground beside Master Law, grabbed him and tried to pull him clear. "Come on!"

"No," Master Law said. "My son...!"

Big Kung's eyes locked on Boklao. "Re-remember what I told you... anything happens to my father and... name of heaven... spend my last breath taking yours..."

The stern of the junk teetered over them.

"Help him!" Master Law pushed Boklao.

"Once—" Big Kung coughed blood, too much blood and too fast. "—in your damned life just do the right thing!"

"Help my son, please!"

Boklao closed his eyes, cursed out a prayer, and then dragged him away just as the stern tore free and crashed down over them.

詠 春 傳 說

"Only to die," Panther-King said. "To die and to take the shame of your death with you into the next life!"

A dreadful calm settled over Wingchun. The emptiness inside her burned hot and white and her eyes smoldered open.

Panther-King howled and launched her up and over. "If not out then off you go!"

Kwang and Mr. Tao and Auntie zoomed by... They gave way to the endless heavens and then the earth, hurtling back at her...

Wingchun spun and flipped around, got her legs underneath her, and slammed down onto the platform. Tendrils of hair, dark and loose, swirled across her face. Then she was across the platform and at him. Her hand touched his sternum and her palm stamped.

He staggered back, his leg twisted on the wet canvas, and he toppled off the platform and into the mud below.

"She—why bless Kwang's Buddha—she won!"

"She did." Mr. Tao said. "She really, really did! She won!"

"No!" Panther-King slammed his fists into the ground. "She did *not!*"

"Knock-out or knock-off," Mr. Tao said. "That's the tradition."

"But there was no knock," a lump-headed bandit said. "He slipped!"

"All that matters is the off, and Kwang saw that—all of Donglai saw that!"

"You have no sight but what I allow!" Panther-King swatted them back. "No traditions but what I dictate!"

The crowd jeered and began to pelt him with refuse.

"Can you feel it, beast?" Auntie said. "They no longer fear you—a greater power has come."

"Power, Little Grandmother? You would know power?" He grabbed the platform, wood cracked and canvas tore. "*This is power!*"

The platform buckled and began to crash down beneath Wingchun even as Panther-King drew his fist back, a raging mass of muscle and bone, ready to smash the life out of her as she fell.

But Wingchun didn't fall. She simply walked towards him as balanced atop the crashing platform as jagged mountain posts... And then she reached out, her arm a snake parting water...

"It's... it's not possible!" Panther-King staggered back around. "You're just a girl! You cannot beat me!"

He struck again, Wingchun dispersed again, and this time she flicked her leg straight up between his. "Wrong."

Panther-King's face imploded, his knees buckled, and he toppled head first into the muck.

"You *are* beaten."

詠 春 傳 說

Boklao held him fast, tried to stop him from crawling back towards the banks, towards the smoke and ruin.

"Don't—"

"Let me go! I have to tell him—we have to regroup."

"You can't," Boklao said. "Now please—"

"You don't understand, the Law family has to hold the line! I have to tell him. He's—"

"Gone."

"Gone? What do you mean, gone? Gone where? Where could he go? He—"

"Died."

Boklao felt Master Law shatter beneath him.

"No..."

"He died saving you." Boklao kept pressure around the saber-sized shard of wood that jutted from Master Law's thigh. "Now please, don't move."

詠 春 傳 說

Auntie soared back up the mountain.

"Wait!" Wingchun scrambled after her. "What are you doing?!"

"I could ask you the same..."

"Donglai was celebrating—celebrating for me!"

Auntie arched a brow. "And that is what matters to you, the celebration? That is why you did all this?"

"No, of course not, but I *was* victorious..."

"Your swollen face, your broken ribs—that is victory?"

"I'm standing, he's not. What else is there?"

"What indeed..."

"Will you please slow down!"

Auntie broke through the sea of clouds and then stopped dead.

Wingchun scrambled to stop her beside her. "What is your problem?"

"Those stars just now emerged in the heavens," Auntie said, "the constellation in face of the Devil..."

"The one shaped like a sieve?"

"It is called the Girl."

"It... it is?"

"Yes, and it heralds the coming of the Dark Warrior."

20
The Sea of Clouds

There was no sun above the rebels, no clouds, no sky, just the endless white of mourning... A week later, the junk broken up and carted away, and every last one of their bodies recovered, the rebels trudged in procession up the cold, wet ridge.

The money had been put in the bowl, the water bought. What family elders remained had washed, and what friends survived had wailed. There was no time or place for visitations, no silk to shroud the dead or pearls to fill their mouths, but paper fans had still been set in their right hands to comfort them and willow branches in their left to keep away the demons.

Piebald Chan walked in front and scattered what little money they had to buy the goodwill of the spirits. Others followed with cobbled instruments, and the incense pavilion upon which they sacrificed what food they could spare.

The place was auspicious enough, in full accordance with wind and water, even if that wind was now filled with their cries and the water, their tears...

Five-Metal Yang and Lai Bang led Big Kung's simple casket. Master Law followed, clothes torn open in grief, iron-gray hair now shocked white. Mrs. Law and Little Kung came with him. Woodcutter Mok led Butcher Ngao's casket next, widow and son behind.

"He made it," Boy Ngao mumbled. "He made it on the boat..."

And then came the others, so many... so few...

The families wore robes of sackcloth and the friends, armbands. Everyone was there... Everyone but Boklao and Kwai...

Big Kung was laid to rest between the large stone that would be his monument and the two smaller stones that would mark his end.

"My son..."

Little Kung glanced up. "Father...?"

But Master Law's eyes remained on the grave. "My first son..."

詠 春 傳 說

The wind wailed cold across the mountain and snow swirled down over the spires only to melt the instant it touched Wingchun's skin.

"I can feel your look" She alighted from the jagged Plum Blossom Posts. "But you know that, don't you?"

"Of course, girl," Auntie said from her perch, cross-legged on the steps. "The same way I know everything—by what is within."

"Then why, if you already know everything, must you keep asking?"

"Because I would have you know. I would have you say it."

"I said it—I have to go back."

"Lanchow is no more."

"The town may be gone but much still remains."

"Ruin remains and what is in that for you?"

Wingchun looked up and her hair streamed dark against the paleness of her skin.

"Vengeance."

"Girl..."

"What, not righteous enough an act for you?"

"Righteousness cannot be found in any act, only in intent. If your heart is filled with ego and selfishness, if it is done for you and you alone, then it is like the utter destruction of the inferno and you will never find peace, not in this life or the next."

"Peace is not what I'm trying to find..."

The devil turned, his bone robes flared, and his burning eyes blazed...

"That enemy is beyond you, girl," Auntie said. "The Lama will not take you to be his concubine, he will take you to hell—or worse."

"What could be worse than hell?"

"Keep on beating and sharpening a blade and what will come of its edge? If even heaven and earth cannot endure such violence, how can you hope to?"

"I can... if you complete my training."

"Your training *is* complete."

"My father taught me Miu Sun's combination of O-Mei Twelve Postures and the Shaolin Snake Shape Fist. That's two of the three. You know Shaolin Crane and the Wutang Eight Palms. That's also two of the three. If I can put them together—"

Auntie stood. "That system was never finished."

Wingchun swept up and around her. "But it can be. The shapes of Shaolin, changes of Wutang, and power of O-Mei... The Fist of the Elders can be finished now—with me."

"Your father did not want that." Auntie crossed her arms. "Not for himself and certainly not for you."

"I'm not my father, you've known that from the beginning, the same way you know everything." Wingchun knelt down. "I understand now— Panther-King wasn't a victory, it was a test."

"One that almost killed you..."

"One that almost had to..."

"You don't know what you're asking..."

"I do. I leapt and I spread my wings but I can't soar high enough, not yet. The Dark Warrior is coming, you said so yourself—the Girl faces the Devil in the heavens. Well I have to face him here, now, and to do that I need your help."

詠 春 傳 說

The moon ebbed new and then flowed again almost full. Boklao stood in the rain and stared at the river, and even though the burnt, broken husk of the junk had been carted away, he could still smell the ash and the blood... It lingered all the way down the mountain, across the skeleton of the bridge to the ruin of the town, and on and on across the South, to an older, deeper ruin... Ash and blood...

"And all of it—" Boklao held up his hands. "—on me."

"Where have you been?"

Boklao's nostrils flared. "Little Kung..."

"It's been almost a month and—! Wait, why are you wearing the forest-demon robes?"

"They fit."

"My father's had everyone looking for you, do you know that?"

"Of course, I got half his people killed, half his sons..."

"What are you talking about? You saved him, same way you saved my mother and me. You didn't kill half our people—you saved the half that are left!"

"Saved the limb to kill the body... The vagabond saw that, so did your brother. They saw me for what I really am."

"A hero!"

"A selfish, arrogant fool who came all the way across the south chasing the dream—the fool's dream—of a boy who should have had the good sense to die when he was supposed to."

"I know just exactly what you mean."

Boklao closed his eyes. "Master Law..."

He was still in the torn sackcloth, bandaged but still bleeding, and he limped, the weight from his injured leg stooped over a cane. "I too chased a dream... or rather, let a dream chase me. I saw the chance to regain some semblance of the glory of my ancestors from the days of Ming—a reckless, utterly short-sighted chance, which brought us only to the bitter edge of calamity..."

Little Kung's face bunched up. "Am I the only one here who remembers the small matter of the *Ch'ing Army!* Neither of you invaded us, occupied us, oppressed us! Neither of you did anything but follow the path of the brave man and true, of the martial hero!"

"You don't understand," Master Law said. "You're a child..."

"I'm your son!"

"You are your mother's son—"

"What...?"

"—and she needs you now."

"You need me! My place is with you!"

"Your place..." Master Law hung his head. "Green dye comes from blue but is even more highly prized... We take care of them so that... so that..."

"I'll take care of you," Little Kung said. "I'll be a good son!"

"But you'll never be my *first* son. Every generation since before we came here from Fukien, it has been father to first son. It was my legacy and the legacy of my ancestors. It was Big Kung's legacy."

"And now it will be mine!"

"I don't want that for you, just as your brother never wanted it for himself."

"What about what I want? What about me?"

"You? You will go home, back to the caves…"

"The caves aren't my home…"

Master Law turned away. "They are now."

Little Kung stomped off. "I'm telling!"

"Listen," Boklao said. "There's—"

"I wanted to thank you," Master Law. "For what you did."

"No," Boklao said. "What I'm saying is you don't know—"

"I do, I remember. Bits and pieces, I admit, but I remember Big Kung telling me… telling me what I should so long have known. He was always so quiet around me, and only now do I realize it was because I deafened myself to his screams…"

"Big Kung did his filial duty. He did what was expected of him."

"He did what I demanded he do… and how he must have hated it and hated me because of it. It was a burden he could not bear and it crushed the life out of him in the end."

"He wasn't crushed by your burden, and he didn't hate you—he understood. At least, I think that's why… that's why he had me pull you out instead of him."

"You…?"

"Couldn't carry the both of you, and he insisted. He… he was right. He sacrificed himself to save you, while I was busy sacrificing all of you just to damn myself—"

"What…?"

"If I had just cut down a couple of polers the junk would never have come free, never have leapt the banks, never have made me have to choose…"

Master Law's cane clattered against the rocks.

"But the Ch'ing captain was there, in my face, challenging me, and I… I just couldn't let it go. I—"

Boklao's vision burst black and white. Mud… He was in the mud… His head throbbed and his jaw felt heavy as a rice bag and Master Law loomed over him, fist twisted out and first knuckle extended like the eye of a phoenix.

詠 春 傳 説

Snow frosted the desolate courtyard of the Green Snake Temple and clumped along the barren branches of the plum trees that lined its stone tiles. Wingchun stood beneath the rising sun, cowled in indigo, eyes closed and breath deep.

And then the snow erupted.

"I move first," Auntie said.

Wingchun's hand leapt up to parry. Snake Parts the Water. "I join. I arrive first and my touch tells me your center, your intent."

Auntie bent her arm and hacked with her elbow. "I continue."

Wingchun's other hand sliced up and her leg wedged in. Crane Seizes the Fox. "I intercept. I position myself to close your line and cut off your offense."

Auntie stepped to regain the angle. "I adjust."

Wingchun's waist twisted and her hand shot out. Snake Pierces the Bamboo. "I dart in. I penetrate with my own attack before you can recover."

Auntie went with her, dipped down and turned her arm to swallow the strike. "I retreat."

Wingchun followed, one hand dispersing like a snake's head, the other twining like a crane's wing. Yin & Yang Palms. "I stick. I ask the way and you tell me how to defeat you."

Auntie's hands dropped and her cheeks rounded. "They say it is difficult for a student to find a good master, but it is even more difficult for a master to find a good disciple. How fortunate I have been to have found eight of the very best…"

"Seven… You said you had seven disciples?"

"Eight is a far more auspicious number, don't you think? I am especially proud of the last two—a mother and her daughter…"

"Mother and…? You mean—?" Wingchun dropped to her knees and bowed her head. "Master!"

"Up!" Auntie pulled her. "Please, girl, get up!"

詠 春 傳 説

"Down!" Master Law kicked him. "Damn you, boy, stay down!"

"If only—" Boklao spat blood. "—If only you'd done this the first time…"

"I gave you every chance to prove yourself, and not just to me. I gave you every chance and this is how you repay me?"

"Told you…" Boklao stumbled back up. "Told you from the very beginning—"

"What I did not want to hear! They say not to trust a man's words only his deeds, yet your words were all I ever should have trusted! A lesson learned in the most utter desolation!"

Boklao's head snapped back, and he splashed down again into the muddy ground.

詠 春 傳 說

Wingchun's head remained bowed as she was lifted back up from the stone tiles, but Auntie took her by the cheek and nudged her around, and when she did, Wingchun saw the white-clumped plum trees, but it wasn't snow on their dark branches—

"They've blossomed…" The petals were small and tightly packed, silver blushed pink in the center. "To think something so beautiful could mature in the midst of such harshness…"

"Indeed." Auntie's eyes twinkled. "Your father and I used to argue about that very thing…"

詠 春 傳 說

Little Kung grabbed his father by the wrist. "What are you doing?"

Master Law shook him off. "You were sent back to the caves!"

"I—"

"You what, circled back around again so that you could spy?" He glowered at Boklao. "To have hoped something noble could be carved from the midst of such rotted wood… but I should have known—the rot would only spread!"

"What does that even mean?"

"It means that from now on you will learn only the medicine and live only the long life of your grandfather!"

"But not of my own?" Little Kung said.

"Some believe that to enter the temple and question the rites—to question anything—shows ignorance," Master Law said. "Others believe to enter the temple and question the rites—to question everything—*is* the rite."

Master Law grabbed Little Kung by the scruff and tossed him aside. "Do not mistake me for one of those others, boy. For you there will be no further questions!"

詠 春 傳 說

"There are two schools, you see." Auntie pulled Wingchun closer. "The gradual school believes enlightenment can only be realized step-by-step, moment-by-moment, through the deepest of meditation and the strictest of cultivation. The sudden school, however, believes enlightenment can come all at once, through the slightest snippet of sutra, the briefest instant of reflection."

"Which did my father believe?"

"Both."

"And you?"

"I believed he should have picked one and stuck with it, but he insisted on walking the center, the mean. So very stubborn... He thought he could sew the seeds but leave them buried."

"For how long?"

"Forever, if they would remain so. And if not, until such time as they could not..."

"Until now..."

Auntie huffed. "You know, it's possible the Young Snake might have been far wiser than I ever gave him credit for..."

Wingchun smiled. "You could come with me, you know."

"You are not the only one who has begun an awakening, girl. There is still a task that awaits me as well... one I can no longer afford to delay." She glanced up. "But you could come with me?"

"No, I can't..."

"Because you must have your vengeance..."

詠 春 傳 說

"This is our reckoning…"

Boklao spun through the rain—

"Every path we have chosen," Master Law said, "every step we have taken, a bead slid across the abacus to count out our sins. Belief, intent, reason—none of them factored. Results and results alone determine what price must be paid…"

—and splayed out across the rocks.

"You saved me instead of my son…"

"Challenged the captain when all I had to do was stop the junk…" Boklao stumbled up again. "I used every chance to prove myself, to show us both—"

Master Law advanced on him, phoenix-eye outstretched. "I could kill you with a touch."

"—warrior is nothing," Boklao said. "If he doesn't fight for the good of his people…"

"You said you had forgotten…"

"I did, all of it."

"Too easy an answer, boy."

"I've forgotten everything."

詠 春 傳 說

"Remember what I told you."

"The hidden box, I remember…"

"Not just the box, girl."

"I remember, really."

"Vengeance—"

"For me and me alone," Wingchun said, "utter destruction of the inferno, never know peace and all that…"

"Not all. I have given you my robes, girl, take this as my bowl—vengeance can also be in accordance with nature, it can be tempered by mercy. It can be as the storm that restores harmony and brings rejuvenation and renewal, just as the extirpation of death can offer the chance for enlightenment in the next life."

"I'll remember, I promise."

Auntie faced her. "Then go before I change my mind and decide to keep us here forever."

詠 春 傳 說

Master Law turned his back. "Go, before I change my mind and end things here once and for all."

詠 春 傳 說

Wingchun raised her indigo cowl and flew down the mountain into the sea of clouds.

詠 春 傳 說

Boklao pulled on his dark green shroud and raced up the mountain into the sea of clouds.

21
Fragments of River & Lake

Master Law limped through the curtain of water that streamed down past the cave mouth. Lightning flashed. It lit the gray jags of limestone and the even grayer jags of his face.

Five-Metal Yang saw him, grunted, and hustled over.

"Not now," Master Law said.

"But we... we lost another one."

Thunder echoed beyond the mountains.

"The Ch'ing?" Master Law said. "Did they—"

"No, I told you, there are no Ch'ing left here, not that your scouts can find."

"Then...?"

"Stonemason Sek. He went out with us but—"

"But never came back..."

"He told Mok he wouldn't. He told him... He told him that we shouldn't worry..."

Master Law sighed. "It comes as no surprise."

"Sek was one of your first disciples, he took the oaths alongside me and Lai Bang!"

"After carving all those funeral monuments, he vowed never again. He... Sek comes as no surprise."

"Well he makes four now. Five if you count—"

"I don't."

"Boklao was valuable."

"He was costly."

"Master—"

"Take your scouts out again as soon as possible."

"Again?"

"And again and again—ten-thousand times if you have to! Take them out... Take them out until you have found the Ch'ing you cannot find, the ones hiding, the ones waiting..."

"Waiting for what?"

"For me to make another mistake."

"Now just hold on one—!"

"You cannot blame my husband for his lack of faith, Mr. Yang, not when others lack so much faith in him..."

Master Law stiffened. "My wife..."

Mrs. Law was still in sackcloth, like him, and propped against the edge of the back chamber—the farthest she'd ventured out since the funeral.

"We need more food," she said. "Blankets and medicine as well, but food most of all."

"We already shared out what few crumbs were left," Yang said. "Our men—"

"Can't share just a little more for their sick and their wounded, for their children?"

"I didn't say that, mistress. I wouldn't. But our brotherhood is—"

"Broken," Mrs. Law said, "and the only thing left for any of us now is to care for the pieces as best we can."

"Broken, maybe," Yang said, "but like the lotus, even when the stem snaps the fiber still binds. And, with respect, it is our brotherhood and our men who *are* caring, who are standing guard and protecting. We're the—"

"Fools. All of you."

"What? How can you—?"

"Master!"

Woodcutter Mok burst through the curtain of water, Piebald Chan slung over his shoulder.

"Bandits, master, they must have surprised him!"

Mrs. Law hitched up her tattered dress and rushed over. "Is he..."

Master Law checked Chan's eyes and felt for his pulses. "Alive... He's alive..."

Chan groaned. "They... they took the horses..."

"It doesn't matter..."

"Boy Ngao's making sure," Mok said, "but Master, they've taken all of them."

"None of that matters!"

"How can you say that?" Yang ripped off his splint. "Where're my hammers? Those misbegotten sons-of—I'll chase them to the very summit itself!"

"No, what you will do is go get Little Kung and whatever bruise-and-fall wine can be spared, and—"

Mrs. Law gaped at him. "What did you say?"

"The bump on Chan's head—the new one—it will require—"

"No, not Chan—Little Kung! Why must Yang go get him when *you* just went out and got him?"

Master Law sighed. "We had an argument, he was upset when I told him to come back here and—"

"Told him? You were supposed to drag him! You, who know his sons so very well, had an argument with Little Kung and told him to do something—the son who never did anything he was told...!"

"But he's here, he has to be! He's—"

"Out there right now... Goddess of Mercy—he's out there right now, with bandits and... and who knows what else! My last son..." Mrs. Law staggered back against the cave wall. "You have to find him!"

Master Law swung around, beyond gray, beyond jagged. "Yang, get your hammers!"

"Find him!"

詠 春 傳 說

Mist swallowed the mountains and the bamboo, cut the deep teal away like faded layers of a paper landscape until Boklao couldn't see more than a few steps ahead.

"Story of my life..."

Fukien to Siuhing to Lanchow to here, and nowhere left to go...

"My masters home below which we sit and talk now..."

Nowhere but up...

Then the clomp of steel-shod hooves echoed all around him and ebon shadows shot through the white mist.

Boklao put his back against the bamboo. Couldn't be Ch'ing—to lead a horse through a monsoon, around fissures and crags, they'd have to know the mountains well. They'd have to be born to them.

He circled around, tried to get a look, and—

"Not very impressive."

The voice was a chitter above the wind. And it was close...

Boklao stilled, let the forest-demon green of his shroud camouflage him while his eyes scanned east to west...

"Not if you're all the mighty Heaven & Earth Society has left to send after us. I mean you're fast, I'll give you that, but to slink from the water so by your very lonesome..."

Echoes and shadows... His nostrils flared... And a voice stunk full of wine and meat...

"I don't come from the water." Boklao shifted to another bamboo. "Not now, not ever."

"Interesting answer—for a rebel."

Boklao shifted again, continued his way around. "Poor hearing—for a bandit..."

But the voice shifted with him. "We hear arrogance well enough. We hear the deafening arrogance of rebels who say we're all part of the same Brotherhood of River & Lake—of everyone who travels the margins— even as you force the rest of us three paces behind..."

"Don't much care how you travel as long as it's away from me."

"You had everything just handed to you—tables and beds... and wives to fill both. You had everything while we were left to beg and steal and eke out what little we could from what scraps you left us. And when your arrogance finally brought the Ch'ing crashing down around you, you didn't even have the decency to reap your karma like brave men and true. No, you fled. You fled up the mountains, *our* mountains, and you brought them here with you!"

The stench billowed up behind him, and Boklao stepped out to face it. "Listen very carefully because I'm not going to tell you again—I'm no rebel and I'm sure as hell no brother. I'm not anything... not anything but Leung Boklao."

Laughter broke through the mist and, with it, a short, thin man cloaked and hooded in sepia. "Well, Leung Boklao, whatever you call yourself, whatever you say, you *are* something. You are Flying-Monkey's newest messenger boy and you are going to deliver my warning to whatever's left of your little Heaven & Earth Society. If they thought what I did to that old piebald was—"

"Chan?" Boklao stepped closer. "What did—?"

"Ah, you do know them, marvelous! Then I trust one look at your pulped face and mangled body will be all that the rebels need to realize they are no longer welcome here, that the Eight Immortals belong to me now!"

Boklao's hands clawed open. "Not any more."

Flying-Monkey laughed louder. "You hear that, Iron-Scalp? This one thinks he has some fight in him!"

A stocky man with a crusted, callused head lumbered out to the left of Flying-Monkey, snorted, and pounded his fists together.

"Iron-Scalp is a man of few words," Flying-Monkey said, "but Rascal Kwai—"

The bamboo rustled and then went still.

"—usually isn't?" Flying-Monkey shrugged. "Well, Crazy-Goat—"

A lanky man with a battered, broken chopper shambled out to the right, spat, and gnashed his two remaining teeth. "Just wants to see if rebels bleed red as their sashes!"

詠 春 傳 説

The Eight Immortals Crags, milky jade fringe atop dappled turquoise sash, didn't emerge above Wingchun. She emerged down onto them so fast it was almost as if she could fly... Everything was so clear, so vivid, so—

"—Broken!"

She skidded to a stop, her indigo cowl snapped back, and an ebon shadow clomped up over her, neighed, kicked the air, and then crashed back down and clomped off into the mist.

But the voices grew louder. Wingchun cut towards them.

"We must have gotten all turned around. Please, we didn't see you until—!"

"Until you rammed into our rightfully stolen property?"

"You cost us a horse, little man, but don't worry, we're businessmen, we'll give you the chance to settle up…"

"Please, we're lost, we're just—!"

"This can't be happening…!"

The rain fell away and the mist thinned. A cart was knocked over in the mud and people huddled against it—a man, a woman, and a girl… A family—

Screaming.

Wingchun closed.

Three men spread out around them. The first was no-nosed, with a face smashed flat as a tofu square, ears wedged at the corners. The second was bowlegged, his head round as a kumquat and jaundiced very nearly as orange. The last one was pockmarked, his skin saggy like bread taken too soon from the steamer. Their clothes were ragged and mismatched, just like the weapons they carried—a shovel, a pitchfork, a hoe, edges ground sharp…

The mother shook. "Can't be happening…"

"Take it!" The father shoved a handful of trinkets at No-nose. "Take everything we own, just let us go!"

He didn't understand the futility…

"We will." The trinkets scattered across the mud. "We'll let your wife go first!"

"Please!"

Bowlegs' pitchfork swung around.

"NO!"

詠 春 傳 說

Iron-Scalp's feet churned the mud, he bent at the waist, jutted his head out, and charged. Crazy-Goat's arms split the mist, he arched back, swung his chopper high, and leapt.

Boklao side-stepped and stuffed Iron-Scalp's head into the ground, angled and kicked Crazy-Goat back into the bamboo.

"Your style," Flying-Monkey said. "It's like something destined for the opera… so entertaining!"

"Be with you in a few seconds," Boklao said, "entertain you up close."

"And so optimistic! In a few seconds, you'll be dead."

Iron-Scalp wheeled around. Crazy-Goat rebounded. Boklao tried to flank them but he slipped. Rocks tumbled down the slope behind him and plummeted into the mist far below...

Boklao cursed and circled away from edge. Iron-scalp charged in again. Boklao dodged and kicked him in the face but he just looked up, chortled, and then slammed into Boklao.

"That's right," Boklao said, "you're called Iron-Scalp..." The force of the charge drove him back towards the slope. More rocks tumbled behind him but Boklao latched onto Iron-Scalp's wrists, dropped down, turned, and twisted. "Not Iron-Arms..."

Cracks echoed through the mist but Iron-Scalp's scream drowned them out.

Then Crazy-Goat's wail joined the cacophony. "I'm going to slice you open and boil your guts for soup!"

Boklao snapped left and the chopper grazed past his chest. "You're fast," he said. "Strong too... And you have that whole 'crazy' thing going for you..." Boklao snapped right, the chopper splattered down into the mud. "Not too big on the control, though." Crazy-Goat yanked the chopper up but Boklao caught it, spun it back around, and buried it in Crazy-Goat's belly. "I know how that can be."

Crazy-Goat slid from the blade, a willow-leaf saber leapt into Flying-Monkey's hand, and he was on Boklao, hacking and slashing and stabbing.

Boklao barred with the chopper. "What, no more talking?"

"Face-to-face, blade-to-blade," Flying-Monkey said, "let's see what you can really do!"

Flying-Monkey's big eyes peeled bigger, his thin mustache rippled up, and he grabbed the chopper at its cross-piece. Boklao grabbed Flying-Monkey's saber right back. They snarled and spat and pushed and pulled each other across the mud.

"Look at you," Flying-Monkey said. "Your legs are so narrow, your bridges so short, but your power's all wide and long... It's like you're trying to mash together two conflicting approaches—" The tip of his saber slipped through and bit into Boklao's chest. "—Leaving me all these wonderful cracks!"

Boklao fell back and the blade slid up and lodged itself against his collarbone. He clenched his teeth, let go of the chopper, and grabbed onto the saber with both hands. He strained to keep it away, even as his head inched back over the edge of the slope...

The blade bit deeper and the mist thickened.

"A few seconds," Flying-Monkey said. "This won't take even half a—" And then he stiffened and his big eyes peeled huge.

Boklao tilted his head. Flying-Monkey listed and, behind him—

"Little Kung!"

His small hands were clutched around the chopped and his eyes bore into Flying-Monkey. "Get away from him!"

Flying-Monkey blinked, and then he reached around, yanked the chopper from his back, and turned on Little Kung. "Filthy, stunted mother—!"

Blood leapt from Boklao's shoulder but he latched onto Flying-Monkey and held him tight. "Just... just realized something—"

Flying-Monkey turned back. "No...!"

"—monkey's can't fly!"

And then Boklao bucked his hips and heaved them both over the edge and down the slope.

詠 春 傳 說

The cry ruined any chance for surprise but Wingchun hadn't thought about that. All she'd thought about was getting the bandits away from the family. And with a yelp, No-nose did just that.

He charged at Wingchun head-on, shovel low. Wingchun yielded, back leg bowed and front drawn. The attack came fast but she shed it with her right hand and with her left, touched No-nose on the chest.

He flew back, smacked into the cart, and splashed into the mud.

Wingchun glanced at the family. "Go! Quickly!"

Bowlegs slashed at her with his pitchfork. He was tall and his weapon was long. Wingchun flowed back, her face an inch from the tines... and Bowlegs overstepped. She slapped the pitchfork away and, once joined, she cut in, chopped her hand into the side of Bowlegs' neck, and then yanked his head into her knee, rotated her arms over, and slammed him to the ground.

Then she turned and her hands rose, coiled and furled...

"Turtle!" No-nose staggered up. "Rotten bastard of a turtle!" He rubbed his chest and worked the grip of his shovel. Then he exchanged glares with Bowlegs and... hesitated. "Take him!"

"What?" Bowlegs gaped. "You take him!"

"We all take him!" Pockmark spat. "Together!"

They streamed around her in the mist and the bamboo. and she wait-ed for them, for their feet to splash through the mud and their weapons to all but pierce her... Then she contracted, twisted and turned like a snake's body. The shovel whizzed by, the pitchfork rattled past, and the hoe cracked down beside her. Then she expanded, untwisted and returned like a crane's wings.

No-nose splattered, face balled up in agony. Bowlegs crumpled, pal-lor almost green. And Pockmark thudded down on top of them, stiff as overcooked dough.

詠 春 傳 說

They tumbled, Boklao's head over Flying-Monkey's heels. Then they hit the mud and began to slide.

Knocked back and forth by the bamboo, they punched and kicked and wrestled for top position. Flying-Monkey got it first. He brought the willow-leaf saber up—

And they smashed into a jagged spur of rock.

Flying-Monkey howled and Boklao snarled, and they tumbled again, faster and more furiously.

Boklao flipped them over, butted his head down into Flying-Monkey's nose, and followed up with elbow after elbow. "Still... still entertained?"

Flying-Monkey shifted, grabbed Boklao's face, and shoved it towards the saber. "Still unimpressed!"

The slope leveled out but their speed didn't. The veins on Boklao's neck popped and his muscles knotted, and he strained to keep out of reach of the cold, wet blade even as Flying-Monkey puffed and frothed, and forced it closer and closer until it tasted Boklao's cheek.

Boklao growled and shoved back hard. Flying-Monkey snickered, rolled suddenly the other way, and reclaimed the top. He swung his sa-ber up again. Boklao grabbed for it, jammed his knees in between their bodies, and kicked.

And the slope fell away beneath them.

詠 春 傳 說

Wingchun gazed from her hands to the fallen bandits and back. Another test...

Her heart pounded. She took a long, deep breath.

Not apart, not detached, not numb, and no longer empty... The haze was still there, the bitterness and the rush, but it wasn't dull this time. This time it sizzled.

Then the wind changed and the mist curdled into fog.

The bamboo thrashed above her.

Wingchun's head snapped up.

The fog swirled, mud came splattering down, and another bandit, hooded in robes dark as the night, came splattering with it.

He rolled up, his face hidden completely in shadow, even his eyes— everything but the cold, wet saber that glinted in his hand...

詠 春 傳 說

Little Kung peered down the slope at the trench that zigzagged its way through the greenish-brown muck into the fog far below.

"Careful, boy, it'd be a right shame if you were to trip and fall and break your noodle-thin neck..."

Little Kung's face bunched. "Kwai?"

His wide brimmed, coarsely woven hat was low and he flipped a flying dagger back and forth between his fingers.

"I would ask you just what you think you're doing here, if the answer wasn't so pathetically predictable..."

"I was following Boklao and I lost track of him for a while but then I heard the noise—I heard the fighting—and I found him again only there were these bandits—who I think might have stolen our horses—and, anyway, he was beating the—"

"Boy..."

"—out of them but then he got stabbed somehow so I plucked this chopper from the mud and stabbed the bandit right back! He... he tried to come at me but Boklao pulled him, well... pulled them both straight down the mountain and—"

"A breath, boy, take one!"

"We have to do something!"

Kwai flipped the flying dagger again and a sneer flashed across his gaunt face.

"We do indeed."

詠 春 傳 說

Boklao rolled with the fall but as he came back up the world continued to spin around him. Clearing... He was in a clearing and something—a cart or wagon—was broken in its middle... And Flying-Monkey was already up across from him, a cowled shadow wreathed in fog, his saber out, and a body at his feet, so still, so... small...

"Little Kung..."

Boklao waited for the red and the salt and the iron. He waited for his control to slip away... and he welcomed it.

詠 春 傳 說

Wingchun let the first falling bandit's saber splash down into the mud, stepped over his small body, and met the second.

Or tried to.

His power was overwhelming. He forced Wingchun back until she was finally able to change angles, cut him off, and leave him to slip and slide past her.

But he adjusted too fast, spun around and attacked again. She moved with him but she couldn't keep him off-balance long enough to finish...

詠 春 傳 說

Boklao kicked but his leg was jammed. He punched but his arm was stuck. He flailed and stumbled and wailed away again and again. The world pounded with his heart. His rage built and built.

Boklao roared and exploded up.

詠 春 傳 說

"Iron Tiger Cracks the Mountain..."

Wingchun twisted and turned, flowed not so much around his attack as through it.

詠 春 傳 說

"Snake Threads the Bamboo..."

Lightning split the heavens. Boklao glared up, his shroud splattered across his face. Deep indigo fluttered above him and arms spread out like the wings of a crane, light and lithe, and filled with an almost transcendent grace...

詠 春 傳 說

Thunder shook the earth. Wingchun gazed down, the hood of her cowl buffeted against her face. Dark green swirled below her and hands opened like the claws of a tiger, wild and free, but at the same time so certain, so... different...

詠 春 傳 說

Faces ashen beyond porcelain, beaten past weathered, their eyes locked, black jade kindled more turbulent than any storm.
Wind howled. Lightning flashed. Thunder boomed...
And their hearts jolted.

詠 春 傳 說

Little Kung latched on to the last stalk of bamboo and skidded to a stop just as the slope fell away beneath him.
"Bok—!"
Kwai shoved him aside. "Quiet, idiot boy!"
"What the—?"
Flying daggers hissed past his head.
A deep, dark form billowed below.
And the flying daggers struck.

22
Second Sons

Shreds of red silk fluttered away in the wind, an enormous, hook-backed blade flashed in the lightning, and Master Law's Kwan halberd slammed down with the thunder.

"What are you doing?" Mrs. Law said. "Come back inside!"

"When I first heard the Ch'ing were coming for us," he said, "the mountains seemed so small, so low. Now, when I must go out and find our last son, their vastness goes up and on forever…"

"Yang will find Little Kung!"

"Yang is not Little Kung's father."

"Perhaps, but he's not my husband either."

"I will not have you lose him."

"And I will not lose either of you!"

"You don't know what you're asking…"

"But I know what you owe me."

"A son…"

"Two sons!"

"I—"

"Don't say you understand, you couldn't possibly."

"I should have listened to you, we should have fled. I... I was such a fool! I tried to reclaim my life—the full life of my youth—and in so doing lost the only half I had left!" He shook his head. "I never loved my work, healing people, helping people, did you know that? Did you know that it was always the second choice for me? Since I was a child sitting in my fathers shop, watching him treat his patients, it took every ounce of concentration I could muster... The chimes would ring and the people would come in and every one of them—every one—would leave better off than when they arrived, and do you know the only thought that consumed me? When would they finally leave us alone so that we could go back to the boxing!

"My father had hands that brought back the spring. He loved taking their pulses, looking at their tongues, their eyes, feeling their skin... He'd always know just exactly the right medicine while I've always struggled to figure it out, struggled beneath the weight of his legacy, just as Big Kung struggled beneath mine!"

"I can't," she said. "I just—It's all I can do to even stand out here and talk to you right now..."

He turned and looked at her but she looked away.

Then Boy Ngao ambled towards them. "Master!"

"What is it?" Mrs. Law said. "Is it Little Kung? Is he back, is he here? Is—"

"No, not Little Kung, but—"

An old man with a huge belly and a sallow, bean-bald head emerged behind him.

"I... I know you, don't I?" Master Law said. "You're the hermit, Lee..."

"Call me Uncle Lee, Master Law." A smile rolled out over his long, stringy beard. "Everyone does."

"Tell them," Boy Ngao said to Uncle Lee. "Tell them what you told me..."

詠 春 傳 說

The wind sealed, the lightning blinded, the thunder deafened, the rain numbed, and Wingchun flew down the mountain faster and faster.

The man who rescued her, who charmed her, who left her, who spied on her, who traded her.... The man who died for her...

She raced the mountain.

It must be the proximity. She should have known that if she came back, she would bring him with her.

"A memory…"

詠 春 傳 說

"A ghost…" Boklao gazed off into the bamboo.

"He's delirious…" Little Kung fumbled for Boklao's pulses. "Ox balls! Why did I never pay attention!"

Kwai wrenched his flying daggers out from the side of the cart. "I missed…"

"Help me get him back on his feet," Little Kung said.

"I *never* miss…"

"Damn you, Kwai, I—"

Boklao grabbed Little Kung. "You… But I thought—"

He scrambled across to the body writhing in the mud and kicked it over. "Flying-Monkey…"

"What are you doing?" Little Kung said.

Boklao turned down the mountain.

"Where are you going?"

"After her."

詠 春 傳 說

Master Law slammed his fist into the side of the cave. The walls shook, water splattered, and limestone fell in chunks.

"Stop it!" Mrs. Law covered her head. "You'll bring everything down around us!"

"Again," he said. "You mean I'll bring it all down again!"

She shook her head and turned back to Uncle Lee. "How can you be sure the boy you saw was my son?"

Uncle Lee's bushy, white eyebrows crept above his dark-ser eyes. "I've never met your second son, Mrs. Law, but I've met your husband and the boy I saw was him in all but in age."

"And where was this?" she said. "Where did you see him?"

"Down the mountain…"

"Down the… How far down?"

"All the way."

"But... but I don't understand," Mrs. Law said. "Why would he do that, why would he even leave the caves?"

Master Law closed his eyes. "Because they're not his home..."

"No, he... he can't!"

"He can. He is. He's returning to Lanchow."

詠 春 傳 説

The skeleton of the bridge stretched out across the tumult of the Lan River, a long-dead dragon left to rot in the earth, and neither flame nor monsoon could make it clean. Maybe nothing could.

Boklao stood and clenched his fist and felt the tatters of her scarf still bound to it. Maybe nothing was ever meant to.

Their eyes met.

Fire flared. Water flooded.

She called out his name.

She accused him.

And she was gone.

詠 春 傳 説

Their eyes met.

Wood stabbed and steel slashed.

He called out her name.

He reached for her.

And he was gone.

The drizzle sparked over the wreckage, a phoenix dying in the heavens, and neither monument nor eulogy could ever bring it peace. Nothing ever could.

Wingchun strode through the town, its beams broken, its bricks pierced, its people spilled out... The Fai children were strewn from one end of the market to the other, Fire-blower Fo torched and spat out across them... And the crowd, young and old, men and women—everyone Wingchun had ever known—were piled together and trampled into the muck, an endless, senseless mass.

And the stench...

Her hand flew to her mouth and she wretched.

The feelings were overwhelming, but she didn't deny them and she didn't bury them. She let them fuel her.

Central Mountain took her to West Gate, to where the shop had once stood. The doors lay in the mud at her feet, ripped from their hinges and their gods torn and fled. The dining room was buried beneath her bedroom, and her bedroom beneath the roof. The kitchen was the same, cracked shingles atop the crushed furniture of her father's room, and the shelf that had once been in its corner...

Wingchun knelt down, offered a prayer to the shards of Koon Yam's statue, and then sliced her hand through ceramics and wood, and pulled out the box hidden beneath.

It was small but heavy. She brushed away the muck and ran her fingers over the black lacquer and the semblances of cranes at play in their mountain grotto until she found just the right spot... Then she pressed and a seamless lid clicked open...

詠 春 傳 說

The town wasn't changed, it was mutilated—the landmarks not disappeared but destroyed, the direction turned to chaos... It revealed nothing hidden by light or dark, and everything hidden behind the face of man.

Boklao circled around to Red Fortune Alley and there it was, its walls razed and its windows put out—the Yim Family Tofu Shop.

The gates were toppled, the fence charred, and the old, gnarled tree burned down, and it took Boklao barely a step before he was up and over and into the courtyard.

"Master Fong!"

He threw off his dark-green shroud and fell to his knees in the center of the tiles. "Master Fong, you were right! All this, all my fault! I killed those Ch'ing at the river and just like you said, your town and your daughter paid the price!"

He knocked his head. "I'm everything you said I was, everything you tried so hard to leave behind—single-minded, selfish... If only I'd stayed away, if only I'd stayed buried beneath the bodies of my friends, drowned in the blood of my family, burned in the fires of my home, then maybe... maybe the same wouldn't have happened to you and yours!"

Pounded his fists. "I traveled so far, so long, the years, the miles—they lost all meaning... I did things... things I never thought I'd do. I spied, I stole—all that and more. I thought in my heart that it was right, that it was justified... but that's just what I told my heart..."

Clawed his fingers. "If only I'd died when I was supposed to, then your town would still be here, you would still be here, *she* would still be here."

Closed his eyes. "I loved her from the moment I first saw her, but she died too, died without ever knowing..."

"She may have... but she knows now."

The shadows slipped away, the clouds parted, and she glanced over at him, caught in the radiance of the midday sun.

Grace and beauty, power and passion, tragedy and terror... Boklao's heart stopped, the world stopped. Everything, every other thought, every other desire fell away and only she remained.

"Wingchun..."

詠 春 傳 說

Master Law's sackcloth robe sloshed back and forth across the muddy limestone. "We should have heard by now!"

"Yang will..." Piebald Chan winced and adjusted the poultice on his head. "Yang will find him."

"You should be resting..."

"I should be sipping tea and honing calligraphy, but it seems I must learn to live with disappointment at least a little while longer. You, however. should trust that Yang will send word soon, if he doesn't burst in here at any moment, Little Kung bound and gagged over his shoulder..."

"Forgive me if I do not share your optimism, old friend."

"And forgive me if I point out it's usually *your* optimism that is shared, old friend."

"Not any more."

"Need I remind you, Brother Law, that you are still our leader?"

"No more than I need to remind you, Brother Chan, just where I last lead us..."

"Oh, it was your torches that burned down our homes, your spears that murdered our families?"

"No, but it was my decision to attack that junk, to turn around and charge us right back into those torches and spears."

Chan's face soured. "I just realized something, just this very moment—you don't blame that Boklao boy for letting Big Kung die, do you? You blame him for letting you live."

"I blame myself, is that what you wanted to hear?"

"The very last thing."

"There were so many other choices I could have made! I should have!"

"And then you would have faced other adversity. We all would have."

"You can't be sure of that."

"But I can be sure that you did what you were supposed to do. You raised your son according to the ideals and you lead us according to the way. Old friend, there wasn't anyone, Big Kung included, who wouldn't have followed you into the Forbidden City itself if you'd but asked us!"

"I know, old friend, and that's just precisely the problem."

詠 春 傳 說

The wreckage spun, her indigo cowl fell away, and Wingchun strode towards him robed in white, trimmed black and burgundy, and embroidered with cranes in full flight...

Boklao stood and reached out. "I saw you fall..."

She reached back. "Just like you."

Their hands met. "Consumed by flame, flood..."

Their fingers wove together. "Buried by wood and steel..."

"I got back up."

"Me too."

"I should have known," Boklao said. "Should have searched longer, harder... I should have found you!"

"You couldn't. I couldn't even find myself."

"But we've found each other now..."

"We returned to the same place..."

"I never left."

"Why?" Wingchun said. "Why didn't you?"

"I don't know," Boklao said. "Maybe... maybe I had nowhere else to go."

"There was nowhere else I could go."

"It seemed like so long."

"Like time went on forever..."

"But now it's standing still."

"Now it's racing." She looked up at him and her eyes smoldered. "Did you mean what you said before?"

"About—" He swallowed. "About all this being my fault?"

"About me."

"Only thing I ever really meant."

"I didn't think you cared…" She looked away. "You used me, betrayed me…"

"I Asked you before if you'd let me explain, let me make things right. Will you? Will you give me that chance?"

"No."

Boklao almost glanced back but this time she wasn't looking past him, she was locked dead on. "I Understand," he said. "I'll leave right now, I won't bother—"

"No, I mean there's no need."

"—again. I won't—Wait…" Boklao tilted his head. "What…?"

"There's no need to explain. I can see it in you, the same as I could always see it in my father." Wingchun sighed. "That day, when you came down into the dining room wearing his robes, I thought they made you look like him. But it wasn't the robes—it was the pain, the same pain…"

"Exactly the same."

"Exactly…?"

"You don't remember," Boklao said. "How could you, you were barely three years old when it happened. I was five… I was playing kickball with the other boys. There was no warning, nothing at all. I raced back to the village—"

He stumbled up the alley, through oily black smoke and crackling white flame. The square was just ahead. And his father—

"I had to reach my father but constables stamped around, cowered the villagers into the ground, and Forbidden Bannermen tore up the road, body after body tumbled in their wake… I tripped and fell, but still I strained for any hint of my father—"

But all he saw was a defiant man crouched beneath faded rags, ready to rise up—

"Even as the arms of his closest friend—of his sworn brother—stopped him. Then a devil turned, a devil in bone-white robes—"

"The Lama," Wingchun said.

"And his burning eyes blazed—"

"Yield them."

"A spear lashed out," Boklao said. "It sliced me across the side of my head. I screamed—"

"*NO!*"

"There was blood everywhere... Another body fell on top of me. I couldn't move but I could see. I could see my father standing up—"

"*Unstoppable even by the arms of a hundred friends or a thousand brothers—*"

"Your father...?"

"Leung Hong," Boklao said.

"*Twenty-fourth generation disciple of Shaolin—*"

"Blood brother of Fong Dak," Wingchun said, "of my father."

"Killed the exact same night as you mother," Boklao said.

"But then... but that makes you—"

"Leung's second son, arranged some fifteen years ago to one day marry Fong's seventh daughter..."

"Me..."

"Just a few days before..."

"You claimed it wasn't about my father's system," Wingchun said, "that it never was... But if... But then...?"

"You. Only and always you, since the moment I saw you..."

"But we were only children..."

"You were hiding behind your mother's robes but you peeked out and I glimpsed your eyes, your endless eyes, and—"

"You gave me a cricket... The only cricket anyone has ever given me..."

"You smiled."

"And you smiled back. It wasn't just the pain I recognized, it was something deeper—it was you."

詠 春 傳 說

A dozen rebels formed up on the cliff overlooking the Lan River and, just beyond the first wave of bamboo, the murdered town of Lanchow.

Five-Metal Yang sighed. "Sun's out at last, both hammers are finally ready again, and not a damn Ch'ing in sight!"

Woodcutter Mok chuckled. "Hoping to exercise your so recently unbroken arm a little?"

"Work out a cramp, perhaps..."

"Unbelievable," Lai Bang said. "Big Kung was never so flippant about his duty!"

"Yang isn't Big Kung," Mok said. "You'll get used to his style."

"Yang is a merchant, a man of standing like Master Law, like me. I have no need to get used to Yang—he's my brother."

"And me?"

"You either."

"Good."

"You're beneath me."

"What did you just—?"

"We're all brothers here," Yang said.

Lai Bang bristled. "You sell gold and silver, I sell fireworks, and you want me to consider this... this filthy woodcutter a brother?"

"Filthy woodcutter?" Mok said. "Why you arrogant—!"

"I want you to consider your oaths," Yang said, "and I want you to remember that we're not here to squabble, we're here to search out Little Kung and rescue him back to our master."

"Our master's wife," Lai Bang said. "Mistress Law's the one who gave us the rope."

"I'll have you know the Sixth Patriarch was a woodcutter," Mok said.

"I'm surprised they made it to a Seventh," Lai Bang said.

"That's it, your little stick, my giant axe, right here, right—"

"Enough." Yang hefted his hammers and began down the mountain. "We have a boy to find."

"Fine," Lai Bang said. "Sooner we find him, sooner we're done. But if there's any little bit of fortune left us, there won't be a single Ch'ing within a hundred miles..."

詠 春 傳 說

The main body of the third battalion, second brigade, Kwangsi Provincial division of the Constabulary Army of the Green Standard turned up the Northern Road and into the outskirts Lanchow, their three-hundred crimson-tasseled spears assaulting the heavens.

23
The Dragon & the Phoenix

Eagle-Shadow crossed the Kwailam Palace to the hidden gate, opened the secret lock, and descended the spiral stairs to the forgotten cells below. "Old priest?" he said.

"I abide."

"You didn't before."

"Yet now again."

"So quickly?"

"What is time to me?"

"Very little it seems…"

"You grow impatient?"

"I was of the clan of Guwalgiya," Eagle-Shadow said, "of the line of Oboi. I was nephew to generals and lords, and a captain of the Bordered Yellow Banner who tore like thunder across the plains of Manchu! I was all that and more, and yet even now—even now—I lack the base honor of my own name. Tell me, old priest, would you truly experience the full blossoming of my patience?"

The old priest's laughter writhed and reverberated through the chamber, and the terrible presence rolled over Eagle-Shadow. But this time he held his place.

"You think this is funny, old priest?" He scratched down his hook-shaped scar. "You think *this* is funny? It's not just my face, I lost—it's the face of my clan! I guarded tradesmen, I cleared squatters, and I challenged every sick-man Southern boxer I could find. I did whatever I had to do, whatever debasement, whatever horror was necessary, until one day I delivered some wild ginseng and it delivered me..."

"I delivered you."

"I found the Shaolin who defaced me and yet found through him that I wanted more."

"More than his death?"

"More than my life! I want it back, old priest, all of it. I want my station, I want my home. I want my name!"

"Then assuage yourself, clansman of Oboi, nephew of generals and lords. You have practiced your virtue and soon others will become one with their loss."

"The Tao... Instead of answers all you offer is your heathen Tao..."

"The Tao offers far more than answers."

"I am risking everything!"

"What else is there to risk, when everything is what you seek to obtain?"

"You told me that I would believe in you, old priest, but there was no truth to that was there? No truth to any of this!"

"No more truth than fate. Nothing, not in all the universe, but essential nature. We will do as we will do. That is the only truth." The laughter faded and the terrible presence with it. "Now go, attend to your once-and-again master."

"And?"

"And wait for him to do as *he* will do."

詠 春 傳 說

"All this time," Wingchun said.

"Every minute of it," Boklao said. "Every second..."

"Back at the shop, I thought you were making a deal with my father right there, right then. I..."

"Wondered how he could even consider giving you to a spy, a thief?"

"To someone I thought he barely knew, to someone I thought wanted everything but me..."

"Who wanted only you, the one thing your father would never consider, not even after he realized who I was, after he saw me use my father's peerless technique—"

"Iron Tiger Cracks the Mountain..."

"It was only when the Ch'ing left him no other choice... No other choice but to entrust you to a spy and a thief."

"But I don't understand," Wingchun said. "You are who you are, why spy, why steal?"

"Mouths tell ten-thousand tales," Boklao said, "but the fist comes straight from the heart. Almost fourteen years and more miles than I could count, I had to know... I had to know if it was really him to know if it was really you."

"You could have just asked."

"And if your father decided to take you and run again? If he lied to buy himself time?"

"He wouldn't do that."

"Why not, he lied to you, didn't he? Same way everyone in my life has lied to me since the moment that Ch'ing spear cut across my head..."

"What are you talking about?" Wingchun said.

"I must have looked murdered enough," Boklao said, "at least to everyone but Uncle Choy. He was one of the Red Poles, one of my father's closest disciples. He found me lying there beneath all the bodies, pulled me out and took me with his family when they fled to Kwangtung, to the small town of Siuhing.

"They were good to me, especially Second-Son Fu, but I was closest in age to the youngest, Fifth-Son Bil. We trained together, ate together, did everything together.

"I worked hard and Uncle Choy said he was proud of me, but it wasn't pride I smelled—it was fear... Still, he claimed he taught me everything, as much and as well as his own sons, even my father's peerless technique. He said there was no defense...

"That night I was so excited I couldn't sleep. I slipped out to train some more and that's when I felt the house shake like it was caught in a monsoon. Uncle Choy was teaching First-Son Lung... teaching him something he'd never taught me. My lessons—and the lessons of everyone else when I was around—were always as big and bold as the tiger, combining the long arms and dynamic kicks of its Northern heritage with the short bridges and complex footwork of its Southern refuge. Cross Shape Fist, Tiger Taming Fist—those were the sets I learned. What Uncle Choy was teaching First-Son Lung was something else entirely, something closer to your father's Little First Training..."

"The Fist of the Elders," Wingchun said.

"The secret fist," Boklao said. "At least that's what Bil told me when he caught me watching, when he laughed at me and asked if his father had really never told me.

"Uncle Choy said I was family, claimed he taught me everything, as much and as well as his own sons. But there was a dagger hidden in his smile."

"Maybe he was waiting," Wingchun said, "or maybe he just wanted to protect you?"

"The way your father was waiting," Boklao said, "the way he just wanted to protect you?"

"Maybe he *was* afraid... afraid of what you might do with it?"

"I don't know his mind. All I know is that I wasn't part of his family, not really, and he wasn't going to teach me the Fist of the Elders, not ever."

"How can you know that?"

"Because he got sick just a few weeks later..."

"He died..."

"And the day after the funeral, well, let's say Bil decided to show me just how well my father's so-called 'peerless technique' could be defended, how much I was really missing...

"When it was over, Second-Son Fu picked me up. He knew I couldn't stay in Siuhing any more, that there was nothing left for me there, and so he bought me the salt—the freedom to travel—and told me something else Uncle Choy never bothered to—the rumors about *you*...

"I'd lost my father and his system, I'd lost everything. But then, all of a sudden, I was given this gift, this hope that you'd somehow survived as well, that you were somehow still out there. I raced back to Fukien, gave my father what rites I could, and talked to anyone who might know anything, anything at all. Then I began my journey to the west...

"To me," Wingchun said.

"So many years, so many times I got stuck in the same rut... I had to be sure!"

"And so that's why you spied?"

"I intended to fight, to have your father beat into me the proof I needed. But then I saw you there and, well, people can hide a lot but not the way they move. I... I just couldn't take another lie, even if I became one myself."

"Not a lie, just life..."

"What?"

"I understand now."

"It doesn't justify anything," Boklao said, "doesn't excuse what I did. So stupid! I can't ask you to forgive me, not after I caused all this." He cast his eyes across the wreckage. "My recklessness, my selfishness, my fault—"

"You're right."

"I know, all of—"

"I meant about being stupid."

"—it—What?"

"You didn't cause this," Wingchun said.

"I fought those Ch'ing at the river," Boklao said, "and I led that scar-face right back to your father."

"That scar-face hunted my father by name—by his real name—and the Lama hunted with him."

"But—"

"But nothing. The guilt is not yours to carry."

"Then how?"

"Fate, chance... a confluence of events? I don't know. Maybe we'll never know. Maybe we don't even have to. Maybe all we need to know is that it did happen and that it's never ever going to happen again, not to anyone."

"What are you talking about?"

"Nothing, I..."

"You...?"

Wingchun looked west. "Do you hear that?"

"Hear what?"

"A fight..."

Boklao tilted his head. "No, a battle..."

詠 春 傳 說

"Like blind men to the damn matchmaker's!" Woodcutter Mok raced up the rocks and swung his axe wide in an attempt to drive the constables back. "They lured us in, barred the gate, and then swarmed ugly all over us!"

Lai Bang clutched his three-section staff by the middle and twirled both ends to block. "This is all your fault, tempting fate with your... your exercises and your cramps!"

"Yang's cramps! And I just teased fate a little, you're the one who insulted its mother!"

Five-Metal Yang plowed across the mud between them and battered away the spears. "Mok, take the left flank and punch us a hole into the bamboo, if we can reach it, there's a chance we can lose them! Lai Bang, take the right flank and—!"

"And what?" Lai Bang said. "We're outnumbered nearly three to one!"

"That's just more of them to kill!"

"Yes! To kill *us!*"

詠 春 傳 說

Boklao skidded around the bend but this time he didn't need to put his body between Wingchun and the bamboo, and he didn't need to push her. He just needed to keep up.

"Slow down," he said. "The old riverbed—"

"Is pretty much new again." Wingchun cut across the shallow, muddy water and up along the banks. "But the shortcut will still lead us to the Western Road..."

"I know," he said. "We ran this way be—"

Wingchun stopped and her hand lashed out. Steel hissed and buzzed from the bamboo. Boklao jerked back and then her fingers were clamped in front of his left eye, a flying dagger caught between them.

"How did you—?"

She shoved him. "Look out!"

The hissing and buzzing returned three-fold, but Wingchun's arms circled, her white robes flared, and flying daggers splashed down around her.

Then a strangely mottled shape burst out in front of them. "Run, boy, or—" Kwai stopped and stared. "Oh, come on!"

Boklao spun back up. "What the hell—?"

"You're not Ch'ing!" Kwai said. "Why the—wait a minute..." He pushed his coarsely woven hat back and gaped at Wingchun. "A girl?"

Wingchun glanced at Boklao. "Friend of yours?"

"No."

"The damn dagger-catcher's a girl?" Kwai said.

"She's not a dagger-catcher," Boklao said. "She's—"

"Chopstick girl!" Little Kung darted out from behind Kwai.

"Chopstick girl?" Boklao said.

"Never mind," Wingchun said.

"You're alive!" Little Kung said. "I mean, we thought—"

"What are you doing here?" Boklao said. "Following me again?"

"Of course! You were injured and you just ran off, and… and…"

"And you thought you could help?"

"I did before…"

"This isn't before." Boklao glared at Kwai. "And what about you, you certainly didn't come to help…"

"Couldn't take the chance the boy might go and get himself eviscerated without me being there to enjoy, now could I?"

"We don't have time for this," Wingchun said. "The fighting—"

Little Kung jerked back around. "The rebels!"

Boklao grabbed him by the collar. "Don't even think about it!"

"Rebels?" Wingchun said.

"Five-Metal Yang and Lai Bang and Woodcutter Mok and the others," Little Kung said. "My father must have sent them after me, and now—"

"Now, like us, they're trapped," Kwai said, "cut off by three squadrons of the Green Standard. Should have just wrapped us all in a giant red envelope…"

"They're going to be slaughtered!" Little Kung said. "I have to—"

"Get back into the bamboo and hide," Boklao said. "Vagabond—"

"Told you, Leung Boklao," Kwai said. "My name's not Vagabond."

"Whatever your name is, turns out you did come to help after all—to help me create a distraction."

"Like hell!"

"It's that or be the distraction." Boklao turned to Wingchun. "Stay with Little Kung. As soon as we draw off the constables, get him over the bridge and up into the mountains, he'll show you the way."

"He'll show himself," Wingchun said. "I'm not leaving, not again. And don't even think about telling me that I have to. I have a choice."

"No, you don't. There's going to be fighting—something you don't know anything about—and I won't risk losing you, not again, not—" He tilted his head. "What's so funny?"

詠 春 傳 說

Lai Bang dodged a spear but the constable jerked it to the side, smacked him in the face with the flat of the blade, and sent him reeling. Then the constable lunged in and—

"No you don't!" An axe cleft through the spear shaft and then swung around and cleft through the constable behind it.

"Thirteen of them down and only four of us," Mok said to Lai Bang. "Don't think for one minute I'm going to let you go and die and lose us that advantage!"

"Advantage?" Lai Bang said. "At this rate perhaps Yang might still manage to limp out of here alive but, for the rest of us, we need to rout and we need to do it now!"

"You mean regroup?"

"Did I say regroup?"

"No one's going anywhere!" Five Metal-Yang charged through them and into another Ch'ing. "Not without Little Kung! Master Law has already lost one son, we're not losing him another!"

"No, we're just losing him all of us!" Lai Bang launched his three-section staff out its full length. It lashed around Yang and cracked into the constable that was sneaking up behind him. "Little Kung is long gone, he has to be! One look at all these Ch'ing, and do you really think even Little Kung would stay? No one's that stupid!"

"No one but us," Mok said. "We seem to be just exactly that stupid."

"What I'm saying is, if Little Kung has any sense of self-preservation, he's nowhere near—"

"Here! I'm right here!"

Lai Bang glanced back and saw Little Kung clambering up the side of the bridge. "He's right there..."

"I can see him," Yang said.

"Then what are we waiting for?"

"A sign from heaven," Yang said. "That's what it's going to take to stop the constables from hacking us to pieces the moment we try to rout."

"He means regroup," Mok said.

Then, suddenly, the very back of the constabulary lines rippled... rippled, and broke.

"Someone's engaging their flank," Lai Bang said.

"More than that," Mok said. "They're splitting their forces!"

"Who?" Yang's face knotted. "What?"

"What else?" Little Kung laughed. "Your sign."

詠 春 傳 說

A constable howled and leapt off the rocks, spear high up above him. He swung it as he landed and Boklao watched the blade whip down at him like a hammer. Then he side-stepped and tiger-tail kicked the constable into the river.

"Vagabond," Boklao said, "the rebels have reached the bridge! Vagabond!"

Not a hiss but a wail erupted from the bamboo. Three of the constables turned, and jutting from up their arms, along their necks, and in their faces were dozens of chopsticks, their tips whittled sharp.

"Little Kung... Little Kung is with them," Boklao said. "But I don't see Wingchun... Where—?"

He glanced back... and his mouth fell open.

詠 春 傳 說

She tore through them like wind through the bamboo. Her arms twisted and turned, her palms stamped, and constables fell around her like late autumn leaves.

Wingchun closed her eyes—

詠 春 傳 說

—And the Lama's eyes blazed open.

"Master?" Eagle-Shadow said.

"They have beaten the grass—"

"The governor's forces?"

"—and startled a snake..."

"And what will you do?"

Bone-robes flared, the Lama was gone from the chamber, and the narrow lanterns flickered and went black.

"Cut off its head and drink down its blood as I have done every single one before."

詠 春 傳 說

Five-Metal Yang bowed and Little Kung tumbled from his shoulder and splashed down at the entrance to the caves.

"Second son, found and bound as ordered, master."

Little Kung struggled against the ropes.

"Hey! I—!"

"Not a word, boy." Master Law glanced around. "You left with a dozen men, Yang, yet return with barely half... And every one of you wounded..."

"There were three squadrons of the Green Standard waiting at the Lan River," Yang said. "They ambushed us the moment we crossed the bridge. I doubt even this many would have made it back if not for..."

"For what?"

Mok chuckled. "A sign from heaven..."

"Boklao," Yang said. "It was him, I saw him. He gave us an opening and we took it, we cut our way to the bridge and didn't look back."

"Lai Bang looked back," Mok said.

"Filthy woodcutting piece of—!" Lai Bang bristled. "Only to make sure we weren't being followed!"

Master Law looked at him.

"We weren't..."

"Boklao does not give you an opening," Master Law said, "not by himself."

Mok nodded. "The vagabond might have been with him."

"It wasn't just the vagabond," Little Kung said. "It—"

"What did I say about words, Mankung?" Master Law gestured at Mok and Lai Bang. "Put him in the caves. Put... put everyone there, and then prepare the wounded for treatment, yourselves included."

They bowed and did as he said.

"Yang," Master Law said. "You're sure no one followed you back?"

"Master?"

"Even Boklao?"

Yang huffed. "I asked for him to—forgive me, master, I did—but he just turned away... He turned away, yelled something, and raced off into the bamboo."

"What did he yell?"

"Wingchun."

詠 春 傳 說

"Whoa…"

Wingchun's nose crinkled. "So you keep saying…"

They were together amid the shattered courtyard of what had once been the Yim Family Tofu shop.

"Disciple of the White Crane Nun, Wumei…" Boklao shook his head. "It's just…"

"Let me guess—whoa…?"

"You look the same but you're not, not at all. What I just saw you do, I… I still don't believe it." He stared at her. "You're unmistakable even when I can hardly recognize you."

"And I'd recognize you without looking. The same inside, even if the outside has changed…"

"Has it?"

She touched his hair. "Unshaved and unbraided…"

"Don't like it?"

"I like it very much."

"Good."

She turned, her arms wide. "This place…"

"When I suggested we get gone, this wasn't exactly where I had in mind."

"Right under the Qing's noses?"

"The last place they'll look but the first they'll see…"

"Good."

"Wingchun, I know this is your home but—"

"But it never really was, not for me, remember?"

"Because you never really understood what it was to have a home."

"Not until I lost it… It wasn't where I came from but it is where I *became* from. This is where I learned to walk and talk, to grind tofu and serve it. This is where my father taught me the first two parts of the Fist of the Elders, and it's where I'm going to teach you all of it."

"The—? You—? Now just hold on one damn—!"

"Boklao…"

"After everything that's happened…!"

"Because of everything that's happened."

"I can't."

"You have to. I need you to." She opened the Little First Training. "We'll start with the meridian palm."

He backed away. "We're not starting with anything, especially not with something I've known since I was about three."

She angled a brow. "Did you now?"

"Come on, a palm strike? We're talking the secret system, I can't even imagine how complex the theory must be..."

"No, you can't. That's the secret."

"I don't understand."

"Neither did I, not until I fought with it."

"I've fought plenty, need an abacus to count the times..."

"Life and death, when your arms shake, your legs feel like they're stuck in the mud—"

"Blood races, it's all you see, all you taste, your breath gets hot and high, everything slows and narrows, and—"

"It's like you're floating and falling at the same time, only the most instinctive actions are possible, the—"

"Most simple..."

"There are so many systems," Wingchun said, "some based on the writings of General Sun or the *Book of Changes* or the *Sutra*, all complex and intricate enough to consume the life of a scholar, and all utterly useless in the face of a real enemy."

"But the Fist of the Elders," Boklao said.

"Can be written on your palm, simple and direct, as the essence of all things." She held up her hand and extended her arm. "Our bridges are straight so they will not shake, our postures are stable so they will not falter, and our theory is essential so it will not fail. It is the littlest of training, the smallest of ideas... But why am I telling you this, you've known it all when you were—three was it?"

He tilted his head. "About..."

"Show me."

"Show you?"

"Hit me... before I hit you."

"Listen, crazy girl, I'm not going to—"

Her palm pressed against his chest.

He chuckled. "Ouch?"

"That wasn't the hit."

"Then—"

A wave surged through him and Boklao flew across the courtyard, smashed into the fallen balcony rail, tumbled down the back steps, and collapsed.

Wingchun stood over him. "There are degrees of knowing."

"Must run in the damn family..."

"Some systems throw like a nail dart," she said, "sharp but light. Others swing like a hammer, heavy but dull. Both are dead, expended in the moment of their creation. The Fist of the Elders notches a nail and drives it in with a hammer."

"Your bridge makes the path," Boklao said, "and your body, the power..."

"And understanding begins..."

詠 春 傳 說

Master Law paced back and forth across the narrow, winding tunnel, his robes splattered with so much muck now that they flickered a corroded green beneath the dwindling lanterns.

"Answer me, boy!"

Little Kung's face bunched up. "Answering would require words, father, and you said—"

"It would be a grave mistake..." Master Law's face fell. "It would... It..."

"I know how worried you and mother were," Little Kung said, "as worried as you've always been about me—not the least little bit."

"I sent Five-Metal Yang out to look for you, boy! I sent a dozen rebels, so many of whom will never come back, to—"

"Do whatever it was you told them to do. It could just as easily have been to fetch your old teapot or—"

"Into the Forbidden City itself..."

"—slippers or—what?"

"Never mind."

"Of course—never mind, never heart! Only Big Kung, only your first son. He's the only one you ever cared about!"

"Cared to death, very nearly the both of you... And now—"

Master Law stiffened.

"And now...?" Little Kung said. "Now what?"

But Master Law turned and limped off towards the clearing.

"Fine!" Little Kung wriggled harder against the ropes. "But you can't keep me tied up forever! You—!"

Then he caught a glimpse of Woodcutter Mok and Lai Bang, axe and three-section staff ready, and the other rebels fanned out around the arms and armor of the Green Standard...

24
The Inner Gate

Boklao pierced both hands forward, bent down, then swung back as far and as fast as he could, to very edge of collapse. Then he breathed out, pressed his palms down, and brought his feet back together.

"Not bad," Wingchun said from where she perched, cross-legged, atop the wreckage of what had once been the tofu-grinder.

Boklao tilted his head. "But not right..."

"Better than the last time, at least."

"I meant the routine. Something's missing..."

"The changes of Wutang, the power of O-Mei, and the Snake and Crane arts of Shaolin, melded by the wisdom of the elders themselves, and yet Leung Boklao thinks something's missing?"

"No..."

"Good."

"Leung Boklao knows something is."

Wingchun laughed.

"I feel it," Boklao said. "I do, really—the changes, the power, the arts—all good, all great. It's just..."

"Something's missing?" Wingchun said.

"You know, the dispersing and the twining—"

"The two seeds."

"—too unbalanced, like heaven and man without the earth to support them. It opens and it transforms, but into what? It doesn't complete the cycle."

"Let me guess, Chi Sim had an essence to his Tiger Shape as well?"

Boklao extended his hand, elbow folded and palm turned down. "Taming Arm—it closes and collapses, seals power away like a beam locks a gate. After you intercept an opponent's attack, before you dart in with your own, it would let you break their defense, let you use half the effort—"

" '—To achieve twice the results.' Of course."

"Heard that before?" Boklao said.

"I've taught you the legacies of Miu Sun and Wumei," Wingchun said, "and of my father and mother. My legacy. But you carry Chi Sim's legacy with you as well. My boxing will forever be just that—mine. While you can use it, I hope, to gain some small enlightenment, the big enlightenment has to be your own. One essence, three essences, ten thousand... Snake and Crane, Tiger Crane, whatever. In the end it will be just you and whether or not you can use it."

Boklao smiled. "Yes, master."

"Master...?" Wingchun angled a brow. "Are you making fun of me?"

"Of course not."

"I didn't think so..."

"It's not polite for a student to make fun of his master..."

"Boklao!"

"Wingchun..." His smile faded. "Why did you come back here?"

"I told you, there was nowhere else I could go."

"You could have gone anywhere, maybe everywhere. So many different places, so many new and exciting people... it sounded so romantic to you once."

"To a skinny little girl, in a tiny little town, stuck out in the middle of nowhere..."

"And now?"

"Now... I don't know." She took a breath. "But I do know you've learned everything I can teach you. All that remains is for you to realize it."

"Really?" He crossed his arms. "And what remains for you?"

She gazed up towards the mountains. "The others."

"You mean the rebels..."

"I mean the survivors of Lanchow, my neighbors, my friends. I need to see them."

Boklao shrugged. "So go see them."

"And I need you to come with me."

"Can't."

"Don't worry about Law. It won't matter to him, not once he realizes—"

"It'll still matter to me," Boklao said. "Besides, there's someone else I need to see..."

詠 春 傳 說

Plumed in studded-metal armor, taloned with a long, curved Wo saber, and crested red as blood, the Lieutenant of the Green Standard was every inch a hawk in mid-strike.

Master Law pushed past Five-Metal Yang. "You must know that coming here means your death."

"Yet it remains my duty," the lieutenant said.

"Death is a duty where you come from?"

The lieutenant extended three fingers out from his hand. "I come from the water—from River & Lake. Death is my only duty."

"He's... He's a rebel..." Lai Bang folded his three-section staff back into a crutch. "Inner Gate..."

"Nothing gets by you," Woodcutter Mok dropped his axe and collapsed back into the mud. "Least not after it's made all completely obvious..."

Master Law bowed. "Fok, my old friend."

Fok bowed back. "I'd almost forgotten... I've heard it pronounced Huo for so long, I'd almost forgotten the sound of my own name in my own dialect..."

"How perfectly appropriate," Piebald Chan said, "for one who's forgotten his own people as well."

"Chan," Master Law said, "Fok is our sworn brother."

"No," Fok said. "Chan is right. I failed to warn you about the Forbidden Bannermen moving against Lanchow. I—"

"Had no way of knowing," Master Law said.

"It was my duty to know."

"And here I was just warming up to the whole 'death is your duty' thing," Chan said.

Master Law glared at Chan and then turned back to Fok. "You warned us about the junk and about the Territorial Bannermen. That failure was *mine*."

"Not according to the Kwangsi Governor," Fok said. "That's why I had to risk coming here directly. His report to the Leungkwang Viceroy blamed the loss of his junk and troops on the Shaolin, on their threat here in Lanchow not being completely eradicated."

"But it was," Yang said. "They eradicated the whole damn town!"

"You don't understand the politics. The Leungkwang Viceroy contends with that mad Vietnamese General who tests his strength to the south, and the Wankwai Viceroy ever-eager to absorb more territory to the north. If the governor shows any weakness the viceroy will replace him in the most painful and bloody sense of the word imaginable."

"That's why the governor sent those three new squadrons of the Constabulary Army to Lanchow," Mok said. "Isn't it?"

"No," Fok said. "That's why he's sent twenty-five."

"That's... that's a full battalion," Chan said. "That's *three hundred men!*"

"And they deploy tomorrow at dawn, with a Colonel of the Territorial Banner in the lead."

"A banner colonel?" Yang said. "Why in the hell would a banner colonel be leading even a battalion of the Constabulary Army?"

"Because he asked to," Fok said. "Because the Territorial Bannermen sent before were lead by a banner major, were led by—"

"His son," Master Law said. "His dead son..."

"The governor, however desperate, needs only show the viceroy that Kwangsi remains firmly under his control," Fok said, "but the banner colonel—"

"Wants blood..."

"He does, and he will do whatever it takes to get it. He will empty the Kwangsi Armies if he has to."

"T-to what end?" Lai Bang said.

"To our end," Mrs. Law said.

Master Law turned to his wife.

"You should not be out here," he said.

She stayed on Fok. "That's right, isn't it?" she said. "They will finish us and they will depopulate the whole county to do it."

"The whole prefecture." Fok bowed to Master Law. "I'm sorry, old friend. I'm supposed to be leading the scouts... So many people here crammed into so little cave, if I'm gone too long, if I'm not there to draw them away..."

"Of course." Master Law bowed back. "Thank you, old friend."

"They wouldn't," Yang said. "The whole prefecture—they couldn't, could they?"

"They can and they will." Mrs. Law said. "They've done it before."

"To combat pirates in the Taiwan Straight," Master Law said. "They depopulated the Fukien coast. Tens of thousands died... More... The rest fled into Kwangtung, and here, to the deepest backwater..."

"To death," Mrs. Law said.

"No." Wingchun alighted into the clearing. "Not yet."

詠 春 傳 說

Kwai slunk low through the shadows just beyond the clearing. His strangely mottled robes and well-honed skill made him all but impossible to see or hear—

Boklao's nostrils flared.

—but not to smell. "Find out anything interesting, vagabond?"

Kwai glanced up under the rim of his coarsely woven, conical hat, a flying dagger suddenly in his hand. "I'm not telling you again, Leung Boklao, my name's not Vagabond."

"No, I know who you are now." Boklao bent over him. "Who you really are."

"Took you long enough—"

"Bandit."

"—to figure it—What?

"You're a damn bandit."

Kwai chuckled. "Close as the air, far as the heavens..."

"You've been working with them the whole time."

"Whole time I've been in Kwangsi..."

Boklao glanced back at the rebels in the clearing. "So your debt to Law?"

"Got caught up on the end of an unfortunate misunderstanding is all..."

"The beaten and left-for-dead end?"

"Don't remember the details—I was quite a bit past drunk at the time. Suffice it to say Law stumbled over me—quite literally—while gathering herbs and—"

"He took you back to Lanchow and healed you."

"All right and proper."

"And in return he had you join his rebels…"

"More associate with than join, really. He wanted information from the mountains and I wanted to skip all those annoying oaths."

"To save you the trouble of having to break them later…"

Kwai inclined his head. "Exactly right."

"You like shortcuts," Boklao said. "That's good."

"Come again?"

"I want information as well and, much as I'd love to, I don't have time to beat you near-death enough first to get it."

詠 春 傳 說

"Daughter of Fong Dak," Master Law said, "disciple of Wumei… Your story, it's… Well, it's just—"

Wingchun sighed. "Whoa…?"

"At least we know who helped make our opening," Woodcutter Mok said.

"Yang's sign?" Lai Bang said.

"What? Who?" Yang said. "You mean *her*?"

"You saved my people," Master Law said to Wingchun.

"No," Wingchun said. "We only bought you some time."

"We?" Yang glanced around. "Boklao's here with you?"

"Always, just not here, not now."

"Then that begs the question, Miss Yim, of what exactly *you* are doing here, now?"

"Mrs. Law…" Wingchun's face softened. "You well?"

A tear fell down Mrs. Law's cheek, soiled and unpainted. "Not the least little bit."

"I know how you feel."

"Beaten and broken? Almost a hundred of us gathered here after the massacre of Lanchow, now less than half remain…" She took a deep breath. "Some fled, most dead, others so injured they may as well be… We're like an old mortar too long beneath the pestle, Miss Yim, unable to take much more, perhaps not even a single grind… You know how that feels, do you?"

"I know you can't hide, not anymore."

"No, but we can still die, can't we? That's why you're here, isn't it? Because we've gotten so terribly good at dying..."

"I'm not here to ask you to die." Wingchun said. "I'm here to beg you to live."

Mrs. Law scoffed. "If only we fight for you, right?"

"If only you run."

"What...?"

"I'm begging you to run. To take only what you can carry, and to run until leg or land fail you."

"Don't you think we've considered that?" Piebald Chan said. "That we've considered everything, even scattering ourselves to the four winds? But the Ch'ing will just chase us. They'll chase us for as long as they have to. They'll whittle us away one-by-one, day-by-day, until there are no rebels left."

"But the Ch'ing aren't looking for rebels, are they?" Wingchun said. "Not really."

"They're looking for Shaolin," Mrs. Law said, "But we don't seem to—" She stopped and stared at Wingchun.

"No," Master Law said. "I forbid it!"

"With respect," Wingchun said. "You can't forbid me anything. All you can do is what I tell you to do—take your people and run."

"No way," Yang said. "There's no way I'm running, not even from an entire battalion, not when a girl's staying behind to fight."

"If you don't—"

"What, I'll die?" Yang shrugged. "I don't have much left in this life anyway, I might as well clench my teeth and charge into the next, claim what chance for honor I have along the way. If death is coming, I'll meet it with fists raised and eyes open."

Mrs. Law snorted. "And head empty."

Master Law sighed. "But heart full."

"What the hell," Mok said. "Dying young saves having to live up to all the distinction and wisdom that are supposed to come with age..."

"Dementia and bladder-failure more likely in your case," Lai Bang said. "Still, if you're finally going to get yours, I'd kill *myself* if I wasn't there to enjoy it."

"I don't believe this," Mrs. Law said. "There is no discussion here! Yang's not our leader, none of you are, none of you speak for us!"

"You're right," Master Law said. "That burden falls to me."

Mrs. Law looked at him, her eyes trembling.

He turned away. "I'm sorry, I'm so sorry..."

"What...?"

"I can't make this decision. I won't, not for any of you. The daughter of Fong Dak—the heir of Miu Sun and Wumei—stands before you. Stand with her if you will. Flee if not. For myself, I'm done."

詠 春 傳 說

Kwai watched the rebels break up and wander back to the caves, and then a sneer flashed across his face. "Wouldn't know it to look at them but the bandits are as old as the rebels, as the water margins. Some share the same roots, protection turned to predation, care to competition, raising money to stealing it—the very reasons I joined up with the Panther's Head when I arrived here. But, as I soon figured out, true bandits aren't bred, they're born. They claim their territory and demand their tribute, they—"

"I don't care about the social romance," Boklao said, "I just want your leader's name."

"How very General Sun of you... Up until recently the bandits in these mountains were led by a beast of man called Panther-King."

"Until recently?"

"About a month ago he up and disappeared. No one knows where. Of course, there are stories..."

"What stories?"

"Usual stuff— Ch'ing sent this or that famous general to arrest him. It varies with each telling." Kwai shook his head. "There's even this one crazy rumor that some little market girl got all warrior-attendant on his..." He stopped and blinked. "Wait one damn—"

Boklao shook his head and chuckled.

Kwai's face curdled. "Don't tell me...!"

"I won't, now go on, who's the new leader?"

"Flying-Chimp's trying something fierce. His little brother, Flying-Monkey, was making every effort to upstage him, though, what with stealing the rebel's stolen horses, but you went and made him lose enough face that it's all weak tea again and the fools are about to declare open war on each other."

"Real tight-woven group you have there..."

"Panther-King was a firm believer in the Confucian ideal," Kwai said, "and he made it his habit to rip the arms off anyone who didn't conform to his particular notion of it. Now that he's gone—"

"Everyone and his martial-uncle is claiming to be the one true inheritor—including Rascal Kwai."

"Please," Kwai said. "It'd be mine, bowl and robe, in a moment if I had even the slightest little speck of interest..."

"But what, too much responsibility?"

"Too much visibility. Besides, true power is never found on a throne..."

"True power is found behind it..."

Kwai smiled. "Ancient wisdom."

Boklao scoffed. "And just as hollow."

"Do tell."

"Say you manipulate yourself behind the bandit throne, then what?"

"Amass wealth."

"And then?"

"Spend it on wine and sing-song girls..."

"And?"

"More wine, I don't know! What else is there?"

"Homes and tables and wives and everything else not stolen or eked or forced three paces behind."

"And what the hell's that?"

"The future."

詠 春 傳 説

Third-Daughter Chao lay so limp, so pale... Mrs. Law wiped her brow. "Cold, but still alive..."

"Her tears have just run dry." Widow Pang looked across the children, the elderly, the wounded. "All our tears..."

"I'll try to bring some more food," Mrs. Law said.

"And wine," Grandmother Ngao said. "A drop or two would help us forget the rumbles in our belly. For a while at least..."

Mrs. Law nodded and then turned back down the dank tunnels to the barren stores. The lanterns had burned dead and Mrs. Law had to feel for the large rice bags, for any that might still bear even a catty of weight...

"Let me help."

Mrs. Law clutched her chest and stumbled back. "Goddess of Mercy!"

Wingchun emerged from the shadows. "I didn't mean to frighten you."

"No, of course not," Mrs. Law said. "Just like you didn't mean to commit our people to one final act of insanity back in the clearing..."

"I had no control over that, over anything that happened before, no more than I had control over what made it happen. None of us do."

"How very convenient..."

"How very not."

"So you came to talk but not to take responsibility for your talk. Fine." Mrs. Law hefted a bag, swung it around, and dumped it against the side of the tunnel. "You tell me you have no control over what happened before, and I suppose that must be fine as well. But what about what happens next, you certainly seem to have control over that, don't you?"

"Not enough."

"How can you say that? How can you be so casual about life and death?"

"I'm anything but casual." Wingchun drew closer. "I see what's inside you now—the emptiness of your son's loss, the rage taking his place..."

"You see a reflection," Mrs. Law said.

"Maybe... Maybe that's why I know you have to put aside the feelings. You have to put them aside or they'll consume you."

"You'd have me deny them, you'd have me bury them?"

"I'd have you accept them."

"As you have?"

"Yes."

"When inside you I see anything but acceptance?"

Wingchun's eyes kindled. "Now who sees a reflection?"

"I see the loss of my son," Mrs. Law said, "and I see the loss of what little I have left. But you... you have nothing left. What you've set in motion can end only in death. And... and I think that is precisely what you want. You'll never see your family again, not in this life, so I think you've decided to charge headlong after them into the next."

"You have no idea..."

"Well that makes two of us then, doesn't it?" Mrs. Law clucked. "You're just a girl. Just a girl playing at being a general and you're going to get every one of us killed."

25
Return of the Ch'ing

Boklao gazed back down the mountain, through the lattice of bamboo, and out across the full vastness of the south.

"The future?" Kwai snorted. "I'm supposed to believe you give a damn about the future? And what are you going to do if I don't, drop a burning junk on me? Or is that only for the one's who do believe?"

Boklao shook his head. "More daggers..."

"Better little bits of wood and metal than whole bloodied bunches of people, don't you think?"

"But still from hiding, still from the shadows."

"Hard to convince others, isn't it, when you can't even convince yourself?"

"I am convinced."

"Why, Leung Boklao? Why now? Everything you've ever done has been for you and you alone."

"Just like you."

"That's right! So why should this time be any different?"

"Because it has to be. Because—" Boklao bit down hard. "Because there's a whole battalion of the Constabulary Army forming up in the ruins of Lanchow ready to—"

"Wipe out a backwater filled with people who never meant anything to you?"

"To wipe out the one thing that means everything."

詠 春 傳 說

Wingchun leant against the cold, jagged mouth of the cave and looked up to the heavens, and beyond the glare of the afternoon sun, to the Girl and the Devil drawn ever-closer together...

"Bad enough I'm stuck in here," Little Kung said. "No reason *you* should be as well."

Wingchun angled a brow. "You don't look very stuck."

"Ha! My mother may have untied the ropes, but father went and found a spare ox-yolk and just dared me 'to so much as glance outside'..."

"They want to keep you close." Wingchun held out her hand and water drained down from the limestone and filled her palm. Then she closed her fist and the water squirted from between her fingers. "They don't understand."

"You... you really are different, you know that?"

"Always have been."

"No, this is a different different."

"And what kind would that be?"

"The kind that... that can fly across rooftops, maybe?"

Wingchun almost laughed. "Do you see any rooftops left around here?"

"Bamboo tops then! You could do that now, right? Float across the sky like in the martial hero epics?"

"Chase dragons out of the sea and drag the Great Sage down from his mountain?" Wingchun sighed. "I'm just a girl."

"That's not what the rebels are saying. They're saying you must fight like a—Well, like maybe even better than my father..."

"They're saying that?"

"Yes, and that's why... That's why I want you to teach me. Teach me so I can fight better than my father as well."

"Fighting fragments and separates, it's as much losing as winning."

"What isn't?"

Wingchun crossed her arms and leant back against the limestone. "Tell me about it."

Little Kung leant opposite her. "There's nothing I can tell, not to you, not anymore. Not—Well, maybe just…"

"Just what?"

"You remember that story? The one I was—so embarrassing—the one I was acting out back at the bridge when you came to do your laundry?"

"The one you liked."

"I don't like it anymore."

"Because it's not just a story now…"

"Because I've seen the real fire giant now, I've seen what it's like when real things burn… But I've also found out how it ends—"

"Little Kung…"

"—the fire giant loses. He loses to a girl."

"To a *princess*," Wingchun said, "and let's not forget the small matter of a golden pagoda to the head…"

"Doesn't matter," Little Kung said. "He loses. That's how it ends."

詠 春 傳 說

Five-Metal Yang cursed and stomped into the bamboo and began to rummage through the underbrush. "Supposed to cleave with it, not throw it, that's why it's called a meat-cleaver, not a meat-thrower! Throw it at the first enemy, what have you got left for the second, for the third? So much like his father, I should probably just blunt the damn—" He stopped and looked up. "—thing…"

"Wingchun asked me to talk to you," Boklao said.

"What's there to talk about?" Yang said. "We're seizing the final initiative. Figured you of all people would appreciate that strategy."

"I appreciate striking first, but it's based on the proper conditions and the right timing."

Yang sighed. "And you're here to tell me that those conditions aren't met and the time's not now?"

"No. I'm here to remind you that's not the only strategy…"

詠 春 傳 說

Kwai raced up the bamboo-covered ridge, past the fissures and around the crags, until an older cave came into view.

"The future…"

Fires burned unabashed at the entrance, horses bucked in a ramshackle pen just beside, and bandits, tattered and grimed as the mountain, stomped and drank and howled out their defiance to the night.

"I'll give him his damn future…"

詠 春 傳 說

There were less than a dozen of them at first, rebels still well and able enough to join Five-Metal Yang's last stand. But then them some of the less-mortally wounded emerged from the caves, some of those just a little too young or too old. And then the women, Hakka first, then Jong, and even the Han…

"They claim they've watched their men train long enough it's almost like they've trained themselves," Master Law said from the shadows at the edge of the clearing. "They claim that if, through their sacrifice, their children can make it just a little bit farther, their family names can go on just a little bit further…" He shook his head. "They have no more conception of what is about to happen than you."

Wingchun stepped up beside him. "The depth of my conception may surprise you."

"I can't give you what you want."

"What makes you think you know what I want?"

"What makes you think it's not exactly the same thing I want?" he said. "But I'm not your father and you're not my son. There's no absolution here, not for either of us."

"This is not about absolution."

"No?"

"It's about reason."

"For your father's death, for my son's? There's no reason in that, not in any of this."

"I wish that were true," she said. "It would make things so much easier, it would let the burden slip from our shoulders like baskets from a pole… But it's not. You know it's not."

"First you tell me what I don't know, now you try to tell me what I do… What is it you want from me?"

"To lead your people. That is, if you even remember how."

"You have no idea just how terribly I remember."

"I do. I can see it in your eyes, same way I could see it in my father's…"

"I told you," he said. "I'm not you're father."

"You're right," she said. "My father understood in the end."

"So did my son."

"You know that?"

"I do now…"

Wingchun slipped off into the deeper shadow of the bamboo. "That's the reason."

"For their deaths?" Master Law called after her.

"For everything."

詠 春 傳 說

Mrs. Law felt Third-Daughter Chao's forehead again.

"Before she was cold and now she burns…"

"The sickness is taking her." Widow Pang checked the other children, the other elderly, the other few left in the caves. "Taking all of us…"

"Come," Mrs. Law said. "We should finish loading the carts."

"I can't," Widow Pang said. "I'm not going… not with *you* at least."

Mrs. Law stared at her. "You…"

"My family died for Heaven & Earth," Widow Pang said. "How could I face them in the next life if I was unwilling to do the same?"

Mrs. Law turned to Grandmother Ngao. "Talk to her, talk to all of them," she said. "You're their elder, they'll listen to you."

"Listen to what?" Grandmother Ngao said. "Boy Ngao was all I had left and now he's gone to follow River & Lake same as his damn fool father, and if I had any measure of strength or sight left in me, I'd be going with him, and with Pang, and with all the wine that bastard Yang snuck away!"

"You're mad, every last one of you! I'll ready the carts by myself if I have to!" Mrs. Law fled the dank tunnels to the cave mouth and the fire that smoldered all but out, the last warmth she would ever know.

"Drink tea?"

She clutched her chest but this time stumbled straight down. "I-I can't take this, not another grind, not another touch!"

"Just a little." Master Law pushed a cup at her. "Please."

She pushed it away. "I don't drink tea anymore, not even a little."

"Since when?"

"Since I had that bad feeling. You know, the kind I have so many of, the kind you've grown to quick to dismiss..."

"My wife—"

"You told me to put on the water and you promised me that everything would be okay, that by the time it boiled we would be sharing a pot of silver-needle, laughing and counting the greens as a family. You promised me and... and I haven't drunk tea since even if, every day, I put the water on and sit and hope that somehow, someway, by the time it boils..."

"I've taken everything from you, haven't I?"

"Not my emptiness, not my rage... At least that's what *she* said."

"She...? You mean Wingchun..."

"She said I needed to control my feelings or they would consume me, even though when I looked at her, when I looked into her eyes..."

"It frightened you," he said. "It frightened all of us."

"Then why do they follow her?" she glanced out at the rebels. "Why don't they see it?"

"They do, and if it frightens us, well, they can only imagine what it will do to the Ch'ing."

詠 春 傳 說

Wingchun moved through the broken courtyard of the tofu shop like the monsoon never ended. Still soft, still supple, but her strength surpassed any muscle or bone he'd ever seen, and her intent... Boklao shivered.

"Just a couple of months," he said. "It seems impossible..."

"It would be," she said, "if I didn't have a lifetime behind it. But my hands were forged like knives and now those knives are sharpened..."

Her palms slashed the leaves from the bamboo, they blew past her face, and before they could even begin to fall, her fingers pierced them through.

"You've never held a knife," she said, "how would you know?"

"I know," she said, "because they're just like hands..."

"Crossed through Heaven & Earth..."

Wingchun's nose crinkled. "What's that?"

"The meaning of your Little First Training."

"The meaning is to change the tendons, exemplify the concepts, and train the paths and the power."

"The *symbolic* meaning."

"I told you, this system is functional not symbolic."

"There are layers to everything." Boklao said, "or does my master not remember the origin of her own name?"

"Would you please stop calling me that? And of course I remember—it's the name of Wingchun County, the name of place where my family lived... and died..."

"And the name of the hall in the Nine Little Lotus Temple where the Fist of the Elders began... and almost ended..."

She angled a brow. "Not a coincidence?"

"A code," he said, "or the first and last characters of it—always speak with determination; never forget the Han nation; and again will return the spring."

"Again will return the spring..."

"The symbol, it's what made me realize—"

He stopped and tilted his head.

"Boklao?"

And then he dashed off into the twilight.

詠 春 傳 說

"Made you realize what...? Boklao—!"

Wingchun began after him but he was already back, a smile cut wide across his face.

"Hands," he said.

"Hands?"

"Hold out your hands!"

She did and he filled them with his own, and then she felt a flutter against her palms.

"Figured I'd made you wait long enough since the last one," Boklao said.

"A cricket!" It skittered up across her knuckles and then crouched as though ready to jump.

"Careful," he said. "It'll get away."

"Nothing's getting away from me." She relaxed and yielded. "Not any more. Not if I don't want it to."

The cricket chirped and then bristled and skittered back around.

He chuckled. "Not everything's so easy to tame..."

She glanced up at him. His once-white bandana was long gone and the dark indigo of his clothes was streaked through now the red of dried blood... His nose was still bent, his face more weathered than ever, but his eyes weren't so narrow anymore. They were starting to open even as hers had begun to close...

"You were going to tell me before," she said, " about the symbol, the spring, that it made you realize something?"

"I lost you twice only to find you a third time, a last time. It made me realize the one thing that means everything..."

"You, realize something?"

"Don't make fun, reality will kick me back down soon enough."

"What reality?"

"That River & Lake is about to flow red again with blood," he said. "And it's only kindling for the flame..."

She huffed. "So dramatic..."

"What you're doing, what you're planning—"

"To charge headlong into the next life to meet my family again...? Been there, transcended that."

"Wingchun..."

"The rebels aren't a means to an end for me, they're a hindrance."

"And the Lama, what's he?"

"Boklao..."

"He'll come. After tonight, he'll come, he'll have to. You know that. Hell, you're counting on it." He shook his head. "We'll have a week, maybe two."

"No, not a week, not even a day—only now, only tonight. My thoughts are current and I'm not counting on anything."

"Well I am—I'm counting on you to let me handle it. I'm counting on you to leave the Lama to me. And don't even try giving me any of that 'this enemy is beyond you' nonsense either because he won't be, no one will, not if they come anywhere near you..."

She smiled. "So sweet..." Then she turned her hand again and, this time, let it stiffen. "Oh, would you look at that..."

The cricket chirped triumphant, leapt up into the night, and was gone.

"Hey," he said, "I warned you!"

"I know, but just think—now you get to catch me another one."

"Another one?"

"I'm not waiting fourteen years again."

He sighed and turned back towards the twilight, but then the ground began to shake and wreckage tumbled down around them.

She looked out.

"They're here..."

詠 春 傳 說

Rank upon rank of the Constabulary Army of the Green Standard—almost three-hundred strong—stamped their way up South Gate Street and into the ruins of Lanchow.

詠 春 傳 說

Across the river, up the Eight Immortal Crags, at the edge of the ridge, Widow Pang and the other women hefted winter gourds high overhead and then hurled them down at the cross-pattern marked out below.

Past them, in the clearing before the caves, Boy Ngao and the other men twirled their blades around and swung them at thick bamboo poles wrapped in wet cloth.

Sabers and swords and axes cut through them like they were flesh and bone, but for the ten-thousandth time, Boy Ngao's cleaver bounced off.

"Of all the stupid—!"

He swung again and was rebounded again, and the flat of his cleaver smacked him in the nose.

"Ow!" His eyes watered, he grabbed his face, the cleaver spun to the ground, and the dull edge promptly stubbed his toe. "Ow! Ow! Ow!"

Five-Metal Yang took him by the shoulder, settled him, and pressed the cleaver back into his hand.

"I-I didn't throw it this time, I swear!"

"I know, I saw, but you have to keep trying. You have to cut."

"I am trying! But, I swear, I don't think my pole's even really bamboo!"

"You're a butcher born and bred, boy, just like your father and your grandfather before you. If you can cleave through pigs, you can cleave through Ch'ing, and you can damn well cleave through this little twig. Now try again."

Boy Ngao nodded, scrunched up his face, raised his father's cleaver, and brought it down.

詠 春 傳 說

Piebald Chan joined Master Law in the shadows at the edge of the clearing.

"Yang's a good captain," Chan said.

"But he's no general," Master Law said, "and indulging their delusions does them no favor."

"His plan is sound, old friend, and that is favor enough, yes?"

"His plan?"

"Have you not heard it?"

"I have no wish to…"

"The constables will not deploy until dawn," Chan said. "Your—my apologies—Yang's rebels will move in just after dusk, use that… that thin blade of time to slip into Lanchow through—"

"The same tunnels we used to slip out…"

"The monsoon will have flooded them, of course, but limestone has a thirst not easily quenched. They will be passable, if barely, and they will give Yang and the others the chance they need to—"

"Sacrifice themselves," Lieutenant Fok said.

Master Law spun around. "Your battalion, has it deployed early? Are you—"

"No," Fok said, "I'm not here to warn you, not this time…"

"Then—?"

"I'm here to beg you."

"Beg me?"

Fok stepped aside and a small boy of no more than eight years peeked out behind him. "My son."

Chan frowned. "I thought the Ch'ing stationed their constables in other provinces to make sure they would suffer no family attachments?"

"They do, but I was still unmarried when I was sent here from Fatshan. I made friends with a local merchant and he had a sister of appropriate age… She died the very same day our son was born and, so, I'm all he has left. If anything happens to me tomorrow…"

"It won't," Master Law said. "How can it when you have an army behind you?"

"*They* have an army and from behind is exactly how! I will not take the life of my brothers-by-blood and so, tomorrow, I will fulfill my only duty." Fok placed his big hand on his son's tiny shoulder. "But I will not leave him, not alone, not in their world."

"You want him to come with us when we flee," Master Law said.

"I want you to take him—"

"Beyond the four seas if we have to," Mrs. Law said, joining them in the shadows. "We can take both of you. We can…" She gazed out across the rebels. "We can take everyone."

"I'm of the Inner Gate," Fok said, "just as they are of the Outer. We are all children of Heaven & Earth and I can no more abandon the cause than they could, than you could. It's our way. But I too would have my son and my lineage continue."

"We will care for him like one of our own," Master Law said.

"As one." Mrs. Law glanced back. "Little Kung!"

"Fine!" Little Kung stomped out from behind a thick patch of bamboo. "I'll get the ox-yoke…!"

"Later," Mrs. Law said. "Right now you need to hurry up and introduce yourself to your third brother."

"My what?"

Master Law nodded. "Your first duty."

Little Kung blinked and then darted over to the boy and bowed. "I'm Little—" He took a breath. "I'm Law Mankung."

The little boy returned the bow. "Fok Bochuen."

詠 春 傳 說

Higher still up the jagged spires of the Eight Immortals, in the clearing before older, deeper caves, the statue of Koon Dei, Patron of War, stood on a small altar adorned with a red lantern and a bowl of rice flagged five times in red.

Flying-Chimp turned his lumpy head and scowled at Flying-Monkey. "They all paid up?"

Flying-Monkey held his ribs and winced. "In silver."

"Then get on with this."

"Can't wait for them to meet their new leader, can you?"

Eight bandits walked out, bamboo hoops big as a man lugged between them.

"You see before you the Gate of Heaven & Earth," Flying-Monkey said. "If you are true, follow through wood—"

The eight bandits raised their knives.

"—Or fall beneath metal and be left to rot in the earth."

The initiates hurried through the hoops.

"Now lead through fire."

A torch spun end-over-end and fell onto a long, oiled banner.

Flames leapt unabashed into the night.

The initiates stared, paralyzed, until the eight men with knives advanced and drove them through.

When the screams faded a large bowl of wine was brought out and each of the initiates was cut across the hand.

"And join with water." Flying-Monkey said.

One-by-one the initiates squeezed blood into the wine and cast after it paper blessings inscribed with their former names. When they were done, Flying-Monkey grabbed the bowl and poured it out into the fire.

"The smoke carries the past to the heavens," he said, "even as the ash returns the present to the earth. Now the future will blossom for new men, for brave men and true!"

Flying-Monkey bowed and stepped to the right, and the initiates looked up at Flying-Chimp. Then Flying-Chimp bowed and stepped to the left.

And Kwai stepped up between them. "Yes... the future..."

詠 春 傳 說

Boklao strode bright into the dusk, through the shadowed alleys, towards the market square, until the sun burned down fully behind the mountains. Then he slowed and stopped and tilted his head...

"You come to a fork in the road."

The voice was still somewhere between wind and water, but no longer elusive. Boklao turned to the old women, robed and capped at the edge of the ruins, and a smile cut across his face.

"I know you now."

"Do you?"

"Same way that I know all things, Great Lady."

"All things?" She shook her head. "Not hardly, not even as much as I might have hoped."

"At least I realize now where my path truly leads."

"You anticipate, but realization exists only in the moment and that moment has yet to come."

"I'm not going to break my promise," Boklao said. "Not ever again. Falling's all behind me, the landing, the crushing someone else beneath me..."

"Not all of it," she said, "and not everyone."

"What...?"

"Are you afraid now?"

"Yes."

"Good."

"What's going to happen?"

"You ask me?"

"I ask the coins."

Her cheeks rounded and she cast. "Waiting," she said, "the pitfall of water above the strength of heaven. True strength requires nurturing and, if acting in danger is to be avoided, if the trap is to be overcome, then true strength also requires the proper timing. You cannot presume, cannot be impetuous—you cannot count on the slimness of chance or on action without all limitation. You must believe, must take the true Yang of water and return it to the palace of heaven. Only then will you have crossed the great river and awakened the golden elixir. Only then will the sun and moon be truly merge."

Boklao bowed. "Thank you."

She arched a brow. "For the vague generalities couched in alchemical gibberish?"

"For her."

詠 春 傳 說

Wingchun stood dark after the dusk and stared over the wreckage of her town, her home, until the heavens were finally swallowed by the utter blackness of night. Then her gaze settled.

Before death yet long past life, in the chill of last evening gale, her body remained and her spirit now with it, and she dreamed of nothing and no one but her singular purpose...

"Like the moon blinding itself against the endless surface of the lake..."

The voice was a writhing whisper, nothing at all that could be ascribed to a hermitage high among the Miu and Yao peoples of the mountain.

"Uncle Lee...?"

"Interesting times, Miss Yim," he said, "or does that still sound like just a word?"

"You're keeping me..."

She began past him.

"Of course." A smile rolled across his sallow, bean-bald head. "The days have grown even shorter now, haven't they? Shorter than they've been in a very long time."

"I'm afraid so."

"Are you really?"

"No," she said. "Not the least little bit."

"You *have* changed, I don't think even you realize how much. Not yet."

"Why are you here?"

"Not for the tofu." He glanced across the wreckage. "Not anymore."

"Not ever," Wingchun said. "Not really."

"This used to be a place of dragons, Miss Yim, did you know that? They held the Middle Kingdom in their talons, shaped it, molded it... Then winter descended and the dragons took slumber. But nothing lasts forever. The heavens weep, the earth floods, and very soon now the dragons will awaken..."

"As the snakes coil and the cranes take flight..."

"Do they now?" His bushy white brows cocked. "Then Darkness has finally given way to Contention and the heavens rise dangerously above the water. Harmony is fully violated, truth is fallen, and the battle begun. Absent the Great Sages, the bounds of temper poison and the plots and schemes manifest at last."

"You have no idea how little any of that means to me," Wingchun said.

"Well, well, look who's all dressed up in her mother's robes..." Uncle Lee laughed, a terrible sound, and his indigo cowl cracked open to reveal emaciated flesh that crawled in wrinkled layers over a grossly distended belly, and an eight-trigram medallion that glinted with ancient menace. "Interesting times indeed."

26

The Plum for the Peach

"There was this man who lived next to the sea," Five-Metal Yang said to the rebels spread thin atop the cliff. "Well, almost. Between his farm and the sea there was this huge matter of a mountain...

"The man loved the sea and hated the mountain that denied him the sight of its waters, the smell of its salt, the sound of its waves, the touch of its breeze... But he was too poor and too off-putting to ever be granted better land, and so every day he worked his fields, and every night he stood at his door and raised his fist and cursed the mountain.

" 'You're crazy,' his wife said, 'it's a mountain and you're only a man. What can you do?'

"Seasons turned and the years plowed on, and a day came when the sun was hotter and the air was thicker and the mountain loomed higher than ever, and the man finally had enough of it. He took his shovel, climbed to the very top of the mountain, and he began to dig.

"The man filled his bucket, carried it down, dumped it out, and then went right back up to fill it again and again and again for a day and a night.

"Eventually, his wife came to find him. 'What are you doing?' she said. 'We have fields that need tending and you waste your time here, digging away at the mountain?'

" 'Not digging away at the mountain," the man said. "Digging away the mountain!'

" 'But why?' she asked him. 'Whatever for?'

" 'Because I love the sea!

" 'You miserable bastard! We'll starve and you'll grow old and die and the mountain will stand the same as ever. You're just a man and it's a mountain, what ever can you hope to accomplish?'

" 'I may be just a man but I can dig! I may grow old and die but I have sons who will dig long after me, and they will have sons who will dig long after them, and on and on until the end of generations—until the mountain stands no more! I may be a man but it is just a mountain!'

Yang's deep-set eyes locked on each and every one of the rebels in turn. "Too long has the Ch'ing mountain denied us the sea of Ming," he said. "They are legion and we have been whittled down to only a few, but they are corrupt and we are brave. They are all but invincible and we need still find our strength of old, but they are faithless and we are true.

"We may die." He shook his shaggy head. "No—we *will* die, but in a place and time of our own choosing, charging into the next life in honor and in righteousness! We will die so that our children will live and our lineages will endure!"

Yang crossed his multifaceted hammers high overhead. "Sons of Heaven & Earth, we *will* die this day but we will *not* be forgotten, and as we lead others will follow, on and on until the end of generations—until the Ch'ing mountain stands no more!"

詠 春 傳 說

"There were these two brothers," Kwai said to the bandits, old and new, gathered around him. "The elder was a brute and a bully. He used his strength to torment the younger and, when their father finally died, he used it to take the full inheritance, to take every coin and spot that should have been shared right and proper between the both of them.

"Driven from his land the younger brother wandered for months, begging, stealing, doing whatever he had to do just to survive. Then, one day, he heard rumors of this martial master, this old priest in hermitage at the very top of the mountain.

"So the younger brother climbed and climbed until he reached the very tip top. He found the old priest and he bent right over and knocked his head against the rock. He offered his service, to carry water and fetch food, to damn-well dig dung holes if the old priest wanted, if only he could learn how to fight, how to take back what was his.

"And—probably just to shut him the hell up—the old priest finally agreed.

" 'Tell me what to do,' the younger brother said. 'Tell me how to begin.'

" 'Begin?' the old priest said. 'You've already finished. Go on then, home with you now.'

" 'But... but my elder brother, if he sees me, he will charge at me!'

" 'Then you clench your fist and charge at him right back.'

" 'With what, every ounce of my weakness and contempt?'

" 'No, with the very same righteousness and fury that drove you to seek my help.'

" 'What help? Master, please!'

"But the old priest just turned away.

"More dejected than before, more pathetic than ever, the younger brother went.

"And when he returned home, his elder brother was there waiting for him, their father's saber in his hand and a sneer ripe across his face.

"With no other option, the younger brother did just as the old priest told him to do—he clenched his fist and he charged.

"Their father's saber faltered, the elder brother's sneer spoiled, and he broke and fled.

"The younger brother reclaimed his coin and his every spot of land and what's more—he regained his honor."

"Touching," Flying-Chimp said. "Really. And just what are we're supposed to be in this little story, the younger brother?"

"No..."

"Then what?" Flying-Monkey said.

Kwai spat. "The fist."

詠 春 傳 説

The rickety old carts groaned but the sick and the wounded piled up inside them groaned louder. The children who could still walk milled about, their eyes empty, their faces streaked.

"Hurry up!" Grandmother Ngao jabbed at them with her walking-stick. "Stop crying, stop juggling your shoes, and—Buddha's belly!—stop stopping!"

Little Kung stared after the departing rebels, so brave, so true, so completely without him...

Then he was grabbed by his ear and dragged back to the carts.

"Ouch!"

"Don't even think about it," Mrs. Law said.

"How come Boy Ngao gets to go?"

"Boy Ngao is five years your senior and twice your size—!"

"Twice my width!"

"—and he doesn't have me for a mother!"

"Lucky him! But mother or not, I *will* think about it. You may be able to stop me from doing what I'm supposed to be doing, but there's no way you can stop me thinking about it!"

"Supposed to be doing? You mean the way Big Kung was? We're not going to make the same mistake again, not with you!"

"Big Kung wasn't a fighter. He was good at it but he hated it. All he ever wanted to do was medicine but he was forced to fight anyway. All I want to do is fight to protect my people and you're going to force me right into medicine. You *are* making the same mistake again, and I'm going to hate you every bit as much as he did."

"Good," Mrs. Law said. "If you're hating me, that means you're alive, and while you are, consider this—maybe your people need more from you than just to fight for them."

"Like what?"

"Like why don't you ask your third brother?"

"Bochuen?" Little Kung glanced around. "Where...? Oh, come on, he's not hiding back in the caves again, is he?"

"Isn't it your duty to know? If you can't even take care of one person, Mankung, how do you ever hope to protect us all?"

詠 春 傳 說

Master Law emptied the supplies into the final wagon and then wiped his hands, stared down the cold, gray mountain, and sighed.

"Dusk," he said, "when time stretches out in every direction and we become trapped... trapped between beginning and end, between life and death..."

"Between the charge of the Army of the Green Standard," Piebald Chan said, "and the sons of Heaven & Earth that will meet it…"

Master Law hung his head. "Meet it alone…"

"No, not alone." Chan clicked open a pale green case and his King Ngok sword tasted its first air in over a dozen years. "Just because you won't lead, old friend, doesn't mean that I can't still follow—" He raised the double-edged blade in salute. "—one last time."

詠 春 傳 說

Night fell, the heavens opened again, and the rain crystallized and covered the dark wreckage of Lanchow in a pale white shroud.

Wingchun gazed out from the narrow alley beside the Jade Garden Teahouse at the sentries who spread down Glory Street and Central Mountain Main from one end of the market to the other. Beyond them, patrols wormed their way through the town, but it was the main body of the Constabulary Army, the ones who infested the square, that she focused on.

"Asleep at last." She began to move. "It's time."

Boklao held her back. "Not yet…"

"What are you waiting for?"

Torches flared above them and the Azure Mountain Hall, and above the broken rooftops of the Vast Beneficence Apothecary Shop and the Five Treasures Guesthouse at the north end of the market.

No—Wingchun's eyes slivered—not torches but wine jugs plugged with rags and set alight…

They rose high for a moment, and then hurtled down to the square below and burst in the water… but not water—oil spilled out from the constables' own stores…

Fire raced across the market, cut it north from south and the sleeping constables in two, and then split east and west and cut them off from their sentries.

Boklao smiled. "For that…"

詠 春 傳 說

Yang and the strongest group of rebels slipped out from the tunnels beneath his jewelry shop and swept over the least-strong group of constables—the sentries on Central Mountain Main.

"Kill fast and kill furious." Yang smashed one hammer into a constable's groin and then, when his mouth gaped open to scream, fed him the other. "We need to press the advantage for as long as we have it!"

Lai Bang twirled both ends of his three-section staff, clobbered them into heads and limbs and anything else he came across. "Advantage? You mean the whole minute until the patrols hear this clamor, run back, and skewer the lot of us?"

"Sounds about right." Woodcutter Mok ducked low, spun, and cut a constable off at the knees. "Presuming they skewer you first..."

"Shut it, the both of you," Yang said. "If all goes according to plan, the women will delay the patrols long enough so that, by the time they get back, the sentries will be dead and we'll be re-enforcing Chan."

"Marvelous," Lai Bang said, "considering just how often anything goes even remotely according to one of our plans..."

詠 春 傳 說

Widow Pang and the least-strong rebels, their wine jugs depleted, plucked up sundered bricks and bits of stone, and jagged pieces of metal and shingle, and peered down from the rooftops at the middle-strong constables—the patrols that wormed their way back towards the square.

"Ready, my sisters," she said, even though the other seven women couldn't possibly hear her. "We've given them back their fire, now we give them their destruction!"

詠 春 傳 說

Piebald Chan and the middle-strong rebels emerged from the tunnels beneath the apothecary shop and fell on the strongest constables—the encampment set in the market square.

"They dwarf our number, but they're roused to chaos and divided by flame!" Chan's steps wobbled but the tip of his King Ngok sword pierced steady. "Take out as many as you can before they regroup, commanders first if you can arrange it!"

Chao Jeet raced down the constabulary ranks and stabbed again and again with his double-crescent spear. "If it's all the same to you, I'll take out the closest first!"

"Closest to what?" Boy Ngao scrunched up his face and brought his father's meat-cleaver down. "To taking *us* out?"

詠 春 傳 說

For the second time, Lanchow dyed the heavens black, choked the earth red, and filled the night with screams.

Wingchun glared at Boklao. "You told me you talked to them!"

"I did," he said. "I talked to Yang and Inner-Gate Fok. Talked to them all about the strategy for the attack."

"This isn't what I wanted!"

She began towards the market.

"I know." He began after her. "But it's what all of us needed."

詠 春 傳 說

"Hell is a river," Master Law said, "and the Jade Record describes its course down through Ten Palaces.

"In ancient days King Yanluo stood in greeting before the Mirror of Reflection to grant the compassion of rebirth to those whose deaths were unjust. But the Jade Emperor has demoted him now to the Fifth Palace, and so he sits atop his bow-shaped tower and all he grants is one final glance back at the families left behind, bent in grief and broken in mourning, silently cursing their memory and name..."

The carts bounced up the narrow mountain pass, their wheels banged against the rock, and the wounded moaned.

"Go on," Little Kung said. "What happens to those who make it to the Sixth Palace?"

"They face the judgment of Biancheng," Master Law said, "flanked by the scholar who gives summary and the demon who bestows punishment."

"And no one makes it past them?" Bochuen said. "Do they?"

"That's enough," Mrs. Law said. "They don't need to hear this."

"The children asked," Master Law said.

"Not all questions require answers, especially not the questions of children!"

Master Law held her gaze. "This one does."

Mrs. Law sighed. "Some few do escape... escape all the way to the Tenth Palace, the seat of the Goddess of Mercy herself..."

"What does she do?" Third-Daughter Chao said.

"She soothes them and wipes their spirits clean, and then she sends them on to the next life."

"She sends them on to Those-Who-Preside," Master Law said. "To Life-Is-Short, darkly laughing as he tests his saber, and Death-Has-Gradations, brightly wailing as he tallies their every sin. They're the ones who send us on to the next life, ugly and misshapen, or as dogs or pigs, or creeping, crawling things."

"Only those who—" Mrs. Law looked at him. "Only those whose faith is weak..."

"Who have failed in their duty..."

"But the strong ones, the ones who do what they have to—those who do it no matter what—are reborn as the most auspicious of men, as higher beings..."

"As women?" Third-Daughter Chao said.

The boys glowered, the girls blushed, and Grandmother Ngao hooted.

Mrs. Law stopped and her cart creaked still. "And what I have to do is accept that..."

"Keep moving," Master Law said. "We can't waste any time, not when every moment of it is being purchased by our bravest and truest, by everyone—"

"Not everyone—" Mrs. Law reached into her cart, hand trembling and eyes filled with tears.

"What?" Master Law said. "What are you doing?"

The final shreds of red silk flittered away in the half-light.

"—not yet."

詠 春 傳 說

The patrols raced back towards the smoke and flames of the market, their spears down and their eyes fierce... And then they rounded the corner and the sergeant's eyes bugged wide.

"Robes like bone!"

He reeled back and the constables behind him scrambled to stop.

Wingchun turned.

Bug-eyes squinted. "A girl... Nothing but a girl..."

His spear shot up again,

Wingchun's hand leapt, lightning flashed, the spear splintered, and his eyes bugged huge.

詠 春 傳 說

"Have to love it when she does that." Boklao smashed the butt of a constable's spear back into his buckteeth. "Well, maybe not *you*..."

Two more spun at him. The first was big-jawed and the second beak-nosed. Boklao's pulse raced and his breath grew high and hot. He blocked a second spear with the shaft of the first but his shoulder gave out and a goose-quill saber slashed at him...

But Wingchun was there. She dispersed the saber with her left arm and chopped the saber-man in his ribs with her right. Then she switched hands, jammed with her right wing and sliced him in the throat with her left palm. The saber-man sputtered and gurgled and staggered back, and Wingchun turned to Boklao. "Are you—?"

"Okay. I'm—"

"—able to finish?"

"What? Of course I—!"

"Then do it."

Boklao ducked under another saber slash and then knocked away Beak-nose's spear. And the whole time he could feel Wingchun coil around him, light and lithe, ungraspable and unstoppable. He kicked the saber-man back and then swung around to meet Beak-nose...

詠 春 傳 說

Wingchun soared past a spear and then twisted under and around Big-ears' saber. And all the while, she could feel Boklao steady in her midst, wild and strong, unrelenting and unyielding. She sent the spearman flying and then reached out for Bug-eyes.

He jumped back and began to circle. "Took us by surprise is all, you putrid, stank—!"

Wingchun remained still, her knees turned in, one hand tracking him like the head of a viper.

"—this time you'll be taking something else!"

He kept talking, circling... stalling!

Wingchun stepped back just as spears shot passed her on both sides. She reached out and grabbed them, added to their momentum and unbalanced them, and then twisted and turned up and around.

Cracks echoed through the square but she was already coiling into two more.

詠 春 傳 說

Birds and beasts and reptiles and insects cried out and abandoned the bamboo. Even the earth seemed to recoil.

And steel-shod hooves tore again up the thinly etched path.

詠 春 傳 說

Little Kung spun around but, just as fast, Mrs. Law latched onto his ear again.

"Ouch! Would you stop that, I'm not going anywhere!"

"You can't warn them, idiot boy, not in time!"

"I know!"

"All you can do is die and—what do you mean you know?"

The ground stopped shaking and the pounding faded.

"I was wrong before," he said. "You can't stop me from doing any more than you can stop me thinking. I can still fight, not with the others in Lanchow maybe, but here and now." Little Kung glanced at Bochuen. "I can do my duty and protect my people, every one of you that's left."

Mrs. Law looked at him. "Could it be that your father was actually right about you, right from the very beginning?"

"That I'm not his first, never his favorite?"

"That, after he opened your lessons, after the very first time he taught you his boxing, your potential would be boundless as the heavens."

Little Kung rolled his eyes. "For nothing but trouble, right?"

"For more. He even... He even called you his Divine Fist."

"He called me *what*?"

"You are your father's son, Mankung, and while you may think that means your destiny is in fighting, it isn't." She pointed him west. "Your destiny is in leading."

詠 春 傳 說

The flames ebbed and sputtered, and a constable howled and leapt through from the south side of the market to the north.

Chao Jeet caught him on the end of his double-crescent spear and drove him back. "I knew there wouldn't be enough oil," he said. "Now what are we going to do?"

"Just hold on!" Piebald Chan ran two fingers along his blade, shot up on one leg, parried down, and slashed out, his swordplay achieving the perfection his calligraphy never had. "Yang and the others will be here soon!"

"But we'll still be outnumbered!" Boy Ngao fell back against the wall of what had once been his family's butcher shop. "What can Yang do?"

"Give them one of his 'farmer and the sea' speeches," Woodcutter Mok said.

Lai Bang followed Mok out from the wreckage of the apothecary shop. "Good idea, it got us to throw our lives away pretty fast!"

"Not fast enough," Yang said. "Not the two of you at least!"

The rebel forces—the bare score who remained—joined together as the fire failed and the rest of the constables—still over ten score strong—snorted and spat and formed up in front of them.

詠 春 傳 說

Wingchun slipped past both sabers, looped her legs behind the constables' feet, and hooked her arms across their throats. Their bodies snapped back and their legs flipped up and over and smashed straight into four more of their comrades. The six of them tumbled out into the market square and Wingchun flew after them. It felt as though through the flames...

"The rebels are going to be slaughtered," she said.

Boklao bent down and a constable's spears slashed across his jacket and plunged into a second constable beside him. The first constable gaped. The second glared. Boklao's hands swept up and chopped into both their necks. The spear fell but Boklao hooked it with his right foot and kicked it up. His palms shot out and the shaft smacked into the face of a third constable and then rebounded. Boklao caught it.

"We're here now," he said. "That changes the odds."

"Not enough." She gazed across the town. "We're splitting up."

"Not likely."

"You let the rebels in, now you have to get them out."

"And what about you, what are you going to do?"

"I'm going to give you the opening."

"Listen, crazy girl, we're not splitting up, we—wait! Wingchun!"

But she was gone, down the street and into the smoke and chaos, and before he could follow—

"Boklao!"

"Not now, I—"

Five-Metal Yang grabbed him, spun him around, and pointed him up the Eight Immortals.

"Bannermen!"

詠 春 傳 說

"Go." The Lama's eyes blazed towards the ruins of Lanchow. "Find the Shaolin and drive him to me!"

Eagle-Shadow bowed, his scar twisted, his ebon steed shot past the Lama's pale mare, and the Forbidden Bannermen spread out behind him like the wings of some great raptor taken hunt.

詠 春 傳 說

The rebels faltered and the constables surged.

"No," Boklao said.

The ground shook.

"How did they get behind us?" Five-Metal Yang said.

"Forget how," Piebald Chan said, "it's how many that matters!"

Woodcutter Mok squinted. "Thirty—at least..."

"But that's... that's more than a squadron," Lai Bang said.

The pounding became deafening.

"No." A smile cut across Boklao's face. "Not bannermen..."

The leader was far out in front, on an ebon horse but not in steel plates—just strangely mottled robes and a coarsely woven, conical hat...

"Son of a—!" Yang shook his hammers. "I should have known, we all should have known! Just when we teeter over the brink, you sever the last bond of River & Lake and show up to kick us over the edge!"

"Only thing severed here, Shaggy, is the last of your wits." Kwai pulled up in front of them. "We're not here to fight you—"

Bandit horseman thundered past—

"—we're here to save you."

—and plowed into the constables.

Kwai tilted his head. "Galls, doesn't it?"

Their spears not set to receive the charge, the steel-shod hooves trampled the constables through. Mud, blood, and gore splattered across the flames, and bodies shot up between the horses only to be hacked and smashed back down by their bandit riders.

Boklao tilted his head back. "Vagabond—"

"For the last time, Leung Boklao, my name's not Vagabond."

"Kwai—"

"Lankwai. Leung Lankwai."

"Leung...?"

"I hated you from the moment I saw you but I didn't realize why, not until you introduced yourself to Flying-Monkey." Kwai said. "Should have, though—no one in the whole clan has ever been any damn good."

"Don't trust him," Chan said. "He'll turn on us any minute!"

"If I were going to turn on you, Splotchy," Kwai said, "you'd know it by your view back from the next life."

"Why, then?" Yang said. "Why do this?"

Kwai poked his chin towards Boklao. "Ask him. He's the one with all the delusions, the one who still has hope..."

"Enough," Boklao said. "We work together now because, if we don't, we die together now. Yang, have your rebels keep the constables contained for Kwai's bandits. A charge doesn't do much if it doesn't have something big to crash into. Kwai—"

"Let me guess, charge?" Kwai scoffed. "What I said before, boy, about you being all General Sun, you know what sarcasms is, right?"

The bandits pulled their horses up and began to turn, but the ground ahead of them kept shaking.

"You have more men?" Yang said. "You're attacking both flanks?"

"What are you talking about?" Kwai said. "Do you think for one minute that if I had more men, I wouldn't have put them between me and the pointy end of the constables?"

"But then—" Chan's sword dropped. "But if they're not yours then..."

"Then it's really them this time." Yang's hammers slipped down. "Really bannermen!"

Boklao froze. "Forbidden Bannermen..."

詠春傳說

She passed the sign of the Yim Family Tofu Shop, scorched and half-buried in the mud, and walked out into the heart of the courtyard.

The wind boomed. The air froze.

Then she turned, white robes snapped, and eyes of burning flame locked.

Her blood boiled.
And Wingchun faced the Lama.

27
The Tenth Palace

Boklao stared down West Glory Street towards Red Fortune Alley. "Not a week, not even a day... She knew it, she counted on it! Nothing gets away from her anymore—" *She turned her hand again and, this time, let it stiffen.* "—not unless she wants it to!"

Kwai circled his horse around. "What the hell are you not-making-sense about now?"

"Don't you understand, if the Forbidden Bannermen are here, then he's here too... He's here now!"

"He who?" Five-Metal Yang said. "Who's here?"

"The Lama."

"They're going through the outskirts," Chan said, "sweeping their way in!"

"Driving," Boklao said. "Driving her! I have to go, I have to find her before—!"

"REBEL!"

Boklao glanced back.

One of the constables broke away from the pack, tree wide—at least twice as wide as Boklao—and clad in black enameled armor, crowned with red plume, and burnished with a golden lion in mid-pounce. No... Boklao's head tilted, not a constable... His pulse quickened.

"Colonel of the Territorial Banner..."

"Dog!" The colonel kicked Lai Bang off the tines of his immense tiger-fork and held it up. "This was my son's, born back to me with the proclamation of his murder! I call you out now, rebel leader, whether you have the courage to face me, or the simple cowardice to die prostrate like the dog you truly are!"

Boklao turned back towards Red Fortune. "I know what I truly am."

But the banner colonel cut him off. "You're not going anywhere, rebel leader, not until we've had our reckoning, not until your head decorates the gates of Yanluo!"

"He's not the rebel leader—" Shadow burst across the flaming sky, constables blew back in pieces, and a massive hook-backed blade flashed through the heavens and slammed down into the earth. "—I am!"

Chan beamed. "Buddha's name be praised!"

Yang bowed. "Master!"

And Master Law brought his Kwan halberd up and around. "Go," he said to Boklao. "The banner colonel is mine!"

詠 春 傳 說

The Lama stood out against the swirling snow like a corpse on silk. His stillness was every bit as horrifying, but his eyes... for the first time Wingchun saw something unrecognizable in them—something worse than hell...

"You're a girl..."

"I'm a woman."

"A child..."

"A rebel."

"Not Shaolin..."

"Daughter of Fong Dak, granddaughter of Miu Sun, and disciple of Wumei."

"Nothing. Less than nothing." His breath steamed in the frigid air. "My blade would be wasted on your blood."

"Nothing... Panther-King called me that, others too. Even said it to my-self." She smiled. "Maybe we've all been right. Maybe I am nothing—"

She looked the Lama full in the face, and then she reached down to the sheath hidden against her right leg. String broke, cold steel rang loose, and, with both hands, Wingchun held the knife up. The thick blade was like a cleaver tapered at its tip and polished mirror-bright. Brass arced from the pommel to form the guard and crosspiece, and then leapt up and out like a hook.

"My mother's," she said, "do you remember?"

"I remember how she begged, how your whole family begged..."

"My family..."

"While you watched—while you screamed..."

And Wingchun charged.

詠 春 傳 說

Widow Tsui pitched the melted lump of what had been one of her late husband's countless statues down from atop the Five Treasures Guesthouse. It clunked into the head of a constable and sent him careening.

"Nice shot," Widow Pang yelled from the roof of the Azure Mountain Hall. "Now watch mine!"

She shoved a row of dark gray shingles off the edge. They shattered over another head, one after the other.

"Not bad," Tsui said. "But isn't Chao on our side...?"

Pang winced. "Oh, in the name of—"

Boklao flipped up onto the roof, looked at her, and then leapt across to the Jade Garden Teahouse.

"—heaven...?"

詠 春 傳 說

Boklao dodged the gaping holes and sprinted up the broken beams, high above the combatants and horses that clogged West Glory Street. The hall and teahouse streamed back behind him, the constables and rebels and bandits...

His lungs burned and the ligaments in his legs felt like they would snap. His eyes began to redden, his nose and mouth to fill with iron and salt, but he fought it down, he had to get to her...

詠 春 傳 說

"Back away." The banner colonel said to the constables as he brought his huge tiger-fork across and down. "The rebel leader is mine."

"Collaborator," Master Law said.

"Insurgent," the banner colonel said.

Their voices thundered as one. "Traitor!"

Then their feet shore the snow and mud. The hook-backed halberd shook and its tassel skipped. The spear-tined fork rattled and its tassel jumped.

The banner colonel jabbed right, Master Law slapped it away and thrust left. The banner colonel slapped back and swung around. Wooden shafts clacked and steel blades clanged. Master Law spun and struck with the butt of his halberd. The banner colonel spun and parried with the butt of his fork. They both spun back and kicked out...

Their feet slammed together and the impact sent them flying to opposite ends of the square.

Master Law skidded to a stop in front of the remnants of the South Market Gate, the banner colonel across from him at the North.

"My son," the banner colonel said.

"Killed mine and by mine," Master Law said. "Your son's life cost me the life of my own!"

"A Northern prince for a Southern bastard? Ten-thousand of your spawn wouldn't be enough!"

Their hands tightened, their teeth clenched, and they met back in the center.

Master Law slashed down. The banner colonel whisked his foot away and thrust up. Master Law circled his head around and lunged. The banner colonel skipped back, caught the Kwan halberd between the tines of his tiger-fork, and pinned it into the ground.

Master Law yanked and yanked, but the halberd was stuck.

The banner colonel sneered and kicked high, his leg smashing through wreckage. Master Law let go of his halberd and twisted his left single-knuckle fist up to block, Phoenix Soars to Heaven. Then he shot his right single-knuckle fist at the point just behind the banner colonel's ankle. Iron Needle Threads—

But the banner colonel jumped and switched legs, used the shaft of his tiger-fork like a catapult to increase his height and power, and stabbed at Master Law's throat with the armored toe of his boot.

Master Law leapt back, the banner colonel landed, sneered again, wrenched his tiger fork from the ground, swung it wide, and shot it straight at Master Law's chest.

詠 春 傳 說

The Lama remained still.

Wingchun's hair streamed, her eyes smoldered. Her wrist snapped and the knife leapt up.

The Lama remained still.

Wingchun closed until nothing but an exhalation separated the tip of the knife from the Lama's throat.

Then the Lama's bone-robes parted—

詠 春 傳 說

Atop the cliff above Lanchow, bushy white brows set and dark eyes pierced bamboo and brick and set upon the combat amidst the ruins of the tofu shop.

"You must be so proud, my brother."

A thin, vicious smile rolled across the old priest's bean-bald face. "I am flattered you still call me that, my sister."

"Would you prefer Li Bashan, White-Eyebrow, or here, now, Uncle Lee?"

"You tell me, Lu Sanniang, Wumei—Auntie…"

She stepped up across from him. "Names can be known, but never true names…"

He inclined his head. "Just as the Tao, but never the true Tao."

"And the heart of a man, but never the true heart."

"You know my true heart." His taloned hands spread out from east to west. "As we both know all things since the beginning."

"You have betrayed our ancestors, doomed our descendants, and bathed our land in the blood of our own people…" Her palms folded together, fingers pointed up. "You have manipulated everyone—everything—from the beginning."

"No more than you."

She arched a brow. "What I have done, I have done for the good of Heaven & Earth, for the Han Nation, and the House of Ming. What I have done, I have done for the good of all."

He flattened his. "For the good of all of you and yours, and is that not, in and of itself, evil?"

"You will find no justification in the Tao..."

"I am beyond the need for justification in anything and to anyone, my sister—even you."

"Then why are you here?"

"Why else? To witness the end of my greatest rival..."

"The Lama..."

He scoffed. "My dearest friend..."

She recoiled. "No..."

"This was never about the Lama..."

詠 春 傳 說

The tiger-fork streaked at Master Law. His Kwan halberd was still stuck in the mud, to far to reach, and he couldn't block this, not with a hundred single-knuckle fists...

The three spear-tipped tines sliced through the night and pierced Master Law's once-bronze jacket.

He couldn't block it—

Blood spurted from between his fingers.

—but he could catch it.

The banner colonel gaped. Everyone gaped.

And Master Law stood, chest hollowed, tiger-fork trapped between his folded hands.

Then his hands unfolded and the tiger-fork streaked back. The butt end, steel-bound and bladed, smashed through the banner colonel's golden chest plate, and nailed him into the blazing timbers of the North Gate.

Five-Metal Yang snorted and spat. "That's for Lai Bang, you—"

"Later," Piebald Chan said. "Those Forbidden Bannermen are about to finish their sweep and, the moment they do, the Constabulary Army will rediscover their nerve and, if we're still sitting here, they'll pluck us like the parson's nose..."

The pounding grew louder and louder.

"What do we do?" Chao Jeet said, fingers poking the lump on his head.

Kwai pulled his horse up next to them. "We rout, that's what."

"Rebel's..." Lai Bang clutched his bleeding chest and struggled to sit up. "Rebels don't route..."

"Good," Kwai said. "Then the bandits can use you as cover."

"Name of heaven," Woodcutter Mok said to Lai Bang. "Can't you even die right?"

The pounding reached a crescendo, and the constables shook their spears and began to reform their lines.

The rebels wavered.

Then Master Law's voice boomed down at them from between the stone lions atop the steps of the Azure Mountain Hall. "Sons and daughters of River & Lake! We're bloody and we're broken, but we are not down! Our weapons are chipped and cracked, and what meager fortune we had left is spent, but we are not done! Our lives may be ended but, through our sacrifice, our families will live on! And while we will die, we will not fail!"

Yang chuckled and raised his octagonal hammers. Kwai sighed and reached for his flying daggers.

Master Law leveled his massive Kwan halberd and leapt at the oncoming bannermen. "For Heaven & Earth!"

The rebels cried out and charged after him. "For Lanchow!"

And the bandits blew past on both sides. "For us!"

詠 春 傳 說

The Forbidden Bannermen tore down North Gate Street, their thick-bladed, two-handed choppers high.

The steel-shod hooves of their ebon steeds chomped away the distance in a heartbeat and they burst into the market square just as Eagle-Shadow veered off, down Central Mountain, and towards Red Fortune...

詠 春 傳 說

Wingchun finished her charge, her head up, her eyes flared, and her mother's single knife revealed as two.

"—A butterfly caught in the morning breeze..."

One knife dispersed, the other twined, and the Lama's falchion was trapped between their twin blades.

"How's that for nothing?"

"Impossible!"

She shoved the Lama, kept the dispersing knife hooked around his falchion and sliced the twining knife at his ribs.

The Lama angled and pressed his falchion down to parry, and then thrust back to counter.

Wingchun met him, their blades crossed and their eyes locked.

Metal sprayed, sparked, screamed... Screamed like her family... "You Lama are a disease," she said, her voice a sizzle. "Infecting everything you touch... A scourge—"

"That begs to be healed..." the Lama said.

She hacked at him again and again, until her gaze penetrated the ashen face and burning eyes, and she saw emptiness and rage so deep as to be all but unrecognizable...

Then the blade shifted and the reflection wavered... The reflection in her mother's knives, polished mirror-bright... The reflection of...

"Me..." Wingchun shook her head. It wasn't the Lama she was staring at, it was herself... "What have I become...?"

Her family spread out, her mother and her father with them, and others stretched back and forth across the generations—

Fighting, fragmenting and separating in violence beyond even what heaven and earth could endure...

Screaming... Deafening...Demanding...

Demanding that she not crash back down...

Demanding that she soar...

Then the light flickered and the eyes that replaced hers burned like the inferno, like—

"Hell—or worse."

"What could be worse than hell?"

"Becoming it... Becoming the devil..."

The nightmares shattered and a single, terrible reality fell.

"Is it possible," the Lama said. "Is it possible one of you finally understands?"

"I do..." The emptiness and rage fled and a dreadful calm settled over her. She closed her eyes, the burning hissed out, and, when she opened them again, they gleamed. "True vengeance is not for those who are gone but for those who remain. It is not filled with ego and selfishness, but with virtue and righteousness. It is like the storm which cleanses the land and brings rejuvenation and renewal."

"Delusion!" The Lama spat. "I should have realized the sublime profundity of transcendence was impossible for you and your pathetic kind! You look into the mirror of reflection but all you see is dust!"

"It is you who looks but does not see. In all the universe there is no mirror, no reflection, nothing at all—not even dust."

"There are the charred remnants of your flesh, the ground fragments of your bone! That is where my rejuvenation lies, my renewal—in your death!"

"I bear your condemnation like the sweet dew of morning. Drinking it in, I renounce all." She smiled, dark and bright. "At last, too late, I understand the inconceivable—you may reduce my flesh to char and my bones to fragment, but I am beyond birth or death."

The Lama charged and his falchion scorched the earth. "You are not beyond me! Stare into the burning heart of the hell between this life and the next and you will find me there staring back at you! I am inescapable! I am the inferno! And what are you? Nothing! A child, a girl! What are you?"

High in the heavens a final constellation rose—the twin stars of the End—and Wingchun's knives crossed beneath them.

"Mercy."

詠 春 傳 說

Auntie settled utterly still. "You would face me at last, here, now?"

"Still so confident in the superiority of your skills?" The old priest smirked. "Here, now, you are irrelevant. You have surrendered your seed of the secret system and exposed Miu Sun's as well. In a moment the Lama will strike down your pathetic little disciple—"

"That has not yet been decided."

"You would help her?" The smirk rolled off his face. "Turn your back on me for even the slightest moment and I *will* kill you."

"You will *try*."

"Bah! It matters nothing—whoever survives will be weakened and then *my* disciple will finish them. And then I and I alone will remain, unmatchable by Shaolin, O-Mei, Wutang, or Lama. Unmatchable by anything or anyone—even you."

詠 春 傳 說

Master Law slashed his Kwan halberd wide to cover his people, the mere handful that were left him. "Down the alley!"

Bannermen wheeled around, constables swarmed, rebels fell, and bandits were cut from their horses.

"Come on!" Yang shoved the others. "Quickly!"

"But this alley doesn't go anywhere," Boy Ngao said. "It never has!"

"And... and suddenly I'm back to the routing," Lai Bang gasped from over Woodcutter Mok's shoulder. "We can still make the tunnels and—"

"What, lead the Ch'ing right back to my child, to all of our children?" Mok huffed. "Don't make me drop you!"

"Why the hell are were retreating down an alley that goes nowhere?" Kwai said.

Chao Jeet limped after him. "We're not."

Widow Pang helped him. "I... I don't understand?"

"We're not retreating," Piebald Chan said.

"Then what are we doing?" Widow Tsui said.

"We're making our stand," Yang said.

Master Law let the last few rebels and bandits trickle past him, and then he took position at their head, between the walls of the butcher shop and the stonemasonry.

"This alley has but one way in and one way out," he said. "The Ch'ing cannot surround us, cannot flank us, cannot do anything but come at us a few at a time. They'll still overrun us, but it will cost them down to the last man!"

Footsteps echoed closer and closer.

"Now form up—behind me!"

The rebels whispered their prayers and the bandits their curses.

And the constables swarmed into the alley.

詠 春 傳 說

The world spun around Wingchun and the last of her strength fled. Shadows consumed the corners of her vision, bitterness the back of her throat, and a dull rush swallowed all other sound.

She slumped back, one of her knives still clutched in her hand...

The Lama slumped straight down in front of her, Wingchun's other knife impaled right through his stomach.

Then the ground trembled and a scar-faced monster reared up over her.

Eagle-Shadow vaulted over the fence and into the courtyard, his body robed ebon as his horse, and his chopper stained with the blood of her sisters and brothers...

She couldn't move anymore. She could barely breathe...

And the chopper fell.

"NO!"

詠 春 傳 說

The old priest gazed down and his white eyebrows bristled. "As you said, I have manipulated everything—everyone—from the beginning..."

Auntie closed her eyes and a single tear cut through her serenity. "No more than I..."

詠 春 傳 說

Boklao leapt from the toppled roof and did his best to crush Eagle-Shadow beneath him. But Eagle-Shadow heard his scream, turned from Wingchun, and the wooden shaft of Boklao's spear splintered against the steel blade of his chopper.

Eagle-Shadow's ebon horse bucked, flame and blood whirled by, and they crashed to the ground. Boklao rolled up in a crouch but Eagle-Shadow was already lashing out with his chopper.

Boklao flowed back, the blade scratched just across his throat. Then he twisted and turned in and slapped his hands against the hilt.

The chopper twirled off into the wreckage.

"Impressive," Eagle-Shadow said, "but not Shaolin impressive."

He lurched to the side and his knee shot out. Boklao angled and cut his arm down. Eagle-Shadow kicked, Boklao turned with it and slipped in. Eagle-Shadow stepped and elbowed. Boklao pressed, stuck to him, and—

Eagle-Shadow's other smashed through.

Boklao stumbled back, his ears rang and his head swam.

Eagle-Shadow laughed. "My fists are tempered like meteors, invincible!"

Boklao's nostril's flared and his teeth clenched.

Eagle-Shadow punched. Boklao hooked it and yanked down to force an opening... But Eagle-Shadow's arm segmented, he lurched again, kneed again, kicked again...

In pattern! It was hard to see what with Eagle-Shadow's body all kinds of broken, but it was there...

Boklao timed the next step, the next elbow, and then he slanted, twined the punch, let Eagle-Shadow segment, and leaked through. He touched Eagle-Shadow with his palm—his nail—and smashed with the full hammer of his body.

A clang echoed through the courtyard and Eagle-Shadow's scar twisted. "My body is adamantine as the Bodhisattva, invulnerable!"

"Dead." Boklao shook his hand and then clawed it open. "And this time you stay dead."

"Like Fong did." Eagle-Shadow glanced past Boklao. "Like *she* will..."

Red. Iron. Salt.

Boklao exploded into Eagle-Shadow.

Eagle-Shadow turned the circle. "Pathetic."

Boklao bounced back, wheeled around, and swung wild.

Eagle-Shadow stepped along the diamond. "Not a ripple."

Boklao snarled, smashed the ground, and—

Eagle-Shadow struck from the lotus. "Not even a murmur."

Boklao blasted back through the wreckage.

"Now..." Eagle-Shadow turned and reached for Wingchun. "By whatever tricks or traps, you ended the Emissary. Now I end you and I *become* the Emissary, the gradations of my redemption complete! My station, my home, my name!"

Boklao tried to get to his knees, to stand, but his body cramped and his mind refused to focus for even another second. The rhythm of his life—the pace that hadn't faltered in nearly twenty years—slowed and stopped.

Then it happened. Red thinned white, iron burst like glass, salt stung bitter, and Boklao let go. His mind flew as his body moved on, his breath cooled and deepened, his spirit released—

And Boklao roared.

Eagle-Shadow glanced back. "You should have stayed down, that would have been quick. Now I'm going to break you bone by bone and grind what's left into paste!"

"Your power is rigid." Boklao's arm twisted. Eagle-Shadow stumbled past. "True power is wrapped in softness."

Eagle-Shadow lurched back around, stepped and elbowed.

"Your movement is obvious." Boklao's waist turned. Eagle-Shadow stumbled again and tripped over the wreckage. "True movement is cloaked in stillness."

Eagle-Shadow screeched. His fist smashed into the cracked tiles and the stone burst in chunks. Then he launched himself at Boklao again, his feet tearing the earth and his fists igniting the heavens.

"Your intent is indirect." Boklao's fingers shot out like a spear. Eagle-Shadow breathed in and set his adamantine skin. Then he breathed out and Boklao bent his fingers and drove his knuckles in. Eagle-Shadow's adamantine skin rippled and he gasped. And Boklao smashed his fist through. "True intent cleaves the center."

Eagle-Shadow stopped dead and stared down at Boklao's hand, pierced straight through his chest. "You... But you can't—" Blood poured from Eagle-Shadow's mouth. "I'm invincible... I'm—"

But Boklao was already across the courtyard. "Wingchun!"

"Boklao..." She pushed him back.

"Wingchun, you did it, you avenged your family, both our families! You—"

"Boklao—!"

Bone robes surged up behind him.

"—move!"

And the Lama's falchion split the heavens.

詠 春 傳 說

Constables clogged the only way into—and out of—the alley between the butcher shop and stonemasonry, a frothing, stabbing mass of flesh and steel.

The rebels and bandits narrowed their blurred and blinded vision, hefted their chipped and cracked weapons, cried out to heaven, and—

"Fok!"

Master Law reeled back, his Kwan halberd held out to the side.

Lieutenant Fok matched him, his long, curved Wo saber, holding the constables at bay.

"Get to your tunnels," Fok said. "Flee—quickly!"

"We can't," Yang said. "We won't!"

"You know," Master Law said, "you know for this to have any chance of working the Kwangsi Governor must believe he has expunged all threat to his control. Victory here can come only through our deaths."

"Don't you see—it already has!"

"What are you talking about?" Yang said.

"You are like the golden cicada that has lured the spider from its lair!"

"Yes," Piebald Chan said. "Only to be eaten by the spider!"

"No," Fok said. "Only to shed your skin and leave the spider with nothing to eat but husk."

"Cantonese, you stupid bastards," Kwai said. "Do any of you speak it?"

"You don't have to die here," Fok said, "the governor just has to think you're dead."

"It won't work," Master Law said. "There's no way..."

"There is and it will, just as soon as you leave and I go back and personally report it so to him."

"You?" Chan scoffed. "And what idiot put you in charge of the Ch'ing?"

Fok pointed at Master Law. "He did, when he killed the banner colonel and every other officer in the Fifth Battalion."

"Oh..."

"This can work," Fok said, "but it has to work now, before the Forbidden Bannermen decide to carve their way in here for a look. Nothing can hinder them..."

"You can't go back," Master Law said.

"I have to or the governor will just send more troops. He'll... he'll send all of them."

"If even one of your men betrays you..."

"Then the governor will waste weeks figuring out what is the more convenient truth and you will be long gone, beyond the four seas..."

"Fok..."

"Safe."

"Fok!"

"With my son."

Master Law closed his eyes and nodded.

Chan bowed. "I was wrong about you, brother Fok. You are exactly what the founders had in mind—you *are* the Inner Gate."

Fok bowed back. "Thank you. Now, in heaven's name—run!"

"Yang," Master Law said, "regroup what rebels we have left. Kwai, your bandit army—"

"My bandit army," Kwai said. "Has quite a ring to it, don't you think?"

"—Are welcome to come with us as well. Fok, so are any of your constables who wish it."

Yang's face darkened. "Criminals and collaborators?"

"Southerners, brave and true," Master Law said, "And if we're to rebuild the south, we will need to rebuild its people—all its people."

詠 春 傳 說

Boklao splattered through the muck. The sights and sounds blurred together, colorless and toneless. The Lama's falchion split the heavens. And Wingchun's single remaining knife cleft them back together.

Steel shattered, white shadows crossed, a body fell and a head a moment later... It bounced several times before rolling to a stop in front of Boklao.

Pale beyond death, mutilated by layer upon layer of scars—the Lama's head.

The snow faded and the night fled.

And Boklao scrambled back to Wingchun. "Crazy girl, I told you to let me handle it, I..."

She gazed back at him like she was about to speak but then she doubled over—

"Wingchun...?"

—And began to fall.

"Wingchun!"

He caught her and lowered her down. She felt cold...

"I..." Blood trickled from her lips.

"Don't," he said. "Save your strength."

"But..."

"When you're better. Whatever you have to say you can say it when you're better."

She coughed wet and red. "Sweet boy..."

"Only just found each other..."

"But we did. We did find each other. A moment, an eternity, it doesn't matter..."

"It matters to me."

"The lungs are governed by the metal element," she said. "They hold all the grief, all the pain. Mine held it..."

"Not long!"

"But so very deep..."

"Law's here. I'll find him, find medicine... Your father's ginseng, I'll... I'll..."

"Promise me something."

"Heal you. We'll find a way to—"

"Boklao..."

"No. I can't hide and I won't fight, not any more. The price is too high. You can't ask me that!"

"I won't. Not to hide, never to fight..."

"Then...?"

"Teach."

He blinked. "Teach?"

"The legacies of my Miu Sun and Wumei and Chi Sim. The legacy of Shaolin, Wutang, and O-Mei... The boxing—"

"Wingchun's boxing! Your boxing, your legacy! You're the one who brought the three schools together, who bound them. You're—"

"Just a skinny little girl, in a tiny little town, stuck out in the middle of nowhere..."

"No, a woman enlightened, transcendent..."

"Who taught you."

"When you had no reason to. When you had every reason not to."

"When I had the only reason..."

"But who? Who would I teach, and where would I even begin?"

"Everywhere and everyone who shares the rebel's heart, who can help us achieve the skill and number... Everyone brave and true, so that one day our people won't ever have to hide again, so that one day we can reclaim our land. The Pure Land..."

"No land will ever be pure, not without you in it..."

She clutched her hand over his. "The flowers blossom and the moon is full..." It was—it wept silver even as the dawn broke gold. "You've already come here to my home, now you need to take me back to yours." She reached up and brushed the tears from Boklao's face. "I want you to promise me."

"Wingchun..."

" 'Again will return spring'—you told me that, you told me it reminded you of the one thing that means everything, it reminded you of..."

"Hope..."

"The one thing that means everything, and you shared it with the rebels and the bandits, and now you must share it with the rest of our people..." Her voice faded but her dark, endless eyes stayed locked on his. "Promise me..."

He lifted her up and cradled her in his arms, and then he turned them both away from the town and into the moon, joined at last by the light of the rising sun.

"I promise."

For ordering information and extended and enhanced
Legends of Wingchun content, please visit:
www.legendsofwingchun.com

For more information on the history, training, and application
of Wing Chun Kung Fu, please visit:
www.wingchunkuen.com

René Ritchie is publisher of the internet www.wingchunkuen.com website, author of *Yuen Kay-San Wing Chun Kuen*, co-author of *Complete Wing Chun*, and his articles have been featured in *Inside Kung Fu*, *Martial Arts Illustrated*, *Martial Arts Masters*, and *Martial Arts Legends*. A graphic and web designer, and writer, he works and trains in Montreal, Quebec.

Printed in the United States
95410LV00003B/19/A